I'll Cross the River

C. Hope Flinchbaugh

Destiny Image Fiction an imprint of

DESTINY IMAGE® PUBLISHERS, INC.
P.O. Box 310, Shippensburg, PA 17257-0310

"Speaking to the Purposes of God for this
Generation and for the Generations to Come."

This book and all other Destiny Image, Revival Press, Mercy Place, Fresh Bread, Destiny Image Fiction, and Treasure House books are available at Christian bookstores and distributors worldwide.

For a U.S. bookstore nearest you, call 1-800-722-6774.
For more information on foreign distributors, call 717-532-3040.
Reach us on the Internet: www.destinyimage.com.

ISBN 10: 0-7684-2648-0
ISBN 13: 978-0-7684-2648-9

For Worldwide Distribution, Printed in the U.S.A.
1 2 3 4 5 6 7 8 9 10 11 / 12 11 10 09 08

Dedication

Until the day we are permitted to walk into North Korea and personally hand people food and Scripture, it is the daily drum of the prayer warrior that shapes the destiny of North Korea and calls down the swords of Heaven to Earth. *I'll Cross the River* is dedicated to the precious people whose persistent daily prayers aid countless North Koreans across the Tumen River. I know a few of you and some I've never met. You pray together, alone, or in groups—in homes, churches, or on phone conferences around the globe. Many of you rallied together when I called for an international day of prayer and fasting for North Korea in August 2005. God bless you. I want to honor you on this page for hearing the call to war on behalf of your human family in North Korea! There is one team that I treasure most highly, and they are the mighty women of God who pray for me personally and faithfully every week: Deborah, Nancy, Jennifer Garrido, Carol Lehman, Penny

Drexel, Jenn Patil, and Jane Bryan. You have put swords into the hands of the warring angels over North Korea! I love you!

ACKNOWLEDGMENTS

I acknowledge Jesus Christ of Nazareth as the Son of God and coming King, the Captain of Heaven's armies and the Victor over death, hell, and the grave. Jesus, thanks for loving me and bringing me into your family and enlisting me into your North Korea Love team!

I am indebted to Heidi and Rolland Baker who asked me, "Hope, have you considered writing about North Korea?"

I salute the United States "General" for North Korea, Suzanne Scholte, president of the North Korea Freedom Coalition, founder and president of the Defense Forum Foundation in Washington, DC, and my personal friend who's allowed God to break her heart for the destitute in North Korea. You have taught me *so* much! Thank you! I'm cheering for you!

Special love and hugs to my husband, Scott, and to our three children for your support as I go into "hiding" to write about what God is doing in the nations.

Special thank you to my dear mother, Betty Keenan, and my faithful friends Jennifer Garrido, Cleo Sippel, Jessica Pustejovsky, and Courtney, my home editors and advisors who helped me to prepare the final copy of this book for Ronda Ranalli and her editorial team at Destiny Image.

Sin U Nam, thank you for reading the first few chapters of the Young Soon story and adding your insights into North Korean culture. You are definitely an inspiration to every member of the North Korea Freedom Coalition.

Ronda, you have given your editorial talents and your tender heart, too—a combination that has been refreshing to this writer! Thank you for your enthusiastic support for this book, for weeping with me over the injustices suffered by North Koreans. I have greatly benefited from working together with you on this novel.

When I sought for permission to copy the lyrics from China's *Canaan Hymns* in my book, I was refreshed by the response to my request. A representative of the Chinese sister who wrote more than 1,000 of the Canaan hymns told me, "You certainly don't need any permission for these! I know [the author] quite well, and I know if I ever mentioned copyright or permission she would burst out laughing."

There's a writer who will have a full reward in Heaven! Thank you, Sister, for freely sharing your songs with the world!

All Chinese songs in this book are selected from more than 1,000 Canaan Hymns written by a young Chinese woman and sung all over the world in Chinese churches today. To view a selection of the hymns, go to: www.chinasoul.org/3/cross/script4.htm.

Rev. Henry Gruver, prayer walker to the nations, contributed to this novel his insights on Heaven. Go to www.seehope.com and click the "Heaven" page for more insights on Heaven and how you can get there.

Some Korean words and insights were pulled from a report titled "Thank You Father Kim Il-Sung," documented by the United States Commission on International Religious Freedom. The report can be read in its entirety at: http://uscirf.com/countries/region/east_asia/northkorea/NKwitnesses_WGraphics.pdf.

ENDORSEMENTS

Our friend Hope has given us a rich treasury of stories to pro-
voke us to carry God's healing presence all over the earth as the
waters cover the sea (see Hab. 2:14). We must stand with North
Korea to be a voice for the voiceless and a face for the silent suffering of millions. This book stirs a deep hunger for the light of
His glorious love to break forth in the hardest and darkest areas
of the earth.

Dr. Heidi G. Baker, Founding Director
Iris Ministries

Too often we forget what goes on behind the closed doors of
countries like North Korea. Often things that are hidden from day-
to-day life get ignored by those of us who *can* do something and
make our concerns and our voices heard. Hope Flinchbaugh wants

to draw your attention to the plight of the people of North Korea and hopefully we will all respond.

Kathie and David Walters, Good News Ministries
Macon, Georgia

Hope Flinchbaugh has skillfully interwoven two stories she carries deep in her heart—the beauty of the vibrant housechurch Christians of China and the grossly oppressive and warped society of North Korea, where unspeakable atrocities and suffering occur every day. *I'll Cross the River* will both encourage and challenge you to follow Christ unreservedly and to make an impact on our needy world.

Paul Hattaway, Author of *Heavenly Man*
Missionary to Asia

Through this book, Hope Flinchbaugh has given us a picture of life for the average citizen who must struggle daily to survive in what could arguably be described as the world's biggest prison—North Korea. Her central character, Young Soon, reminds us of the triumph of the human spirit. Emboldened by love, redemption, and forgiveness, Young Soon overcomes in a land gripped with fear, suspicion, and condemnation.

Suzanne Scholte
President, Defense Forum Foundation
Chairman, North Korea Freedom Coalition

I'll Cross the River touches my heart—I am so impressed. I believe this book represents the situation of North Korea exactly so people can understand the most closed country and the lives of North Korean citizens.

Jung Min Noh, Broadcaster/Reporter
Korean Service Radio Free Asia, Washington, DC

I'll Cross the River is a timely and provocative novel based on true stories researched by Hope Flinchbaugh. With stunning accuracy, Hope details the real-life drama and unthinkable choices involved with being a woman in the oppressive communist nation of North Korea. Undoubtedly your heart will be stirred and inspired as you read this book!

Pat Robertson, Chairman/CEO
The Christian Broadcasting Network

This gripping story plunges into the continuing holocaust in North Korea as the mad leader starves and destroys his own countrymen. The author brings you into the courage, humanity, and pathos of Chinese Christians, who risk prison and martyrdom, becoming unlikely heroes, giving rescue and aid to the desperate fugitives who risk their lives to flee this hell on earth.

Charles Stock
Pastor, Life Center

I pray that the story in this book will birth in you the heartbeat of God for this nation. Hope Flinchbaugh—whom I know personally—once again has captured the heart of a nation by going deep into the lives of its people.

Pastor Kathy Balcombe
Revival Christian Church, Hong Kong

I am thrilled that a writer as skilled and as passionate as C. Hope Flinchbaugh has chosen to write on this subject. Because she bases and builds her plots around the testimonies of North Korean refugees, she manages to give her readers a painfully accurate insight into North Korean suffering.

Elizabeth Kendal
World Evangelical Alliance Religious Liberty Commission

Powerful and compelling, *I'll Cross the River* captured my heart with the reality of the suffering of our North Korean brothers and sisters. It is a moving story of bold spiritual courage—I highly recommend you read it, and pray!

Carl A. Moeller, PhD
President & CEO, Open Doors, USA

C. Hope Flinchbaugh has already written extensively about the plight of Christians in China, and this highly challenging and informative book will open your eyes to understand the power of evil and the triumph of Christ and righteousness in both nations. I highly recommend it to the Christian who has the compassion of Christ for these tens of millions in North Asia. I believe it will motivate you to prayer and action as we reach out and help our brethren.

Pastor Dennis Balcombe
Hong Kong, Revival Christian Church
Revival Chinese Ministries International

TABLE OF CONTENTS

PREFACE

While writing news stories for *Christianity Today, Charisma,* and various Focus on the Family publications, I interviewed Christians who are currently hiding orphans inside China—children who were fortunate enough to make it across the North Korean border into China. I personally heard the stories of Christians from several countries, including China, who were imprisoned by Chinese officials for volunteering to safe house North Korean refugees. I held the hands of Korean mothers who sobbed over their young daughters who were sold as sex slaves to Chinese men after reaching China in hopes of food and freedom.

At the time of the publication of this book, China is hosting the 2008 Olympics. Simultaneously, its police officers are capturing starving North Koreans who've crossed onto Chinese land and are presently sending the defectors back into North Korea where they are interrogated, beaten, imprisoned in Auschwitz-style prison camps, and sometimes executed.

> *Pure religion and undefiled before God and the Father is this, To visit the fatherless and widows in their affliction, and to keep himself unspotted from the world* (James 1:27 KJV).

Come with me in the pages of this book and visit the fatherless and widows of North Korea. Be encouraged by the compassionate work of the church of Jesus Christ in China as it struggles to reach out to North Koreans presently hiding inside China. Just listening to this story will help them to know that we care. Share this book with a close friend and peruse the websites listed in the back of the book.

Our human family is suffering. This story is burning in my heart. I'm honored to tell it. I hope you will be compelled to share this story with others. The time is now.

*Speak up for those who cannot
speak for themselves;
ensure justice
for those being crushed*

(PROVERBS 1:8 NLT).

Tanching Village, China

CHAPTER 1

Mei Lin rinsed her empty tray in the muddy water and sloshed toward the dirt bank. The top of her feet rubbed against her wet shoes. She sat on the edge of the bank and took off her shoes and dumped the water out of them, swishing them about in the water until most of the mud was gone, and then did the same with her feet. They emerged from the water wrinkled and raw from the friction of walking all day in the mud. She waited a few moments for her feet to dry, her eyes scanning the rice paddies. The sun was still high, but it was nearing five o'clock. Some people, finished with their planting, walked slowly toward her in pairs. Others were still bent over their rows.

She felt someone behind her and turned to look. Before she could turn completely around, hands went over her eyes. Mei Lin put her hands up to feel the arms of the person behind her.

"Liko!"

She felt the warmth of a kiss on the back of her head.

Liko laughed and plopped down beside her.

"Are you finished plowing already?" Mei Lin asked.

"Hardly," he answered. "I'm finished for the day, though."

Mei Lin took his hands and turned them over. "You wrapped the rags around the plow handle?" she asked.

Liko nodded.

"Fine help that was," she said, inspecting the loose skin. "The blisters look worse."

"No worse than those red things at the end of your legs," Liko teased.

Mei Lin grinned. "Those red things at the end of my legs served me well today, Chen Liko. It's not nice to make fun of them."

Liko playfully picked up her foot and tickled the bottom. "Ooo, sponges," he teased.

Mei Lin looked at her hands. "These aren't much better. A bit chapped, but they will soften again after spring planting. I should be finished with the Kwan quota by the end of this week."

Liko sighed. "I'm afraid it will take me another three weeks to finish plowing. It's taken me five times as long this year without Old Gray."

"I miss Old Gray, too," said Mei Lin. "It will be years before we can afford to buy another water buffalo."

Liko took her tray, stood up, and reached for her hand. Mei Lin let him pull her to her feet. She winced. The bottoms of her feet were tender from standing all day in the paddies. She slid them into her wet shoes and tiptoed carefully, allowing Liko to pull her slowly behind him. Suddenly, she was whisked off her feet and into his arms.

"Whoa!" Mei Lin cried out.

"A free ride to the most beautiful maiden in Tanching Village," he announced.

Mei Lin laughed and put her arms around Liko's neck and lightly kissed him. "Maybe plowing the field yourself is making you as strong as Old Gray."

"You—are as light as a teacup," he teased.

Mei Lin nestled her head into his chest and Liko kissed the top of her head. An elderly couple behind them chuckled and Mei Lin felt her face grow warm.

"Liko, people are watching us," she whispered up at him.

"Ah, they are watching you, Mei Lin, the most breathtaking woman in Tanching and they are envying me—the luckiest man in the world."

Mei Lin smiled. She loved these little outbursts of affection. They both surprised and thrilled her.

Within minutes they were walking through the bamboo near her house—the first one in from the fields and the one farthest from the center of the village. Her grandmother liked the added protection of the natural wall of bamboo between their house and the fields. Amah insisted that the gods placed the bamboo wall there for good feng shui. What she called "added spiritual protection" made her feel better, anyway.

Except for the bamboo, their house looked exactly like all the other houses that followed—that is, alike except for the new addition father was building for Liko's mother. She'd not seen her father so happy since her mother was alive. Liko was glad his widowed mother would be taken care of and, really, even Amah seemed pleased with the arrangement. Father insisted on finishing the addition before getting married, though, and Amah wouldn't stop giving advice on how to build the new room so it would have good feng shui. Amah also insisted that no one had a larger fishpond in Tanching, but Mei Lin thought that Ping's aunt's pond looked larger.

Liko put her down just outside the chicken house. "I should leave now," he said. "Mother promised to make dinner for all of us and bring it to your house this evening."

Mei Lin suppressed a giggle. "Is your mother still trying to impress my father? I don't think she could do anything to change his mind about marrying her. I've never seen him so happy. He's working every day on that new addition."

"I think Mother is trying to impress Amah more than your father."

"Really?" asked Mei Lin. "Amah likes your mother. She seems very happy that she and Father are getting married."

"Ah, yes, but the bride-to-be always wants to please the future mother-in-law. And you know Amah—she's always insisting upon the old ways of China."

"Oh, do you think I should be about this business of impressing my future mother-in-law, too?" asked Mei Lin. A mischievous grin curled her lips and Liko bent over and brushed her lips with his.

"Next year I will be twenty-two. You'd better impress her before then, because I think I shall marry you the day after my birthday."

"Liko!"

Liko filled a couple of water buckets and Mei Lin followed him, hauling the buckets up the hill to water the garden. Within ten minutes they'd watered the vegetable garden that sloped up the hill toward the cow shed. Small snippets of tender green cabbages, peppers, and tea plants poked their heads out of rich broken earth, reaching for the golden sun.

"Look!" said Mei Lin, pointing. At the bottom of the hill between the chicken house and the garden, fuzzy yellow ducklings were following their mother out of the pond heading straight for the chicken coop.

"Perhaps your ducks think they are chickens?" asked Liko.

"Ha! They'll get no grain from Amah unless they lay eggs for breakfast."

"I'll see you in an hour," said Liko. He handed her his empty buckets, then planted a kiss on her forehead and easily ran down the path beside her house that led to the front road. Mei Lin watched him, her heart full of love. Would he skip so happily after she told him her dreams for the summer?

Poydan, North Korea

CHAPTER 2

"Oma, my stomach! It's bad." After calling for his mother, eight-year-old Nam Gil rolled side to side on his reed mat; his face squinted so that the only facial feature noticeable was his small nose.

"Here," Young Soon offered. Slowly she shuffled across the floor. "Take a sip of this good water. I borrowed rice gruel and mixed it in." Every grain of rice had been siphoned out of the liquid, but a hint of nourishment was there, and Young Soon wanted her son to have it first. Obediently, Nam Gil swallowed the watery substance, holding his stomach. He turned on his side and threw up.

"What a waste," Young Soon murmured to herself as she cleaned it up. She would owe her neighbor for this rice gruel but they both knew she had no way of paying him unless the government would come through on the promised rations. Her husband had earned enough points to feed them this year before he died.

Now she had to make every political meeting at the town shrine or the points he worked so hard to gain would be lost.

Young Soon sighed deeply, rinsed her hands, and pulled a tattered blanket over her three-year-old daughter who'd already found sweet relief from hunger in a late afternoon nap.

Compassion welled up inside her and Young Soon gently knelt beside her son's mat and ran her slender fingers through his hair. His black shiny hair was now a reddish color, brittle and falling out—a sign of the deadly starvation that had taken her husband three months earlier and her older sister and nieces last year. Large sunken eyes looked up at her, all light gone from his face. Young Soon ran her finger down the side of her son's jaw. There was a green tint to his skin now; a common symptom of the deadly grass poisoning that had taken the lives of several other village children. His skin tightly stretched down his jaw line to protruding shoulder blades. Young Soon tried to imagine what he would look like had he been fed like she was as a child.

I wish Kim il-Sung were still alive. At least people weren't starving.

Young Soon glanced up at the pictures of Father Kim il-Sung and his son, the Dear Leader, hanging on her wall—fear tingled down her spine. The picture of Father Kim il-Sung was crooked! Adrenaline shot through her and with that energy she sprang to her feet to straighten the picture.

There. Thank you Father, Kim il-Sung.

Her mind went back to the Yap family who was publicly humiliated and sent to prison after their child accidentally knocked the picture off the wall, marring it irreparably. She shivered. *What if Ja is right and the Dear Leader, General Kim Jong-il, or the spirit of his deceased father heard her thoughts? Would they know that the picture was crooked?*

Young Soon dismissed the thought. At least she caught it and the pictures were straightened. For now she had more pressing matters on her mind. She looked at Nam Gil's arms and legs. Twigs.

Narrow sticks. Deep in her heart she knew he could not live on their meager diet for another year.

She touched the small roundness of her own abdomen. She could not imagine how her baby was surviving when she'd had so little to eat the last month. The last two weeks before he died, her husband gave her all of his food so that she and their unborn baby would have more to sustain them in the first months of pregnancy. Young Soon was proud of her husband's sacrifice. Yet despite such great sacrifice, starvation had seized them all by the throat, choking them on boiled bark and green grass soup.

"Rest here, Nam Gil," she said wearily. "Aunt Ja is coming and we will go to the political meeting. Then we will search for food."

Except for her brother who left Poydan years ago to serve in the North Korean Military, Young Soon had only one sister left in her family. Ja was the only person she could trust now. Every neighbor within three houses of each other was commanded to report his neighbor for spying, stealing, or speaking against the Party. Every-one was under suspicion and only the words of the Dear Leader could be trusted. Ja was a haven of rest, a rainbow in the storm of her life. Without her, Young Soon would have given up by now.

The tremors in her arms and legs began and her head filled with the locusts again, all buzzing, swarming, chasing away her thoughts of Ja. Firespears flew in her middle and, heavy with dread, Young Soon checked on her children one more time and then lay beside her son.

Willing another day's strength into her body, she lay still and watched the dust particles move within the diagonal beam of sunlight at the front window. After a few minutes, the buzzing stopped and Young Soon was able to focus on her surroundings. Except for the door, the room was plain. There were few furnishings—bed mats, a few cooking utensils, and the On Dol stove on the left side as you walk in the doorway. The On Dol stove always warmed her heart and her home. She stretched her trembling legs and smiled at the memories around that old stove. Father used to smoke his pipe after supper and read to all of them from their family chokpo. His eyes twinkled behind the yellowish waft of smoke and the sweet pungent smell of tobacco filled the room. Father read from the old family book that told the wonderful story about one of her father's ancestors who made his living building many of the stoves still used by their neighbors. The stoves, now more than 100 years old, continued to efficiently heat their floors. She remembered Father proudly explaining to Hwan, his only son, how the heat from the stove goes through a tunnel underneath the house and heats the floor. Then they would go outside and walk the perimeters of the house, so that Father could point out the workings of the Korean On Dol stove. Young Soon learned in elementary school that Chinese houses sat on the ground and wondered again how the Chinese stayed warm.

What would Father think of his old house now?

One of Mother's old calendars hung on the wall on the right. The picture of the Dear Leader, General Kim Jong-il, hung on the wall directly across from the front door. She checked to be sure that the portrait of his late father, President Kim il-Sung, was remaining straight. "Thank you Father Kim il-Sung," Young Soon said softly. Sleepily, Young Soon made a mental note to check the pictures again before she left for the political meeting.

~

Young Soon awoke with a start, her heart pounding. Panic seized her. She struggled to get up. She had to get up. She had to move—she refused to allow the hunger to paralyze her. Fear gripped her heart and she stifled a sob. Nam Gil lay still beside her. She struggled to sit up and checked his neck. He was alive. Quietly, she watched her daughter until she saw her little chest rise and fall in even breathing.

The old rice-paper door slid sideways and Ja appeared in the doorway.

"What is it, Young Soon?" asked Ja. "You look ashen. Did I startle you?"

Young Soon shook her head. She was glad for Ja's company, although she didn't say so. About once a week now she experienced an attack that woke her up with a pounding in her heart and wild fear in her mind. But she rarely remembered any bad dreams. It was just a feeling she couldn't shake—a feeling of fright that was at its worst in the middle of the night.

"Ah, I see you've hung Mother's old door," said Ja.

"Just last night, Ja," she finally answered. "I hung it last night—to remember Mother."

Young Soon looked at her sister standing beside the opaque door, imagining it was her mother there again, painting pink flowers and azalea bushes around the edges of the doorframe. Her mother had crushed red azalea petals in a bowl and, using a few drops of water, formed a crimson paste. The colors were faded now, but Young Soon could still see the light pink and dabs of red Mother had swirled about the door with an oxtail brush to make it appear as though one was walking into a room full of flowers.

"What are you thinking?" asked her sister, as she slowly walked closer.

"I was thinking of how much you remind me of Mother standing there in the doorway," Young Soon answered.

"Mother," said Ja with a sigh. Ja knelt beside Min-Hee and stroked her cheek. Min-Hee had been Ja's sole source of comfort since her baby daughter died two years before. "What would Mother think of us now?"

Young Soon sipped some of the watery rice gruel, savoring its taste and washing it through her mouth before swallowing. "Please, take some," she said, and offered the rest to her sister.

Ja received it eagerly. "Thank you." Her hands trembled as she drank. "It tastes good."

Nam Gil groaned and turned beneath his thin blanket.

"Let's go," said Ja. "Before they both wake up."

It was too late—Young Soon knew her son was already awake. Young Soon's legs still trembled with weakness, but love for her children pushed her to drag herself out the door one more time to attend the political meeting. She took her tattered rice bag off the wall. Its only content was a sharp rock that she used for digging grass roots from the ground. Father's shovel was sold long ago for food. She often fantasized of finding a wild red ginseng root, a root that her father taught them would cure all sickness and grow strong healthy children with bright minds.

"Do not bother with the ginseng grown in the confinement of a garden," Father warned. "It is the wild red colored root found in our mountains that carries the ginseng magic."

Young Soon imagined such magic…She would put the root in a pan of water and boil it into a tea. She pictured Nam Gil drinking the tea, and then he would sit up on his mat and smile at her. Her sister said that the grass roots were making Nam Gil sick, but Young Soon felt she had little choice. Until she found the ginseng, she must feed him grass roots or he will starve. Young Soon looked over at her son. Perhaps she and Ja will walk farther today, higher into the hills where the wild red ginseng grew.

"Nam Gil, I will return when the sun goes down. The door is shut tightly. Watch over your sister."

Deep in her heart, Young Soon knew that her son was far too ill to lift his head much less care for his sister. But she hoped her words would breathe courage into his heart. Young Soon hated to leave Min-Hee behind every day, but she had no choice.

As soon as she stepped outside, the dusty afternoon air whipped against her face, playing with her hair and shirt. Walking was a large effort—but every day Young Soon determined she would walk to the political meeting and then walk up the hillside one more time to search for food. Every day she promised herself that she would not stop walking—her children needed her.

Sometimes she imagined Nam Gil and Min-Hee running around in the yard, playing some childish game. And laughter—how she longed to hear her children laugh. But malnutrition and disease had long ago hushed the mirth and amusements of all the North Korean children she knew. Wildlife and birds weren't heard anywhere because they'd all been killed and eaten.

A small barefoot boy squatted in the street, staring at the women as they passed. Young Soon stared back. *Gotchebees. The shame of North Korea.* The police hated them and drove them out of the main cities. The jojang, the coal mine boss, tried to scare them out of Poydan, but there were too many and they were too weak to travel now. To Young Soon, the Gotchebee orphans were leaches that stole the last of Poydan's food from her own children. They were a death mark on her town—a constant reminder that famine had emptied at least one fourth of the houses in Poydan. How pitiful they were last year, huddled together in the dark freeze of winter, slowly starving to death. Young Soon spit on the ground in disgust.

"Go," she threatened him. "Or I'll report you."

The boy turned away. Young Soon and Ja kept walking. Young Soon had neither time nor energy to waste on the gotchebees.

Most of the time, she ignored the gotchebee children—everyone hated hem. For most, their parents died of hunger or abandoned them. A few ran away, looking for a job so they could get food. The government promised to take all the street urchins to safe houses set up by the government. *All the better for them,* thought Young Soon. *And all the better for us.*

Poydan was not a large town, and it soon became obvious that the little beggars would stay until they died or moved out. Everyone wanted them to move out. They were blood-sucking leeches—no parents, no food, just vagabonds that pilfered from citizens and soldiers alike. Worse, they were like cockroaches—tiny little spies that you couldn't see in the dark. They'd lie about anyone to the military police if they thought it would get them a bite of food. Liars and thieves.

Young Soon thought of her own children all alone and shuddered. She mentally checked herself—yes, she had locked the front door.

She had nothing to offer the gotchebees and even less to offer her own children—nothing except to stay alive to love them.

Young Soon pushed the gotchebees out of her mind and walked against the wind past the gray houses toward the hillside north of her village. Each gray house looked like the next in Poydan, although some leaned backward or had vertical planks missing here and there. She liked to look at the corrugated tin roofs. The ginger shaded tin provided the only depth of color against the sandy brown dirt roads and brown splotchy hillsides. The good trees were far away, outside the city. The trees inside Poydan were barren, all the leaves picked and eaten in the early spring, the bark scraped off before summer in the village-wide search for bugs.

As her feet slowly shuffled forward, her mind traveled backward, into the past. Young Soon hadn't eaten beans or even a rat for that matter, for a year. She fondly remembered the day her husband came home with a rat he'd caught while working in the mine. He pulled it out of his pocket where he'd hidden it from the other men. It was their night of great fortune, he'd said. Young Soon couldn't remember its savory taste any more.

She and Ja did not speak. Each saved her energy for walking. Young Soon shuffled one foot in front of the other, all the while imagining the flavor and nutrition of the ginseng root.

Tanching Village, China

CHAPTER 3

Liko took her hand. Mei Lin thought she felt a quiver there, a slight shudder as he touched her. It was June—three weeks had passed since she broke the news to Liko. It was their last night together until autumn—a night to remember during the uncertain days ahead.

The sun was nearly set by the time they reached the bank of the rice paddy. Liko lit the lantern and, after slipping off their shoes, they made their way to the big rock. Mei Lin hung on to Liko's shirttail with her free hand and watched the lantern reflection wiggling and twisting about their feet in the dark waters. Small black rice shoots jutted out of the images and both of them were careful not to disturb the new plantings.

Mei Lin took Liko's hand and stepped up on the rock. She laid her jacket down at the same old spot and waited for Liko to place the lantern on the level area of the rock, and then sit beside her. Without a word, the two of them searched the clear China sky for twinkling stars sprinkled about the moon, now high in the dark expanse.

Mei Lin leaned back on her elbows and watched the stars. Tomorrow, time would separate them physically. But never in spirit. Always, forever, they were bonded in spirit and distance could not rob that from them.

~

Liko watched her, memorizing the outline of her face in the soft lantern light, the tilt of her head. She was like an eagle, poised, positioned, ready to fly.

How does a man protect such an eagle? Clip her wings? Refuse to let her fly?

Liko's throat tightened each time he remembered how she suffered in the Shanghai prison. That was three years ago. Mei Lin was young and defenseless and half the size of the guards who beat her. With all of his heart, he wanted to cherish her and keep her safe for the rest of his life.

She looked up at him and smiled. "You're watching me."

"I like watching you," he whispered. "Although your thoughts seem to be a thousand miles away."

"Not so far away," Mei Lin answered. She sat up and squeezed his hand. They sat in silence for some time. Liko weighed his words carefully.

"I won't stop you, Mei Lin," he finally said. "If I tried, you would consider our village a cage and my arms a leash that tied you to the ground."

Mei Lin looked at him. She couldn't argue—he knew her well.

"You are like an eagle perched on the high crag of a cliff, ready to soar at the next flash of danger across the China sky."

"I will come back to you, Liko," she said. *Unless I get caught starting churches.* Mei Lin bit her lip so she wouldn't say what she was thinking.

"I want to let you fly," he said. "For your sake. But I can't help the longing in my heart. When I close my eyes at night I can still smell your hair or feel your small hand inside mine, and I remember the way the sun dances on the water around you as you work in the fields."

Silence fell between them again. Mei Lin struggled to find the right words, words that would comfort her lover and friend. She was excited about the trip when she spoke to her friend Fei—full of faith for their evangelistic meetings in far unreached villages. For Mei Lin, the thought of an adventure was like oxygen pumping life and energy through her heart and into her bloodstream.

But it wasn't just the adventure—there was more. Much more. Nothing she experienced in her life compared to the thrill of seeing a person's life changed when they believed in Jesus. The whole world looks different to a new Christian. She thought of the prisoners in the cell who accepted Jesus three years ago. Only God could bring real satisfaction to people and she knew the way to God—how could she *not* go?

Yet when she was with Liko, she realized that her decision to travel on this adventure impacted everyone around her, especially Liko. She wanted to comfort him now.

Liko spoke first, his voice tight with emotion. "Mei Lin, I—I will miss you."

Mei Lin leaned her head into his muscular arm. "And I will miss you."

"Where will you sleep at night?" he asked.

"Where God provides," Mei Lin answered softly.

"What if you can't find a house to sleep in?" asked Liko. "I can't think about you sleeping outside, even on a beautiful night like this. What if it rains? Who will care for you?"

"Pastor Wong will lead us to WuMa where we will get the Bibles. After that, God will care for Fei and me," Mei Lin answered. "You must trust him. We both must trust him."

Liko sighed deeply, leaned forward, his arms wrapped around his knees. Mei Lin heard a sob catch his throat and his body suddenly heaved and shook.

"Liko!" she cried, throwing her arms around his back and shoulders. His back was stiff and tense. "What is it?"

"I want to protect you, Mei Lin," he answered, his voice strained. "I wish that I could go instead of you."

"Oh, now that would look good," said Mei Lin. She knelt beside him and tried to humor him into a lighter mood. "I can just see you and Sister Fei traveling all over southeastern China together."

He ignored her attempt at humor. "Do you realize that if no one takes you into their home you will be outside in the rain or cold all alone? What about wild animals? And what sort of men lurk around women who sleep outside in the dark? These thoughts— they have been driving me mad."

She touched his shoulder, but Liko's frame was hardening like rock, impenetrable. His fear was like a wall around him that kept her out.

Mei Lin tried to penetrate the wall. She wondered if this was why he wanted to walk with her tonight—to try to talk her out of going. Mei Lin had pushed thoughts of dangerous animals and evil men to the back of her mind. But Liko insisted on bringing the dangers to the forefront. Her mind raced and silently she prayed to the One who made the earth and skies.

Lord?

She could feel God's presence wrap around her and she wanted to draw Liko into its comfort. But Liko was outside, anguished with the pain of separation and the anxieties of the unknown.

"Liko," she whispered. "Perfect love pushes out fear. You have to let go of the fear."

He was quiet for a moment, his muscular frame silhouetted against the light of the lantern.

"Sometimes I think of that verse and I have comfort. Other times—"

His voice trailed off and Mei Lin rushed to turn his thoughts toward love one more time.

"Fear is our enemy, Liko." This was an old discussion, but one that they apparently needed to repeat once more before she left. "Promise me that every time you are tempted to fear that you will declare your faith for my protection and God's love for me."

His lips swept over her hand briefly and then he turned and looked at her. She shifted so she could kneel in front of him. She felt their hearts lock.

His heart softened at the sight of her, pounded with love for her. Fear wanted to make him crazy at the thought of anyone or anything hurting her again. Yet here, looking into her soul, his faith soared with this eagle woman, flying high above his fears, even mocking them.

Time passed as he studied the young woman in front of him. Silently she waited for him as he flew higher, higher until Liko felt a descending, a settling over his heart. Finally. Finally it was there. He could feel the peace fall like a warm blanket. Then faith—faith was like a magic carpet that carried him high again, high above the dark worries that darted through his thoughts these last few weeks. Faith was what he'd been waiting for, searching for, as he read the Gospels lately. He wanted to *know* beyond all doubt that Jesus not only lived and died and rose again, but he yearned to grasp the bedrock belief that Jesus is here *now*, walking with them in Tanching Village—that Jesus is here *now*, ready to live His life again through Mei Lin as she follows His steps into the unknown. Faith carried him higher and higher until finally he could see with eyes of the Spirit—a place where Heaven was cheering them onward and angels attended their earthly assignments.

He bent forward and lightly kissed the top of her head. Knowing his last words would be the most important, remembered by both his lover and his Lord, he spoke, his mouth close to her cheek.

"I could never love anyone like I love you, Mei Lin. Your faith in God draws me to you like a magnet. Even if the devil looses every wild animal in Jiangxi Province against you, your shield of faith will be like a house of walls around you."

Mei Lin caught her breath, her scalp tingling at the declaration of his confidence in their God. He did it. Without anymore urging from her, Liko was declaring his faith in God.

"If wicked men attempt to touch you or harm you in any way, God will warn you and show you how to escape. You will walk into a village to preach and the blind will see. The deaf will hear."

Mei Lin's mouth dropped open. *I've never seen a blind person healed before. What is he talking about?*

"The demon-possessed will be delivered and the lame will walk. You will go out in the power of the Holy Spirit sowing seeds of the gospel." He lightly waved his hand over the rice paddies before them. "You will return in autumn when these watery paddies are hidden under tall stalks of rice. You will return with a harvest of souls for the Kingdom of God."

The dark water shimmered under the star lights and Mei Lin felt one with its quivering glory.

"Miracles that Jesus performed will happen in your travels. You will go off to some barn or hillside to spend the night in fasting and prayer and return from there the next morning full of the Holy Spirit of God. You will hear His voice and know the direction you should take from village to village. You will know where to stop and when it is time to leave."

At this, Mei Lin's body tingled with the fresh realization of Liko's love for her. All at once she realized that she didn't just need Liko to love her, she needed him to believe in her as well. Liko did believe in her. And he believed in God with her. She was rich—rich in love and rich in heavenly gifts. Tears flowed now. Mei Lin reached for his hand, speechless.

Liko continued. "Jesus, when You left the earth, You said to wait until we are clothed with power from on high."

Liko placed his free hand on her back. "Father, I ask you to clothe my sweet Mei Lin with Your mighty power from on high."

In that moment, God's presence fell upon her in wave after wave after wave. Her spine tingled with holy electricity and a liquid love seemed to pour down through her body. Her head felt as though it was being pushed forward to her knees in front of her under the tremendous weight of glory. Mei Lin felt as though every shadowy thought she'd ever had disappeared, swept away by the liquid love. Suddenly, she knew Jesus as never before. She felt one with His love for the world and one with His love for his Father in Heaven.

The stories of the life of Jesus paraded by her, forming pictures of attainable miracles and tangible teachings. Even Pastor Wong's faith didn't seem so hard to reach right now. It was real. She could touch faith as sure as she could feel the warmth of Liko's fingers wrapped around hers and his other hand on her back right now. The love of God kept coming over her in waves until she thought she would have to beg Him to stop.

Liko was quoting Scripture now. "Go, Mei Lin. Go into the forgotten parts of China and preach the gospel..."

Poydan, North Korea

Chapter 4

Young Soon slowly shuffled down the street with Ja. She was grateful for her sister's company—the daily walks to the political meetings would be unbearable without her. She tucked her face down further into the front of her shirt to shield herself from the flying dust and slid her arm into Ja's. Maybe today they would get money for rice.

Each family carried its own sorrow. Ja's only child died two years before. How can a mother release her only daughter into the earth? Young Soon told her sister Ja that she would not have to attend the meetings because her husband worked in the mine and his attendance was enough. But Ja was cunning and she hoped her voluntary attendance would be seen with favor by the mining boss and perhaps her husband's money earnings would be increased. She promised to share with Young Soon if that happened. Whenever the money came, sometimes a week or a month late, they'd go together to the outdoor market and buy a small bag of rice. Ja's husband, Chul Moo, would go, too, so that they would not be stolen from. That rice would have to last one month.

Time meant nothing. For Young Soon, success was measured by distance. Strength was her valued possession; strength to make it to the center of town where they always stopped to catch their breath, strength to get up from her seat on the floor after the political meeting and ascend the mountain for food...Strength that descended into the ground, rushing out of her legs as she dragged them forward like two heavy tree trunks walking on Center Road through Poydan. Young Soon kept her eye on the dark gray house with the crooked window shutter, the house that marked the center of town.

The sisters made it to the middle of the village and then stopped for a moment to regain their strength. Young Soon looked back at her dirt packed front yard in the distance, imagining fruit trees and vegetable plants and even red azalea bushes. She vaguely recalled these luxuries from her childhood. Her mother had once crushed the red Azalea petals into a crimson paste, put the paste on her fingernails, and then sent her to bed with each finger wrapped in cloth. The next morning she wakened and took off the cloths. Her fingernails were pink! She squealed with delight, proudly showing her father and sisters and brother her beautiful nails.

Good memories. One day she wanted to create good memories for her own children. Most of all, she wanted to hear her children laugh. She shuddered to think that her daughter might never see a fiery red azalea bush or a vegetable garden or a field heavy with rice stalks.

Young Soon sighed. Several other women were ahead of them now, most of them hobbling like so many lame ducks toward the same pond. She again took Ja's arm and walked toward the warehouse that was closely guarded by soldiers. As they approached, the announcer's voice on the government radio station grew louder and louder, touting the Ten Principles of the Party's Exclusive Ideology.

"All who betray the Party should be killed. Disloyal attitudes are like a disease among the people. We believe in Nodongdang, the Workers Party. We must raise up sons and daughters of the Party…"

It wasn't hard to block the rhetoric out of her mind. She knew the words so well, she could have made the announcements herself.

She eyed the soldiers who were everywhere—guarding everything. Where did they expect the starving people to go?

Only to their graves, she thought.

As quickly as the thought came, Young Soon tried to squeeze it out of her mind again. She was afraid to die and worse, she was afraid to leave her children behind all alone in this barren place.

Just before they reached the warehouse, they approached the herd of well-fed guards in green uniforms, berets, and shiny black boots stationed around the cornfield, closely guarding the only real food left in the town. Young Soon watched the earthen ditch on the opposite side of the road. Twice the winds had blown some of the corn scraps across the road and Young Soon and Ja grabbed them before the guards saw. Every time they passed this field, Young Soon paid silent tribute to her brother Hwan. It was this field and the soldiers in green uniforms that inspired her brother Hwan to quickly join the army years earlier. Every North Korean boy had to join the army for 10 years, but Hwan was especially eager and left early.

The day he left, he told their mother, "I must go away to become a soldier so that I can eat the corn that grows in our fields."

Young Soon was glad her brother was eating. They hadn't heard from him in three years now, but it comforted her to think of one person in her family without worrying about them dying. In fact, she liked to imagine all of the grand things that Hwan had eaten as a soldier in the army of the Democratic People's Republic of Korea. She often thought of Hwan sitting at a long table with other soldiers, eating a large bowl of both rice and beans for supper. Father was proud of him and so was she—proud and glad that he had made a sacrifice to join the military earlier than others, thereby honoring their Dear Leader, General Kim Jong-il.

Young Soon and her late husband were loyal to the Democratic People's Republic of Korea. She watched her husband die of starvation five months earlier. She tried to crowd out the horrible pictures of his demise with the better pictures of her brother Hwan defending the General Kim Jong-il, the embodiment of health and strength. The DPRK was honored at her husband's funeral—just the way her husband would have wanted it. The loud speaker proclaimed, "Though this body is deceased, the spirit of the revolution still lives." All of the townspeople chanted the words together until Young Soon could feel the words throb in her heart.

She sighed as she remembered her vow at his death. "I will live as the daughter of the General and Mount Paekdu."

One day she wanted to make the journey that every North Korean was expected to make at least once in their lifetime to Mount Paekdu, the birthplace of Kim Jong-il.

At night, when all was dark and quiet, Young Soon often felt surges of anger at her husband for leaving her here alone and starving. She considered killing herself. But how could she abandon her fatherless children? Watching Nam Gil weaken more each day was greater torture than her own hunger. He was a faithful, good son. All of her family was proud of him. Now most of them were gone. All but Ja and her husband.

Discouragement weighed heavy in her heart. Where was the hope for laughter today? She stopped on the road just then to catch her breath.

"All right, Sister?" asked Ja.

Young Soon nodded.

"What are you thinking?" asked Ja.

Young Soon looked into her sister's eyes, peering deep into the soul of the one person in the world that she trusted with her most treasured thoughts. "I want to hear my children laugh," she admitted.

It was a sacred wish and Young Soon did not want her sister to think she was foolish.

Ja sighed deeply, took Young Soon's arm and began walking again. "A noble ambition, I suppose, Sister."

Young Soon was glad that her sister did not scorn her dream. Young Soon thought perhaps it sounded ridiculous to want her children to laugh when she couldn't even feed them. She hung onto her dream—but first she must find food.

Her thoughts were heavy but her feet would move ahead. Her only hope for survival was a new promise from her late husband's boss—if she attended the two political meetings every day with the workers at the mine, she would be considered for a seven day ration of food each month. She may as well catch a star in the sky as to eat a meal of beans with rice, so she would not let herself be tempted into dreaming of a full rice bowl. She ran her fingers along the seams of the rice bag that once bulged with rice. Today she hoped to fill it with a root or a fresh skin of tree bark to boil into soup for her children. Perhaps the little moneys earned by her husband last year would earn enough to include corn flour or a bit of rice. She'd use the corn or rice to make gruel. The soup would make the food stretch out for more days and bring some nourishment to her family. Every day she fantasized about what sort of food she would receive with her rations.

"Stop thief!"

Young Soon's heart jumped! She looked—just ahead was a man writhing under the butt of a soldier's rifle, clutching green ears of corn in his arms.

"We are starving! Let me feed my children!"

Young Soon gasped. She knew that voice—it was her neighbor, Chung-Ho. Young Soon looked over at her sister. Ja's eyes were bulging with disbelief. The penalty for arguing with a military soldier was death.

"Traitor! Infidel!"

"I only want to feed my children," Chung-Ho cried. "Please, I beg you. Only a few ears of corn."

His eyes were wide and pleading. He looked half crazed and she pitied him. But she knew that Chung-Ho was the type of man who would lie about her and turn her in to the authorities just to get some food.

Young Soon stood beside Ja and watched. Any show of sympathy or remorse would bring them under suspicion with the guards. Young Soon trembled. The coal mine siren blared, whoop—whoop—whoop—. The soldiers carried the man to the office. As soon as the soldiers' backs turned, two old women quickly scooped up the ears of corn on the road and stuffed them in their shirts. Young Soon admired their bravery. And she knew that the women would share an ear of corn with her and Ja tonight—a bribe to keep her and her sister from reporting their theft to the guards.

Tanching Village, China

CHAPTER 5

Restless to begin her journey, Mei Lin slept little more than four hours. She tiptoed out of bed at 4 a.m., lit her lantern, and went outside to the brick outhouse to relieve herself. Sometimes she missed using the convenient toilet at Mother Su's apartment in Shanghai. But she had grown up squatting over a hole in the brick outhouse. Father kept a bucket in the corner so that the human dung could be used to cultivate the gardens. A rice bag held the toilet paper that was later burned outside. All in all, it wasn't so bad.

Back inside, she quietly washed her face and hands, brushed her hair, and changed into her traveling clothes. She'd brush her teeth later. Noiselessly, she pulled her Bible out of her backpack and sat at the kitchen table with the lantern and Bible. First she read John 15, verses that always spoke to her heart about persecution. These Scriptures came alive to her when she was in a Shanghai Prison. Then she turned to Mark 16, the chapter that Liko quoted to her last night. Liko's prayer from the night before washed over her again. Jesus' words burned like fire inside of her, fueled by love—God's love. She thought about her evangelizing trip and smiled. She expected great things, greater things than she'd seen before. Silently, she lifted praises to the One who made the earth and skies. After some time, the sun's rays pushed through the crack underneath the kitchen door. Father stirred, then swung his legs to the floor beside him.

"Couldn't sleep?" he asked.

"Not much," Mei Lin admitted, yawning a little as she stretched her legs in front of her.

Father looked at her Bible, then at his daughter, the warm glow of the lantern light playing at her hair. "You look like your mother sitting there at daybreak with your eyes sparkling in the lantern light."

"Mother prayed before dawn sometimes?"

Father nodded.

Mei Lin knew her mother used to pray before everyone woke up, but she was hoping to draw her father into telling her again. This morning, it helped her to think of praying like her mother. She wanted to feel close to her again before she started her journey.

"Before she went to prison she was usually up before me, sitting at the table reading her Bible and notebooks under the lantern light. You're so much like her, Mei Lin."

Mei Lin felt her cheeks flush under her father's warm approval. "Thank you, Father. I hope to be as good an evangelist as Mother, too."

Father reached for his shirt. "You will be Daughter. Just listen to what Pastor Wong tells you, and then follow the Holy Spirit's voice."

"I will, Father," Mei Lin answered. She went to the stove to start the fire and the tea water, her back to her father, so that he could get dressed. After he left for the outhouse, she readied the pan of water for him to wash his face and hands, and then opened the kitchen door and the window shutters at the far end of the room. The fire was hot enough to begin the rice congee, so she set the pan over the open hole on the stove, mixing the porridge inside of it.

"What are you up so early for?"

It was Fu Yatou, standing at the doorway of her little room, rubbing her eyes in the bright light. Yatou was eleven, but she looked to be about eight. Her small frame hardly looked capable of taking care of Ping's baby, much less Amah's endless list of household chores. Mei Lin even wondered again if her old friend Ping was allowing Yatou to help just because Mei Lin and Ping were old friends. Whatever the reason, Liko felt that this trip would be hardest on Fu and Mei Lin immediately felt compassion for her.

"I was too excited to sleep, I guess," Mei Lin finally answered. "Did you sleep well?"

"I had a dream that you came back," said Fu Yatou. "And we had a tea party."

Mei Lin laughed. "Why, I didn't even leave yet! Oh, Fu Yatou, what did we ever laugh about before you came into our family?"

Fu Yatou grinned, her long nightgown brushing against the floor as she shifted her bare feet on the cool floor. Father came in the door with a stack of wood in his arms.

"Breakfast will be ready in 15 minutes," Mei Lin announced loudly enough so Amah could hear her as she set out a bowl of peanuts on the table. Mei Lin sliced short slender slivers of spring onion and placed them on top of the rice congee porridge. "Do you remember your list of morning chores?"

Yatou stretched her arms high, yawned, and nodded all at once. "Get dressed, collect the eggs for breakfast, bring in the small fire wood from the courtyard, go back out and feed the chickens, start watering the garden until Amah calls for breakfast."

"Good!" Mei Lin was always careful to praise Fu Yatou's efforts. "And what if it's raining outside?"

"Her eggs will get wet," Father teased as he restacked the woodpile.

Fu Yatou rolled her eyes. "I'll put on my rain jacket," she answered. "I'm not that dumb."

"You're not dumb at all," said Mei Lin. "I just want to be sure you are prepared for anything, that's all. And what about Saturdays?"

"Mmmmm. On Saturdays I go to market for Amah—"

"Amah may go with you if she feels like it," Mei Lin reminded.

"Right," said Fu Yatou. "I carry eggs to Mr. Chan to sell at the market. Then I shop for food, come home, and set up the soap and wash basin in the courtyard to help Amah wash clothes."

"And through the week?" asked Mei Lin.

"Help Amah weed the garden and clean house in the mornings, then go help with Han in the afternoons."

"Right!"

Mei Lin frowned.

"What's the matter?" asked Fu Yatou, her eyes wide with wonder.

"I'm wondering if you'll have time to pray or read your New Testament," said Mei Lin. "I want you to stay strong inside, too."

"I won't pray this early," replied the little girl. "But you know I pray every night before I go to sleep. And sometimes I quote Bible verses when I'm rocking the baby to sleep."

Now Mei Lin's eyes widened. "You do? What does the cadre say?"

Fu Yatou clasped her hands together as if delighted with herself. "He doesn't know! But Ping said it's OK."

Mei Lin shook her head. "Be careful, Little One. I don't want you to anger the cadre."

"I'll be careful," Fu Yatou promised. Her face sobered a moment. "I'm going to miss you, Mei Lin."

Mei Lin wiped her hands on the towel and walked over to Fu Yatou, lifting her into her arms. "I'll miss you, too, Little One," she whispered. "I'll pray for you every day. I'll be back in ten weeks. That's only two and a half months."

"Seems like forever," said Fu Yatou, choking back a sob. "Don't forget me."

Tears sprang to Mei Lin's eyes and she turned so Father wouldn't see. "I'll never forget you, Little One. I carry you right here, in my heart always."

"What's the matter?" Amah interrupted. "She broke her leg?"

Mei Lin let Fu Yatou slide down to the floor. "Legs are all fine," Mei Lin answered. Fu Yatou scooted out the door to the outhouse. "How are you this morning, Amah?"

"What does it matter?" Amah shot back at her.

The back of Mei Lin's neck bristled. *Will she ever approve of anything that I do?*

Father caught Amah's attention; his eyebrows winged upward, a silent warning not to persist in a morning tirade against Mei Lin's departure.

Just then, Fu Yatou returned with a basket of eggs, still in her nightgown.

"Girl, what are you doing in the chicken coupe in your night-gown?" asked Amah. "Whatever will the neighbors think?"

Fu Yatou set down her basket and threw her arms around Amah's neck. "I wanted to surprise you," she said.

Mei Lin thought she saw Amah soften momentarily. "Well, I'm surprised all right," she replied.

"This is ready," said Mei Lin, glad to divert the conversation. She used potholders to bring the pan of rice congee to the table, placing a rice bowl, a glass scoop spoon with a curved handle, and a teacup in front of each chair.

After prayer, Father asked, "What time do you meet Fei?"

"I need to be in DuYan by ten o'clock," replied Mei Lin. "We are meeting with Pastor Wong at Pastor Zhang's house." She had already gone over all these plans with Father, but she guessed he needed reassuring.

"Do you have everything you need?" he asked.

"I packed and repacked everything last night," Mei Lin answered. "I know I remembered my hairbrush, toothbrush, toothpaste, soap, washcloth, small towel, two changes of clothes, six sets of undergarments, a rain jacket, the small flowered thermos, a wooden rice bowl, and chopsticks."

"Can't sleep on a rain jacket," said Amah. "What are you going to sleep on?"

"I don't think I have room to pack a blanket," replied Mei Lin. "Besides, it would be so heavy."

"Amah's right, Mei Lin," said Father. "You don't know where you will sleep from night to night."

Amah wiped her mouth with a satisfied look. She was obviously pleased that Father had heeded her advice on the blanket.

Mei Lin hadn't taken a bite of her food yet. Her eyes searched Father's face. "Did Mother take a blanket with her on her journeys?"

"Well, your mother just went to Du Yan Village to stay with friends while she evangelized. Or she'd travel with a team if it was a long distance. You're going to villages you've never been to before to meet people who don't know you. I think it would be wise to take the blanket and maybe the tarp in case it rains."

"Okay," Mei Lin answered. She dared not tell Amah that she would also carry a large red and white plaid rice bag stuffed with Bibles and teaching materials. How would she carry so much?

"What about matches?" asked Father.

"I put a box of matches in the side pouch."

"Are they in something that can withstand the rain?" asked Father.

"I did my best," answered Mei Lin. "We are packing one meal for today and a few meals that will last until we get to WuMa. Fei said we should not take extra food with us because it will only weigh us down."

Mei Lin knew that Father needed to go over all of the details again for his own peace of mind.

"I'll be all right, Father."

"Eat," said Amah, pointing at her full bowl. "You'll need your strength."

Mei Lin smiled. She knew that those words were Amah's show of affection for her. She sprinkled a few peanuts into her congee, picked up her spoon scoop, and took her first bite.

After breakfast, Mei Lin brushed her teeth, using the basin in the dry sink, then carefully put her toothbrush away. Father led everyone out into the courtyard.

Fu Yatou helped Mei Lin fill her thermos with fresh water from the pump while Mei Lin fidgeted with her scarf until it hung perfectly even around her neck. She didn't expect to wear the scarf every day, but today it was important that Father saw it on her.

"We still have this invisible red thread between us," she said, looking into Fu Yatou's eyes. Then she quoted the old Chinese proverb. "An invisible red thread connects those who are destined to meet, regardless of time, place, or circumstance. The thread may stretch or tangle, but never break."

Mei Lin imagined a red thread unraveling from her scarf, stretching out magically to surround Amah, Fu Yatou, and Father. In a flash of memory she saw the same thread float like a kite string to the sky and surround her mother who was peering down on all of them.

Father, unaware of Mei Lin's contemplations, laid a tarp on top of a light blanket, folded it in half lengthwise, and rolled it into a tight cylinder. It wouldn't fit in her backpack, so he strapped the blanket roll on top of the outside of her backpack.

"There," he said. "How does that feel?"

"Heavier," Mei Lin answered. "But I think it will work."

"Let's adjust your straps so that you're carrying the pack lower on your back, not so high and tight about your chest."

Mei Lin let Father adjust her backpack until it really did feel easier to carry.

"Now, you know you can just turn this backpack around and carry it in front if you tire of carrying it back here?"

"I'll do that, Father," Mei Lin assured him. "You've raised a strong farm girl! This is light compared to the large wooden trays full of heavy rice shoots." Father seemed satisfied that she would indeed make it with the blanket added to her pack.

"That toothpaste isn't going to last you ten weeks," said Amah. Mei Lin could still visualize the red thread that went around her shoulders, through her silver bun in the back of her hair. "What are you going to do for food?"

Mei Lin patted the money belt Liko had given her, strapped to her waist underneath her shirt.

"What's that?" she asked.

"A money belt," Mei Lin explained, lifting the hem of her shirt to reveal the waist belt.

"Liko bought it for me at the DuYan Market. He said my money and identity card would be safer there than in my backpack. See? It closes completely so nothing falls out. And it's waterproof."

"Well, what they don't think of," said Amah.

Mei Lin didn't tell Amah that even with the money gifts from a few house church members, she only had 100 yuan to start out on. Their farming village was so poor; most Christians gave food offerings in church instead of money.

Mei Lin looked at her watch. "I should be leaving now."

"Will you stop to see Liko?" asked Father.

Mei Lin shook her head. "We said our good-byes last night, Father. It is difficult to say good-bye in the fields with the whole village staring at us."

Father smiled his crooked smile, apparently amused at her answer.

Mei Lin leaned forward to straighten her backpack. "Fu Yatou, I want one good squeezy hug from you before I leave."

Fu Yatou wrapped her arms around Mei Lin's waist and clung to her. "I'll pray for you every day," she promised.

"And I'll pray for you, too," said Mei Lin. "Our prayers will connect us."

Fu Yatou looked up, her face full of questions as always. "Like the red thread?" she asked.

Mei Lin fingered the scarf. "Yes, like the red thread. The thread is around you and Amah and Father and me, stretching further and further right now while I'm away on this trip. But it will never break. You're stuck with me for life, Little One."

Fu Yatou hugged her once more, and then quickly broke away and stood behind Amah.

Mei Lin bowed toward Amah. "Amah, I hope the next ten weeks will be prosperous for you."

"We will plan your wedding when you come home, Granddaughter," replied Amah. "Li Na and I will be working on the decorations for your wedding while you are gone."

Mei Lin grinned, remembering how hard Liko's mother was working on gaining Amah's approval. But Amah adored Li Na—Mei Lin could tell. "You know we can't marry for another year."

"It'll be less than a year by the time you return, and that's not much time when it comes to planning the biggest wedding Tanching Village has ever had."

"Amah," Mei Lin softly scolded. "I don't need a big wedding."

"Ha! If everyone comes who was at your tea party last summer, it will be the biggest one in years. Then there's Chen Liko's mother and her family, his father's family—"

Mei Lin laughed. "You're way ahead of me, Amah!"

"Just see to it that you come back, Granddaughter," replied Amah. "Be careful."

"I will," Mei Lin replied, and remembering the awful way Amah had seen her leave their home the first time, beaten unconscious by the Public Security Bureau police, Mei Lin leaned over and kissed Amah on the cheek. It felt shocking to do that, but still, somehow, it also felt right.

"My water's boiling," said Amah, and she turned and went into the house.

Mei Lin stared after her, jolted by her grandmother's rejection to the kiss she just gave her.

Father took her by the shoulders. "Your grandmother loves you, Mei Lin. She just doesn't know how to respond to your affection."

Mei Lin shrugged. "I don't understand her, Father. I don't know if I ever will. But I do love her. She still seems so disappointed that I was born a girl. I can't change that, you know?"

"Well, I'm not disappointed," said Father. He drew her close to him and hugged her hard. "I'm proud of you, Mei Lin. No boy could have reminded me of your mother like you do."

A tear slipped down Mei Lin's cheek. She wiped it away with the back of her hand.

"She's here, you know? Right up there, surrounded by a red thread from this scarf."

Father looked up. "I'll miss her more while you're away. I'll miss you both." Father held her out in front of him again. She blinked back her tears and smiled up at him. It was a mystery to her how he could still love her mother so much and yet love Li Na, too.

"I want you to write to us at least once a week, okay?" he asked. "I put envelopes with stamps and paper in your backpack. I even addressed them for you so you would not have to do any-thing but write."

"Ten weeks worth, Father?" asked Mei Lin. "I didn't see you put that in there!"

Father smiled. "I'm still capable of a few tricks now and then, you know. I want you to let us know if you run out of money, OK? And let us know where you are at the end of the journey and we will send you train and bus tickets to come home."

"Father, you can't afford that," said Mei Lin. "God will take care of us, I know he will."

"God can still use your old Baba, now, can't he?" asked Father, his eyes teasing her. Father gave her one more squeeze then let her go.

"You're taking the main road, then the path by the barn and around the mountain?" asked Father.

Mei Lin nodded. "There's nothing to hide on this trip. The cadre thinks I'm going to visit relatives." Mei Lin gave her father one last hug. "I love you, Father. Pray for me."

"Every day, Mei Lin," Father promised as he kissed the top of her head. "I'll pray for you every day, all day long, until you return home to us."

Mei Lin walked through the gate, turning to look at her father once more. He waved just a little. The invisible red thread stretched between them and draped about his fingers. Mei Lin detected a sort of distant sadness in his eyes. She waved back, then shut the latch.

Poydan, North Korea

CHAPTER 6

Young Soon and Ja straightened their hair, removed their shoes, and dropped their empty rice bags just outside the door before entering the meeting room. The room smelled clean and the floors were shiny. Ja paused and bowed deeply before the picture of the Dear Leader and his father as they walked in the doorway of the coal mine meeting room. The slogan, "The Great General, Kim Jong-il, is the Sun in the 21st Century," was etched across the picture. Bowing was habitual. And it was mandatory.

"Thank you Father Kim il-Sung," said Ja. "You have brought life to North Korea." She then turned her gaze to the picture of President Kim Jong-il. "Dear Leader, General Kim Jong-il, you have filled our hearts for you are the Rising Sun."

Young Soon bowed beside her sister. "Thank you, Dear Father, Kim il-Sung. You have taken us in your arms and cared for us as a father cares for his dear child. We are so grateful to you today."

Young Soon heaved forward into a deep bow, a great show of heartfelt emotion for the provisions of their General. Ja wiped away tears of gratitude. The sisters respectfully left their positions and ducked their heads under the low ceiling, then sat on the tiled floor in the back of the dark room. The men used to work ten hours a day, but it was no use anymore. No one could work such long hours on the small moneys they received. Never enough rice. Never a full stomach. But at least they were better off than the rest of the world. It was in the news—the whole world was faltering under the food shortage in the capitalist nations. People in the United States of America, especially, were nearly extinct from starvation. *That's what they get for trying to squash us. Capitalist dogs. Imperialist pigs. We will follow the Great General to the death, no matter how hard the circumstances.* These thoughts gave her some sense of contentment with her own meager rations. At least some of her family was still alive.

All of the men were gaunt and tired, but no one closed their eyes. No one spoke. This was a political meeting and full respect must be rendered or punishment was certain. There was a peculiar tension in the air today—yesterday Chung-Ho had been caught stealing corn. Such offenses were remedied swiftly, so today was the day that the judge's verdict would be announced against the man who stole food to feed his family.

The mining boss introduced the meeting as usual.

"Our Dear Leader, General Kim Jong-il has given us the message. We will protect our own style of socialism. A talbukja is the worst criminal in North Korea and will be dealt with severely."

Young Soon heard the miners talking last week. They said that all North Korean citizens crossing the border to China or South Korea were considered talbukjas, political criminals. There was talk of a group trying to cross, but stories were circulating that whole families were being shot down in the Tumen River that bordered China. Young Soon shuddered to think of such a fate.

"The whole world is still faltering under food shortages, leading to starvation," the mine boss continued. "But our Great General was the first to carry out an extraordinary plan to save the DPRK. At first the capitalist countries resisted our socialistic economics, but the treacherous sanctions of capitalist countries have at last bowed to the Parent General's campaign."

The boss cleared his throat.

Young Soon often wondered if he tired of saying the same things every day. She certainly tired of hearing them, although she couldn't say so. She was afraid to even think the thought because it may find its way to her mouth. She loved North Korea, but the political meetings were full of boring repetition. Her only place of escape was her imagination—something that starvation and death could not take from her. Young Soon trained her eyes to watch the boss while her mind tried to catch that star where beans and rice were part of every day life and the laughter of children could be heard in her Father's house again. Today she dreamed of plunging her stone into the earth and pulling up the red ginseng root that her father loved. She fantasized of finding a patch of ginseng that only she and Ja would share and fine red berries on bushes that used to grow behind her house when she was a child. Two hours passed easily in her imaginary world and, finally, the meeting drew to a close.

"The Great Leader, comrade Kim Jong-il, is the Sun in the 21st century," the boss declared.

Everyone stood to their feet and joined in the final shout.

"Long live the ideologically-sound state!"

"Long live the strong state!"

"Long live our own brand of socialism!"

"Praise Kim Jong-il!" All hands flew into the air, punctuating the word "praise."

"Praise Father Kim-il Sung!"

"Praise him!"

"Praise him!"

Young Soon loved the shout at the end of the meetings. Her heart swelled with love for the Dear Leader and for her beloved North Korea. One thought churned inside of her like a sharp rock in her middle—*Why didn't the boss tell us the verdict?* She followed Ja out the door toward the road that led them to the fields and hillsides where wild grass roots could be found.

Suddenly, a screeching sound came from the loud speaker overhead. "The infidel Lee Chung-Ho was caught stealing from the Great Leader, Kim Jong-il. He is sentenced to death by execution at the police courtyard. All citizens of the DPRK are required to attend immediately."

The national anthem blasted overhead and Young Soon's stomach weakened. She placed her hand on her small abdomen.

"Do not think about the baby now," said Ja. "Come. At least Min-Hee and Nam Gil will not have to watch."

Young Soon sighed. She should be relieved that her neighbor had not been so desperate as to report her or Ja for some made up crime. So many betrayals—friendships broken, families divided, all for hopes of some small coin or food item that was as rare as seeing a bird in the sky. But having to denounce a good neighbor simply because he stole to feed his children seemed grossly unfair. While she loved the Dear Leader, Young Soon wrestled with the unfairness of the famine. The rest of the world was worse off than they, but still she felt trapped by the rumblings of her stomach and the total madness of watching her devoted husband die of starvation. Now—now Nam Gil was sick…Still she held to her belief in the Juche ideology of Kim Jong-il. North Korea would rise above this hunger. Their self-reliance would pay off.

Ja nudged her forward. Young Soon walked, her head down. So much death. She felt sick inside and with all of her heart wanted to run from it all.

People gathered outside the coal mining office in the large cemented courtyard. Uniformed military police roughly dragged the man out into the center of the concrete courtyard and tied him to an execution post.

"Please, have mercy!" Chung-Ho cried. "I love my children!" Soldiers stuffed stones into his mouth and tied his arms and feet to the post behind him. Only his eyes spoke now—eyes wild with terror, searching the crowd, probably looking for his children.

Tears sprang to Young Soon's eyes. Ja put her hand on her arm. It was a warning and Young Soon swallowed hard to show no sympathy for the prisoner.

"Lee Chung-Ho has been found guilty of stealing from the Great Leader. This action is punishable by death."

Three soldiers with rifles stepped forward. Young Soon stared straight ahead with all the others, paralyzed for these few moments by the loud speaker that ran her life.

"Forward!" the Commanding Officer ordered through the amplifiers.

Crunching boots.

"Line up!"

"Ready weapons!"

The click of guns.

"Aim at the enemy!" The voice was louder and angrier now.

"Fire!"

"Fire!"

"Fire!"

"Cease firing."

The man slumped forward. No one moved. A gust of wind scattered a few dry leaves across the concrete.

"You have witnessed how miserable fools end up," the loud speaker blared. "Traitors who betray the nation and its people will die in disgrace. The whole world is still faltering under food shortages, leading to starvation, but the Great General was the first to carry out an extraordinary plan to save the DPRK. All infidels will be punished. The Great Leader, comrade Kim Jong-il, is the Sun in the 21st century."

Young Soon stood at attention with the rest of the people and saluted.

"Long live the ideologically-sound state! Long live the strong state! Long live our own brand of socialism!"

"Praise Kim Jong-il! Praise the Rising Sun of the 21st Century!"

"Praise Father Kim il-Sung. Praise him! Praise him!"

Jiangxi Province, China

CHAPTER 7

Pastor Zhang's house was one of about twelve on the right side of a back street in DuYan. Each house in the row looked like the other, with the back end of each little house carved into the mountainside and the front doors facing the road. Across the street was a dilapidated, abandoned silk factory. Mei Lin hesitated, fingering her mother's scarf that lay softly at her neck and draped over the straps of the book bag on her shoulders. She was on time—ten o'clock. She checked the road for possible onlookers and when it appeared to be clear, she knocked in secret code. Pastor Zhang's mother opened the door and nearly pulled her into the house.

"Mei Lin," she exclaimed after she shut the door. "How wonderful to see you!"

"Hello Mother Zhang," said Mei Lin, smiling easily as she lifted her backpack from her shoulders. "How are you and your family?"

"Very good," she answered. "Fei is waiting for you in the se-cret room."

"Just Fei?" Mei Lin asked. "Isn't Pastor Wong here?"

"No, child. He sent word—Fei will tell you all about it. You look wonderful, Mei Lin. I can see that your marriage proposal has put some color into your cheeks."

Mei Lin felt her cheeks turn warm. "I'll be honored to be Chen Liko's wife."

"What a couple God made in Heaven!" she said, clasping her hands in front of her.

Mei Lin hugged her. "Thank you for your love, Mother Zhang—and your prayers."

Mother Zhang's soft wrinkled hand folded over Mei Lin's and the older woman led her to the little wooden table.

"Here, take this thermos with you into the cave. I just filled it with tea before you came."

Mei Lin smiled. "Thank you, Mother Zhang. You are so kind." Mother Zhang was the most generous woman she knew, and al-ways encouraging—so unlike Amah who frowned upon her every decision. Mei Lin knew her grandmother loved her, but she was al-ways very outspoken in her disapproval of her life choices. In fact, the only decision Amah seemed genuinely pleased about was her engagement to Liko.

Mei Lin laid the thermos aside on the floor and helped Mother Zhang remove a few pieces of firewood stacked against the stone wall by the stove. The whole woodpile came sliding down and there, behind a wooden door, was a hole in the wall that led through a pas-sageway and into the meeting place.

Mei Lin picked up her backpack and Mother Zhang's thermos and stooped, entering the familiar passageway. She kept her eye on the shaft of light in front of her and carefully walked hunched over through the dark, low tunnel, dropping lower as the backpack scraped the ceiling above.

Mei Lin stood erect when she stepped into the secret window-less room that used to be a food storage room. Fei, who was engaged in conversation with Pastor Zhang and his wife, stood to greet her.

Fei was taller than Mei Lin now, her head nearly touching the low ceiling when she stood. She'd cut her hair. Her bangs were short and her hair cropped about an inch above the collar of her light blue shirt.

Fei smiled, her eyes dancing underneath her new haircut. "Mei Lin, how are you?"

Mei Lin smiled in return. "Oh, I am ready to go." Mei Lin hesitated. She had to tell her friend the whole truth. "I am a little nervous about doing so many things we've never done before. What about you?"

"The same," answered Fei as she scooted over to include Mei Lin into their circle of backless stools.

Mei Lin was relieved to finally admit to someone that she was a bit nervous about the evangelizing trip. She and Fei had talked about some details of their trip but really hadn't had the opportunity to make plans as Mei Lin would have liked. Mei Lin was thrilled to have the summer to evangelize with Fei and get to know her. It was Fei that had inspired her to evangelize during her senior year of high school and Mei Lin had admired her zeal for Christ since her first visit to the DuYan house church.

The musty little cave was usually filled with people gathered to worship God. Today it held only the four of them. Mrs. Zhang's hair was graying some and she wore it well over her ears, covering her scar. Mei Lin exchanged greetings with Pastor Zhang and his wife, then pulled up a bench and sat with the little group.

"Pastor Wong wasn't able to come, girls," said Pastor Zhang. "He's been followed by the PSB since last week. He felt that his presence here today would only endanger you as you begin your missionary journey."

"Is he still in WuMa?" Mei Lin asked. "He was going to stay with the Gui family until our Bibles came."

"Yes, he is still in WuMa, but I'm afraid he's not with the Guis. The Guis were arrested last week."

Mei Lin gasped. "Oh, no! Both of them?"

Mrs. Zhang nodded. "Unfortunately."

Mei Lin sighed. The Guis were wonderful people. She had hoped to meet with them again to find out about the orphans she and Pastor Wong and Fu Yatou had visited two years ago.

"What about the Bibles?" she asked. "The Guis were supposed to have the Bibles that we were to take with us."

Pastor Zhang pulled out a black backpack from beside his stool. "Pastor Wong sent you 20 Bibles to begin your work."

Mei Lin glanced over at Fei who was biting her lower lip. Mei Lin refused to let this dampen her faith. "What is the plan?" she asked.

Mrs. Zhang took their hands. "First of all, you must wait to begin your journey. You'll need to leave when the town is busy and people are coming in from the factories and the fields. You will be less conspicuous at that time of day."

Mei Lin swallowed hard. "Okay."

Pastor Zhang pulled a paper out of the front zipper pouch of the backpack and unfolded it. "Pastor Wong sent this map. He has marked five villages that you can evangelize. Of course, the Lord may lead you to go to other villages that aren't included here. We believe that your most important assignments the next ten weeks will come from Heaven."

Mei Lin's throat went dry as Pastor Zhang used a red pen to chart a journey that appeared to go in a large circle heading eastward, then north until it circled southwest to WuMa and finally back to DuYan. She hadn't expected to begin so late in the day—and without Pastor Wong! It would take nearly two hours to climb the steep ravine up the side of the mountain. She tried to imagine setting up a camp so quickly and so close to DuYan.

"What are the small blue lines going here and there?" asked Fei, pointing to the map.

"Water," answered Pastor Zhang. "Try to keep your walks close to the streams so that you are always near a good water supply. You can live for weeks without food, but you cannot live much more than three days in hot weather without water."

"I've never even heard of some of these villages," said Mei Lin.

Pastor Zhang nodded. "Some of them are in the remote mountain areas. Pastor Wong is the only person I know in China with a map that includes these small villages. You will need to be especially careful in the villages that are close to the larger cities."

"What is the blue circle for?" asked Fei.

"The blue circle is around the ZhingCho Village that has a Christian contact in it named Hong. When you get to ZhingCho, ask around the village for Hui Hong. Hong is a Christian. You will give him two of the Bibles because his house church has grown and split into several groups. They will want you to teach there, so this village will be more of a place of rest for you."

"And what about the other villages?" asked Mei Lin. "Does anyone there know that we are coming?"

Pastor Zhang shook his head. "Some of the other villages have never heard the gospel. The house church in WuMa has been praying for relatives and friends in these villages for some time and Pastor Wong charted them on this map so they may hear the gospel. Your evangelizing journey will be an answer to the prayers of many in WuMa."

"The Guis were wise enough to leave the Bibles with another family in the church. When you go to WuMa, you are to gather a pile of stones and leave them on the back doorstep of the Guis home. Do you think you can find it again?"

Mei Lin nodded. "I think so. I memorized the address."

"Okay," said Pastor Zhang. "Pastor Wong will be watching the back door of that house every day. When he sees a pile of rocks there he will know that you are in town. He will leave instructions on where to meet him under that pile of rocks."

"Isn't that dangerous?" asked Mei Lin.

"The Christians have no plans to use that home. I think it will be safe. Also, here is a cell phone number. You may call Pastor Wong from the bus station if you have the opportunity. However, the cell phone number belongs to a family he's staying with and they often change the number when they suspect they're being watched. He wants to use the pile of rocks, so you have an alternative plan."

Mei Lin took the paper with the number on it. The gravity of the situation descended over her. Any one of them could be arrested and imprisoned before the summer was over.

"Memorize the number and dispose of it right way," said Pastor Zhang.

Mei Lin nodded. She recalled the first time she met Pastor Wong in prison. She was a prisoner at the time, too, scrubbing his filthy prison floor. He was passed out on the floor, his fingers swollen to three times their normal size. She'd used the clean bucket water to wash the blood away from his fingertips and soothe the swelling. As soon as Pastor Wong came to himself, he told Mei Lin that God sometimes does not deliver us from prison, but gives us the Gethsemane gift, the gift of enduring hardship and suffering as Jesus did in Gethsemane and on the cross.

"I wish we could send you girls on your journey with a cell phone," said Mrs. Zhang. "One day perhaps we'll have the funds to purchase one to share between our churches."

"Well, the villages these girls are going to may not have electricity," said Pastor Zhang. "A cell phone is useless unless it is charged frequently."

Fei shifted on her little bench, then glanced at Mei Lin. "How will we know whom to talk to in the mountain villages?" she asked.

Pastor Zhang smiled. "A few of the villages may already have heard the gospel. We don't know. It will take you ten days to get to the first village. You will have to hike through miles of wooded areas over the mountainside. I don't know if you'll see other villages on your way or not."

"Ten days?" asked Fei.

Mei Lin was surprised, too. First of all, she did not expect to begin the trip without Pastor Wong. And now to discover that the first journey will take ten days with perhaps no villages to visit in between. She'd never been alone in the mountains like that before.

Pastor Zhang didn't seem to notice their hesitation and continued. "When you get to a village, if you can find a Christian, ask them if you can stay in their home. If you can't find any Christian, then talk to a person you meet and if they believe in the Lord, then ask, 'Can we stay in your home?' We hope they will say, 'Yes, you can stay in my home.'"

"And if they say no?"

"Ask the Holy Spirit to show you where to go," Pastor Zhang answered.

Mei Lin drew a long breath. She expected a difficult journey, but to boldly ask to stay in the home of someone she didn't know would take a lot of audacity. Something else occurred to her that she hadn't realized before—she was relying on going to WuMa first, a town that was familiar to her. She felt fear flush over her and quietly rebuked its power.

"Some evangelists sleep in open fields or barns when they cannot find another place," said Pastor Zhang. "After you are there a few days and you have one convert, ask to meet their neighbors and relatives and then when they invite their families to their home, you can spread the gospel this way. How much money do you have?"

Mei Lin fidgeted in her pocket for her money. "One hundred yuan."

Fei pulled out her money. "I have fifty," she said.

"Good," said Pastor Zhang. "If you're careful, this much money may last you the first four or five weeks. Try to take the cheapest buses or walk. Save your money for food. Brother Hui Hong told

Pastor Wong he would take an offering for you when you arrive in ZhingCho in about five weeks."

"ZhingCho—the village with the blue circle around it?" asked Fei.

"Right," replied Pastor Zhang. He shifted on his bench then leaned forward, his hands clasped in front of him. "Sisters, this journey may be quite dangerous. You may not have a place to sleep some nights or food to eat."

Fei and Mei Lin quickly exchanged glances. Mei Lin thought about the verses she'd read in John 15 that morning. John warned believers that those who love God will have both persecutors and followers. A smile played at her lips. For her, the eternal gain of followers far outweighed the risk of persecution.

"There are risks," Mei Lin finally said. "But that's what it's like to be a Christian in China."

Pastor Zhang smiled. "Pastor Wong told me that God is using miracles right now to bring many souls into the kingdom around WuMa. A man who was sick and near death was healed and his whole family came to the Lord."

Mei Lin remembered Liko's prayer the night before. Her face was all smiles. "That's wonderful!"

"That's not all." Pastor Zhang continued. "It's reported that in a meeting in WuMa, a child who was deaf and dumb suddenly yelled out. When the family asked what was wrong, he said, 'Jesus,' for the first time. His parents and all of their extended family were saved after this miracle."

Mei Lin couldn't imagine being a part of such a spectacular phenomenon. "Pastor Zhang, how does one make such a miracle happen?" Mei Lin asked. "I don't know what to do."

"Jesus did say that we would do greater miracles than He did," said Fei. "But I've never seen a miracle."

Pastor Zhang stroked his chin thoughtfully, stretching and crossing his legs out in front of him.

"I have never seen a miracle like this either, sisters," he replied. "I have seen the sick recover in a matter of days or weeks, but never instantly. And I have seen God answer the prayers of the saints who needed food or money. Yet I've never seen healings or signs or wonders. But it is in the Bible. After talking with Pastor Wong, I believe that it is truly something that God wants to do in China. Even in all of the world."

Mei Lin listened intently. Neither Liko nor Pastor Zhang had told her how to perform such a miracle. She wondered if God expected her to do such miracles. She cringed. *Where do I start? What do I do?*

"We will listen to God," said Fei, interrupting her thoughts. "And we will read the Bibles—we have twenty of them! God's word will help us to understand."

Mrs. Zhang smiled. "Your courage is admirable, girls," she said. "Mei Lin, did you hear God speak to your heart while you were in prison?"

Mei Lin looked into Mrs. Zhang's eyes, her heart full of the bittersweet memory. "Yes, He spoke. He told me that this would be my ministry. I asked Him how it could be my ministry when I was in a prison cell all alone and there was no one to minister to."

"And did God tell you what to do?" asked Mrs. Zhang.

"Not right away," Mei Lin answered. Now she looked at Fei, realizing the point that Mrs. Zhang was trying to make. "He told me several days later by giving me an idea to ask the guard if I could wash floors in the prison."

"Exactly," said Mrs. Zhang. "You ask and expect God to answer at just the right moment."

Pastor Zhang fingered the Bible in his hand. "And remember that if it's in this book, it can be done again—Jesus said so."

"And Jesus said we would do even greater things," Fei put in. Her smile brought courage to Mei Lin's heart. I'm ready!"

"I'm ready, too," said Mei Lin, holding up a map. "Where do we go first?"

"Here," answered Pastor Zhang, pointing to the map. "Ho Ting Village. You'll head east on this road, then northeast, then circle to the left stopping at each of these villages until you come to WuMa. If you spend about five days at each village, that will give you enough traveling time to arrive in Wu Ma in five weeks. Pastor Wong said the first village, Ho Ting, is a ten-day walk from here. You'll need to find a place to sleep along the way."

Mei Lin nodded quietly. She was willing to make such sacrifices.

"We want to pray for you now," said Pastor Zhang. "The Holy Spirit spoke to my mother last night. I will go get her."

Pastor Zhang disappeared out of the cave while Mrs. Zhang helped the girls pack the Bibles deep into their book bags, hiding them underneath their clothing and towels.

Mother Zhang finally hobbled in, the pastor behind her. She bent over until she came to the interior of the room and Mrs. Zhang brought a chair for her. Her eyes were intense and she leaned forward as she spoke. "In Acts 6 and Acts 13, the Holy Spirit instructed the church leaders to send out their missionaries and even their helpers by laying hands on them so that they are sent out in obedience to God and under His authority. You will need the power of God to preach the gospel."

Mei Lin's heart leaped inside of her. She felt privileged to be "sent out" by the honorable Mother Zhang and Pastor Zhang, her son.

"Should we kneel?" asked Fei.

Mei Lin slipped off her stool and knelt. Fei knelt quietly beside her.

Mei Lin closed her eyes. She felt a hand on her head and one on her back.

Pastor Zhang prayed first and then his mother began. "Mighty Jesus, I ask You to grant Your handmaidens, Mei Lin and Fei, Your wonderful power from on high. Oh, Lord of Heaven's armies, send them out today, equipped to preach Your glorious gospel with signs and wonders following."

Mei Lin had never heard such powerful praying. The elder Mother Zhang seemed to command Heaven rather than plead with God for help. Mei Lin trembled, although she didn't feel afraid.

"Dispense angel armies to go, go, go, out ahead of them to prepare the way," she continued praying. "Mighty God I believe they will return with a great harvest of souls for Your kingdom. We ask for protection in the darkness and light on their path."

When Mother Zhang paused, Mei Lin quietly prayed, "Lord Jesus, show us how to use Your wonderful power that Mother Zhang is asking for. Liko believes this will happen, but I don't know how to do it. Help us! I want to preach Your gospel with signs and wonders following."

"Yes, Lord," Fei agreed.

Mother Zhang took one of their hands in each of hers and stared deeply into their eyes. "Daughters, you preach the power of the cross, the power of the blood of Jesus, the power of salvation in His name. Remember, God's word says, 'These signs will *follow* them that believe.' You preach Jesus. Preach and believe and the signs will follow."

Mei Lin nodded, realizing that her heart hadn't yet fathomed what her ears were hearing. Her faith would have to be simple.

"I believe," she answered.

~

The sun's orange disc hung low in the sky when they left Pastor Zhang's house. Mei Lin looked down at her shoes, wondering what they would look like when she returned home in August. She adjusted her backpack, re-checking its contents again in her mind....

Tomorrow she planned to tuck her mother's scarf into her book bag, but she was glad to wear it today. She waved it in front of her, turning it from side to side, letting the warm glow of the setting sun finger the fine silk threads. The center of the scarf showed soft shades of green leaves curved in and out of each other against the aged ivory cloth. The red lotus blossoms floated in a pond of rich blue color at each end. The details were embroidered, not printed, into the material.

"That is beautiful," said Fei. "Where did you get it?"

Mei Lin smiled, still watching the red threads dance on the water pattern as they walked. "It was my mother's." Her voice was just above a whisper. It was certainly the most beautiful item she owned, but its beauty didn't make her whisper. This scarf made her feel closer to her father and mother. This evening she wanted to feel connected not only to her mother, but to her mother's journey. Deep inside she willed her mother's courage to come—it was her heritage. But try as she might, she did not feel brave or courageous or even close to her mother right now. The turn of events had startled her and each step she took toward the steep ravine was a step of courage.

Face your fear, she chided herself. *One step at a time, walk toward that giant.*

She imagined her own mother climbing the same steep slope and wondered if she and Fei were finishing a walk that her mother started.

Fei felt the edges of her scarf. Mei Lin thought her friend looked older with new haircut. Her bangs were high and, although her black hair was cropped short above her collar, the front seemed to naturally flip forward toward her face. Besides, Fei was taller and not as skinny.

"Is it real silk?" she asked.

Mei Lin nodded. "When my father and Amah gave it to me last summer, they said, 'An invisible red thread connects those who are destined to meet, regardless of time, place, or circumstance.'"

"I think that may be prophetic," said Fei as she adjusted her backpack.

"Prophetic?" Mei Lin asked.

"You know," said Fei. "Elijah's mantle fell on Elisha after Elijah went to Heaven. Your mother's scarf falls to you."

Mei Lin smiled at her friend's insight. "A lovely thought," replied Mei Lin. "I was just thinking that perhaps Mother's journey has been passed down to me. But I'd forgotten about Elijah's journey that was passed to Elisha."

"Elijah's journey, but also Elijah's power," replied Fei. "I don't understand it entirely, but there was something about Elisha taking the cloak and not only covering himself with it, but striking the water and seeing it part. He went in the power of the God of Elijah and God met him."

Mei Lin shivered, despite the heat. She'd heard that her mother had started several house churches in DuYan and surrounding villages. Her mother brought Bibles and teachings and literature to these churches. Would daughter follow mother? Or did this journey only belong to her and Fei?

"This way," said Fei, pointing to a dirt path that veered off of the main road and up the mountainside.

Neither of them talked during the steep climb, saving their breath for the arduous hike. Mei Lin's back was soaked with sweat. The backpack rubbed against her lower back, making it itch. Placing one foot high in front of the other, they marched upward for over an hour.

"Thirsty?" Fei finally asked, panting for air. They had reached a sort of landing, the only resting spot on the steep climb.

Mei Lin nodded. The girls stopped, released their backpacks from their shoulders and dropped to the ground. The sun was just above the horizon, but they could see the path well enough. As she drank from her canteen, Mei Lin watched the village below. People shuffled about, some watering their gardens while children gathered to play. Mei Lin saw the white hair of elders rocking just above the ledge of several courtyard walls. She smiled. *I wonder what Amah is up to right now?*

When her heart finally stopped pounding, she cupped a small bit of water into her hand and splashed it on her face.

"We're more than halfway up," said Fei.

Mei Lin drank more from the metal canteen. "Let's go," she said.

They reached the top half an hour later, just as the bright orange disk began to sink beneath the horizon. The steep mountainside ended abruptly and a camp site was in front of them. Charred wood and rocks were surrounded by larger rocks.

"People must climb this mountain for sport, have a picnic, and then return to DuYan before sundown," said Fei as she knelt in the dirt, her hands on her knees. "It's strange. The clearing looks used, but there are no pathways to explore."

"Which means we may be going into woods where no one has walked for years," said Mei Lin. It was getting dark now and they were in the center of a densely wooded area, without a path to follow. They walked away from the ledge of the ravine and Mei Lin pulled her compass out of her front pants pocket. As Fei held the flashlight, she checked her compass, holding it next to the map.

"Pastor Zhang said to head east when we got to the top."

Mei Lin checked her compass again. "That way," she said.

Although the dark woods held its own set of dangers, Mei Lin was glad to begin their journey here. Surely no Public Security policemen were up here, guarding the dark woods or an empty cliff!

Using their flashlights to find their way, it took ten minutes to find the road heading east; only it didn't look much like a road at all. There were two parallel dirt paths with tall grass growing between the paths. It appeared that no one had traveled the road for weeks. Certainly, they were the only travelers on the road tonight. Fei walked on the right path and Mei Lin on the left. The grass tickled her legs now and then, reminding her to step over a bit.

"Do you think we've gone far enough?" asked Fei.

Mei Lin looked behind her. "I think so."

They veered off the path and walked toward the sound of the nearby creek, flashing their lights all around as they searched for a place to camp. Within minutes, they chose a place near the creek and Mei Lin built a fire. Fei spread her plastic tarp on the ground and the girls laid their sleeping bags on top of it. Mei Lin piled sticks near the fire, extra fuel to throw on in the middle of the night. It was warm enough this time of year, but she knew the fire would keep wild animals away from them. Mei Lin swatted at a bug that tried to crawl in her ear. *I wish the fire would keep the bugs away.*

She was not the type to enjoy sleeping outside, but she was determined not to be afraid of it either. The fire gave her some comfort and a sense of controlling her surroundings while sleeping in the middle of nowhere.

Darkness fell and Fei read aloud from her Bible by firelight. Mei Lin swatted at a buzzing sound near her ear, then snuggled down into her blanket, keeping only her feet inside while the rest was flapped back off of her. She stretched her thin legs out in front of her. It felt good to lie down. The fire crackled and popped now and she breathed in the smoky-warm air. Her legs ached from their climb, but her heart soared with anticipation of the journey ahead. Pastor Zhang said it was a ten-day journey to Ho Ting. She wondered what adventures lay ahead and how the Holy Spirit must be preparing people from each village for the gospel. Her mind finally settled down and she fell asleep listening to the crackling of the fire and soothing sound of Fei's voice as she recited Scripture.

Poydan, North Korea

CHAPTER 8

Each day they followed the other villagers farther up the hill than they walked the day before searching for roots, bark, anything they could dig out of the ground. By the time Young Soon and Ja picked the grass today, the sun was beginning to set. Neither sister liked walking home in the darkness, so they tried to hurry home, arm in arm as usual, each with a bag of grass swinging at their sides. She was grateful that the walk home was downhill, at least until they reached the village. Young Soon keenly felt the hunger tonight. *Will the rations ever come in?*

Her body rejected the awful boiled grass. Like Nam Gil, she now threw up almost every time she tried to eat it. Young Soon patted her abdomen and then adjusted her arm so that Ja's sharp elbow would stop jabbing her in the side.

"Have you felt movement lately?" asked Ja.

"Not lately," Young Soon answered.

"Perhaps he is tired, like his mother?"

"Perhaps," Young Soon answered. She could not see Ja's face very well in the dark, but she could feel strength coming from her sister. How she loved Ja! She could not imagine how unbearable Poydan would be without her sister. Mother would be glad to know that they help one another—she always used to tell them to watch out for one another when they left for school as children. Young Soon tried to picture those days again, but jaws of hunger bit at her stomach and her thoughts returned to her own children. What would become of them if—if she died? She and Ja spoke of it before, when Ja's baby was so tiny and helpless. At that time both sisters vowed to care for the other's children should something happen to them. Now—now things were different. Ja and her husband had little food. Her husband may not agree. Many uncles had abandoned their nieces and nephews. Even fathers had left families because they could not provide for them. Young Soon was proud that her own husband had stayed by her side to the death. His example gave her courage to do the same for their children. But the weakness and grass sickness had worsened and Young Soon's thoughts of her children being left alone frightened her. She decided that now was the time to talk to Ja.

"Ja, I wish to ask you something," she began.

"Yes?" her sister replied.

"I am concerned about my children—"

"Ha! That, my dear sister, is an understatement. Isn't this why we walk together each night?"

"What do you mean?" asked Young Soon.

"Young Soon, isn't it your children that cause us to drag our way across town to the political meetings? We do not go for us, we go for the children, for Min-Hee and Nam Gil." Ja waited until she could catch her breath, then they continued to shuffle slowly forward. Finally, she spoke again. "Without your children, I would not have had the heart to continue living after my own little Eun Ae died." A sob caught Ja's throat just then and Young Soon held her arm a little closer. "I had no reason to live."

Young Soon stopped out of respect for her sister's sorrow. "I could not live without you, Ja. I need you now. My children need you."

Ja nodded her head. "I know, I know."

Young Soon squeezed her sister's arm just a little. "Her life here would be so miserable. Perhaps—"

"Don't say it," Ja said. "Don't say it. I do not have one child. Not one."

Young Soon tried to understand. She had two children when Ja's only child had died. She hoped that her sorrow would be tempered in that at least her little Eun Ae was no longer suffering. But Ja's suffering was more intense without her baby.

"I am sorry," Young Soon replied. The two started to walk again. They rarely talked during their food trips because it expended valuable energy. But tonight Young Soon had to have an answer from Ja's lips.

Her heart pounded as she blurted out, "Will you take care of Min-Hee and Nam Gil if something happens to me?"

"Why, of course, Young Soon! We already talked about this. Why do you ask me again?"

"Because—because your little Eun Ae is not here and I cannot return the favor. I have nothing to give you. And your husband—"

"You have given me hope, Young Soon," said Ja as she patted her hand. "And as for Chul-Moo, we have already discussed it."

"Oh, thank you, Ja," Young Soon cried. "I am so relieved. I am so relieved!"

Her sister's promise to help her children brought a ray of hope to her soul. Nothing worried her more than leaving them all alone to survive without her.

They were nearing the village now. Young Soon could see the outline of the cornfield near the police courtyard. A few stars speckled the darkening blue sky as the last strip of orange daylight disappeared over the mountain. Young Soon loved this rugged land. *If only I had a full rice bowl...*

By the time they reached the police courtyard, the half moon was rising in the distant sky above her house. The police were having some sort of party. Small tables and chairs were scattered about the courtyard, the same courtyard where Lee Chung-Ho was shot the week before for stealing corn. The sisters stood in the shadows across the street and watched. There was a stand with drinks on it and a few policemen stood around talking. Young Soon smelled a wonderful fragrance.

"What is that smell?" she whispered.

"Meat," answered Ja. "The government must have given them meat."

"Why? Because they shot the man who stole the corn?"

"Shhhh," Ja cautioned.

The smell of the meat made Young Soon feel crazed inside. She suddenly imagined herself running through the courtyard and grabbing a handful of their party food and running for her life. Ja pulled her arm.

"Don't think about it, Sister. Let them have their meat. If the government gave them food, maybe our rations will be here tomorrow."

The thought of the rations calmed Young Soon. She had labored for weeks to make it to the political meetings to get her rations.

"The Dear Leader will not forget us," said Ja. "Come on."

"Wait!" said Young Soon. Young Soon watched as two of the officers went from table to table and lit small lanterns. The entire courtyard looked beautiful under the lantern lights. It was as though the sky above had fallen down onto the courtyard and settled there, each starry lantern twinkling its small radiance into the darkness. "It's beautiful, isn't it?" Young Soon whispered. "It's as though the stars fell from the sky and settled all around the courtyard." The courtyard was filling up with people and Young Soon watched as the second officer lit another lantern. He hung this lantern on a line that ran across the center of the courtyard. The other officer did the same until an entire line of lanterns dangled above the tables and chairs. Young Soon watched until the officers ducked inside the headquarters to do something else.

She drank in the smell of the cooking meat. Her stomach jabbed her and her mouth watered. She had an awful taste in her mouth. As she and Ja continued their walk home, she tried to take her mind off her rumbling stomach and thought instead about the officers and the lanterns. For the first time since she was a child, she wondered who put the light in the stars? And who hung them up there above the trees? In school she learned that the sun itself was a big star. *Isn't Kim Jong-il the Sun of the 21st century? Doesn't he call himself the Rising Sun? Did Kim Jong-il put the stars in the sky?*

Young Soon clung to her sister, her eyes transfixed on the stars and the distant moon. *A man has the capability of lighting a lantern on the earth. But does any man have the capability of lighting a star in the sky? Does Kim Jong-il really possess this power?* Young Soon adjusted her sack of grass that hung on her arm.

"Who hung all of it?" Young Soon asked her sister.

"All of what?"

"That," said Young Soon, pointing upward. "Who lit the stars and hung them up there?"

Ja laughed. Young Soon savored the sound of it so much that she barely heard her sister's reply.

"What did you say?"

"I said that it certainly wasn't one of those police officers," Ja answered.

They were at her front door now. Young Soon looked one last time at the stars. "Good night," she said into the darkness.

"Good night," answered Ja.

But Young Soon was talking to the stars. After Ja was gone, she glanced once more into the sky. "Oh!" There! A bright star shot across the sky, quickly arched over her town and then disappeared behind the mountain. An exhilarating rush of hope shot through her middle. *Perhaps I will catch a star,* she thought as her eyes watched the mountain where the star disappeared. *Perhaps we will eat from a full rice bowl tomorrow.*

Jiangxi Province, China

CHAPTER 9

"Oh, my legs!" cried Fei. "Do yours hurt, too?"

Mei Lin nodded as she sat up on her sleeping bag and rubbed her calves. "I guess we've been working them hard—three days of continuous walking. I woke up with leg cramps last night."

They were fasting through breakfast, so it was easy to clean up. The girls quickly put out their fire and rolled up the tarp. Mei Lin wanted to get an early start, so they began their walk while the sky before them cast a pink glow over the pathway. Had the path not been carved out, the dense forest would be twice as dark and foreboding. Within time, the pink faded into dazzling sunlight pushing rays here and there through the tree branches ahead.

Mei Lin thought she had never walked so much in her life. The stream became a friend, always nearby, gurgling assurances to them as they walked. By noon, the bottoms of her feet burned from the friction, matching the burning hunger in her stomach. Blisters were forming on her feet.

"Ready to take a break?" she asked Fei.

Fei nodded. She'd been unusually quiet all morning.

They veered off the path to a flat rock by the stream. Mei Lin took off her shoes and socks and wiggled her toes in the air. Fei rubbed her feet in her hands then dangled them in the cool water.

"Do you think they'll toughen up after awhile?" she asked.

Mei Lin nodded. "I think so. Pastor Wong's feet look like tree bark on the bottoms. He said that sometimes his shoes wore out and then he'd travel village to village without any shoes at all."

Fei's countenance fell again. "I'm sorry. I didn't mean to complain."

"You're not complaining, Fei," Mei Lin answered quickly. "I'm just glad we're in this together. I wouldn't want to spend one night out here by myself."

"Do you think we're getting close to Ho Ting?" asked Fei.

Mei Lin frowned. She hated to think about it, but they weren't even halfway there yet. "We have probably six or seven days journey ahead of us."

Fei's countenance fell. "I didn't think we would be in the woods so long."

"We weren't supposed to be," said Mei Lin.

"Our food supply is almost gone," said Fei. "Maybe we should stop to fish in the stream?"

Mei Lin looked up. The sun was high in the sky. She hated to lose a half day's walk to go fishing. So far, the road followed the stream running only yards away from it. They'd met no other travelers and the weather was agreeable.

In the end, her compassion for Fei won out. Perhaps the months of starvation and torture in Shanghai Prison prepared her for this journey. Walking with blisters seemed a small sacrifice compared to starving all alone in prison.

"OK, we can rest here until tomorrow," said Mei Lin.

"My mother packed a little wok with oil and fishing line and a fillet knife. She'd be pleased to know I'm using it."

Fei busied herself linking two sticks to fishing line and hooks, then dug around the bank of the creek for worms. Mei Lin was glad to let Fei do the fishing while she set up camp in the open area near the creek.

Before cooking dinner, the girls took baths and did their laundry in the creek. Mei Lin pushed two Y shaped sticks into the ground and placed a pole in the cradle of the Y's. The girls hung their clothes there near the fire.

In a few hours, the sun slipped below the treetops and the girls fried fish on an open fire. Fei was a good fisherman—she caught enough fish to last them several days! And her spirits lifted considerably.

"You like the fish, Mei Lin?" asked Fei as she put another piece of fish between her chopsticks. "I make it with my mother all the time. She's the one who insisted I bring the little wok and oil and knife for the journey."

Mei Lin thought about the prison rations she had to swallow two years ago. "It's wonderful—anything is better than a few bites of cold kaoliang once a day."

"How did you do it?" asked Fei. "I mean, how did you deal with the hunger?"

"When I felt lonely and scared, I worshiped. Other times the rats came to take my food and I had to fight them."

Fei's eyes grew wide. "You fought rats?" Mei Lin saw her shiver.

"Some of the prisoners I visited wished they had rats to fight. A few of them told me they ate the rats raw just to stay alive."

Fei stopped chewing and her face scrunched into repulsion.

"Sorry," said Mei Lin. "The men prisoners said they tasted good but, for me, the rats and the torture were the worst. To answer your question, Pastor Wong told me about the Gethsemane gift. That helped."

"What's that?"

"He said that endurance is the Gethsemane gift. You experience this gift when, somehow, God gives you supernatural strength to continue glorifying God."

Tears welled up in Mei Lin's eyes and she fell silent. Only the crackling fire spoke for a few minutes.

"What are you thinking?" asked Fei, breaking the hush.

"I wanted to die at the time. I didn't want to endure. I cried that day when Pastor Wong told me about this gift and for the first time I didn't feel ashamed to cry. I cried for my own suffering, but also for Pastor Wong's crushed fingertips and for Liko and Ping. I think—I think I received the Gethsemane gift after that. I had a new grace inside that made the hunger and torture easier to bear."

"I didn't know—that must have been hard. I prayed for you. We all prayed."

Mei Lin nodded softly. "I could feel it."

After dinner, the girls cleaned their utensils in the creek. A few dark clouds gathered above, blocking the sunset. It looked like rain, so Mei Lin pushed long sticks into the ground around them and kept her folded tarp nearby in case they would need to pitch a tent on short notice.

As she settled into her blanket, Mei Lin's thoughts turned toward their missionary work. Now that her stomach was full, her spirit was crying for nourishment! She was hungry to read the Scriptures. She had envisioned the two of them walking into Ho Ting Village full of the Word of God and ready to evangelize. She thought about the prayers that Liko and Mother Zhang prayed, believing God for miracles. She opened her Bible to read Acts 6 and Acts 13, the chapters the honorable Mother Zhang referred to when she laid hands on them and prayed before their journey.

Preach the cross and the blood of Jesus, Mother Zhang said. Signs and wonders will follow them that believe. Preach the cross. Mei Lin pondered her words again as the gray dimmed to black and darkness surrounded them, enveloping her into a deep sleep.

Poydan, North Korea

CHAPTER 10

Ja clung to Young Soon as they made their way to the street. The rations that Ja thought would come the day after the officers' party never came. Young Soon tried to remember the smell of the meat.

The sun hung low in the sky, giving them just enough time to find food before dark. She was glad that the winter freeze was over, but the warmer spring did not bring crops to plant or rain to water the earth and her search for grass and bark never ended.

The two guards in neatly pressed uniforms stood at the edge of the cornfield. She bowed her head as she passed them. Up ahead two elderly neighbors walked falteringly toward the same hill, their heads down. No one spoke as they passed them. The town was quiet, always quiet. No one knows who is a government implant, paid to spy on the townspeople. Years ago, the Kim Choi family was sent to prison—children, grandparents, everyone—because the old grandfather was caught singing a song about Japan.

Suddenly, the loud speaker blared music and they stopped. Young Soon sang. Everyone sang. They all sang the loud speaker music—the National Anthem.

Let morning shine on the silver and gold of this land,
Three thousand leagues packed with natural wealth.
My beautiful fatherland.
The glory of a wise people
Brought up in a culture brilliant
With a history five millennia long.
Let us devote our bodies and minds
To supporting this Korea for ever.
The firm will, bonded with truth,
Nest for the spirit of labour,
Embracing the atmosphere of Mount Paekdu,
Will go forth to all the world.
The country established by the will of the people,
Breasting the raging waves with soaring strength.
Let us glorify for ever this Korea,
Limitlessly rich and strong.

Young Soon was out of breath, so she mouthed the words in the last stanza. No one sang any other song anymore. She and her husband sang the political songs with such fervor twelve years ago when they were teenagers. That's when the rice rations, though small, were steady enough to keep them alive. They believed the loud speaker—they believed the television program at the political meetings. Now Young Soon's stomach told her what to believe. It argued constantly with her mind—her mind was loyal to the Party.

Her steps slowed. Her stomach was hollow and twisted with pain, the kind of pain that took her breath away and landed in her throat afterward. Whenever this happened, she'd taught herself to think about the happier days of her childhood. When childhood seemed too far away, she imagined the airplanes that her father told her about when she was a child—planes that dropped boxes of food from the sky.

I may as well catch a star...

"Shall we rest, Sister?" Ja asked.

Young Soon shook her head, no breath left in her to speak as they walked uphill. Her feet scuffed the dirt road, kicking up dust that went into her shoes. Her energy was lower than she'd ever remembered. She could walk. She had to walk.

Walking was the one thing she could do without the loud speaker's permission. Young Soon put one foot in front of the other and looked back at the loud speaker, daring it to tell her to stop walking. She was too desperate for food to feel anything anymore. Nothing mattered except finding food and walking.

The pain increased. She had to take her mind off of her pain.

When she was little, she remembered watching her mother close the rice door to her bedroom. Within moments, the glow of a soft candle could be seen through the door and Mother would say long prayers to Buddha. When she was small, she wondered why her mother never taught her how to pray to Buddha. Now that she was a mother, she realized that her mother could have been shot for such activity. She was amazed at her courage to do such a thing. Young Soon didn't even tell Ja that she saw Mother praying. If their background was checked, she and Ja would have food rations cut, even though Mother was dead now. Just then a new thought entered her mind—*I wonder if Mother's prayers could help us now?*

A wave of weakness came over her and her steps faltered.

"Young Soon, let's rest," urged Ja.

Young Soon shook her head. "Not now," she insisted. "Later."

Young Soon forced her mind to think about good things. Only good things.

Twenty-five years ago, Young Soon had played with her dolls or drew pictures on fine rice paper her father brought home from work.

Her childhood seemed like a fairy tale now and, on desperately dark days like today, she wondered if all those things really happened or if she'd made them up.

When she was a girl, her great-grandmother told her of a time when food was plentiful and people even ate three full meals a day, rice twice a day, before the Japanese invaded. Young Soon could only imagine such luxury.

More than anything, she longed to hear her children laugh. She had no idea what their laughter sounded like anymore, so she formed pictures in her mind of events that would make them laugh.

She rehearsed the scenes in her mind again and again—airplanes dropping great bags of food from the sky—Min-Hee would surely laugh at that! A new school—oh, that would make Nam Gil laugh. He would come home singing the evils of capitalism and hailing the ideology of their Dear Leader. Perhaps his little face would be full again because his lunches were free.

I need a good deal of imagination to hear laughter again.

Young Soon sighed, inhaling the dry dusty air as she and her sister continued their wordless walk up the barren hillside. She thought of every family member from her childhood days. Famine had nearly swallowed them all. She thought wistfully again of her own mother. What advice would she give her daughters in this hunger trap?

The sisters finally came to the top of the hill. The trees were naked, no green on the branches or bark on the trunk. Ahead of them was another hill, higher than the last. To Young Soon, the hill was as tall as the clouds above them with the stringent personality of the soldiers who guarded the city and the cornfield. But she knew it would be there and she summoned her strength to meet its challenge to climb higher and dig deeper for her supper. Young Soon focused on the tree at the top of the hill. Focus, she told herself. The tree began to swim in front of her and she stared until a dark tunnel formed around the tree. Stars danced—her legs collapsed and the black tunnel swallowed her.

Rural China

CHAPTER 11

Mei Lin bolted upright, her heart still pounding. What sort of dream was that?

The fire was dying out and Mei Lin tossed a few more sticks on the top and stirred the embers.

"What's the matter?" Fei asked in a sleepy voice.

"I had a dream," answered Mei Lin. "It's OK. I'll tell you tomorrow."

Fei rolled over and went back to sleep. Mei Lin was relieved. She needed time to process what she just experienced in the dream. She was in some other country, in a place she'd never seen before. People around her were speaking but she couldn't understand them. She looked down and—she was pregnant! Mei Lin felt for a moment that perhaps it was a cruel trick, considering that she could in no way be pregnant, even if she were married. But another part of her was enchanted with the picture of her swollen midsection. "I have happiness," she said softly into the darkness, imagining herself telling Liko that she was carrying their child.

Mei Lin, you've been in this big forest too long.

But she couldn't pull her thoughts from the dream. In the dream, shortly after she discovered she was pregnant, she was suddenly in labor! Liko was in the dream and he rushed her out of the dilapidated building to where an old broken down car was waiting for them. Liko practically threw her in the back seat and told the driver to go. The driver flew around a circular intersection and down the road. Mei Lin felt afraid because Fei was missing. She cried, "No, go back for Fei." She looked behind her to see Fei standing on the side of the road, waving at them. She wasn't sure if Fei was waving goodbye or waving them to come back and get her. Liko told the driver to go to the hospital fast! Then the strangest thing happened. Mei Lin's contractions came quickly, but without great pain. She felt the urge to push and reached down just below her pubic bone and—Mei Lin savored the memory inside of her—a tiny hand wrapped around her finger. Immediately she felt one with the baby. Although she couldn't see him yet, she knew he was a boy and he needed her and loved her. Then she woke up.

Mei Lin lay in the darkness, cherishing the remembrance of the rounded belly and the touch of the tiny hand around her finger. It distressed her that she left Fei behind in the dream, but then, Fei may have been waving goodbye. She wasn't sure. She wished she could have seen the baby in the dream, but just being pregnant and in labor was such a thrill! She forced herself to forget that she was barren and cherished the dream until she dropped off to sleep again.

The next morning the girls reheated the remaining fish from the night before and then read their Bibles. Fei was quiet again and Mei Lin was glad. She wanted to ask God about the dream. She thumbed through her Bible and read the dreams of Abraham, Joseph, and Jacob. What a thrill it would be to see angels going up and down a ladder! Her dream wasn't that spiritual, but she wondered if it had some meaning.

The more she read the dreams in the Bible, the more convinced she became that God was speaking to her.

Finally, she asked, "Fei, do you think God speaks to people through dreams?"

Fei, who was sitting cross-legged on her fishing rock, looked up at her quizzically. "You mean, today?"

Mei Lin nodded.

"Well, there were plenty of people who had dreams from God in the Bible," said Fei. "I don't know."

"What about today?" asked Mei Lin.

Fei thought for a moment. "I don't know."

Mei Lin grew silent, and a smile glided across her face. *What if?* kept marching through her brain. *What if it were true? What if she was going to have Liko's baby? What if it's the boy whose hand touched hers last night?*

Poydan, North Korea

Chapter 12

Young Soon felt something cool touching her head. But the touch was far away, not close, not next to her skin. *Where am I?* She willed her fingers to move. What's wrong with them? She couldn't find them. *Am I dead?* Panic swept over her.

"Young Soon, you must wake up now. Your children need you." Her sister called.

Nam Gil? Min-Hee?

Another touch. A wet dribble contacted her senses. Young Soon did not know how to command her body to move. It was stubborn and lifeless and somehow outside of her.

Another dribble. Its wetness drew her closer. *More!* She wanted to say. *More!* The dribble continued and Young Soon relaxed. With the calm of a sunrise, her spirit slipped into her body until the shell of thin flesh was filled with all of her, spirit and soul. Light. She felt nothing from the waist down, but she saw light now and there was pain in her chest that went down her torso and into her arm.

Don't let me die!

"Look! She's breathing again!"

It was Ja and Young Soon longed to talk to her. She willed her lips to move. They only parted a bit and let the water into her mouth. It slipped past her tongue and down her throat, watering the sunrise still growing inside of her. Down, underneath the pain, another spirit was there, deeply attached to hers. She thrilled to touch the delicate flower petal—a gentle breath—a living spirit drinking from the spring within her, gripping the light. She held him and drank with him, spirit to spirit, body to body. A boy! She carried a boy! Life! Life is a gift.

"Young Soon, wake up."

Ja was calling her. Young Soon drifted toward the voice.

"Young Soon, Nam Gil wants to talk to you."

Young Soon moved her lips but the sound did not come. She tried again. "I will walk."

"Yes, yes, you will walk," cried Ja. "Do you see Nam Gil, your mother says she will walk?"

Young Soon was settled further into her body now and she was able to tell it what to do.

Open your eyes. There.

Ja's face was in front of her staring at her. "You are awake my sister. Stay awake now. I will feed you some corn gruel."

Young Soon nearly laughed at that. For the first time since she came back to her body, she thought about food! Food was all that one thinks about in this desolate wilderness, yet being detached from her body helped her to see life again—the life of her unborn child, a boy, and she also saw the part of herself that did not need nutrition but coursed through her own spirit and commanded her body.

"Han Chun," she softly whispered.

"What's that?" Ja asked.

Young Soon gathered energy about her to speak again. "The baby—Kim Han Chun, Korean Spring." All of her children carried their father's last name of Kim, but every time she said Han Chun she would remember the day when Ja unwittingly watered the sunrise growing within her, bringing both of them back to light and life. Young Soon knew there was something special about this new little one inside of her. And there was something bigger—someone bigger who gave them entrance into this experience and loved her child. Maybe it was a god…maybe her mother's god. Whatever it was, Young Soon carried a child and she and her child carried a secret, a deep secret that only they knew—Baby Han Chun would grow up to live under a different sky.

"Come, your baby needs some of this corn gruel. Let me lift your head up."

Young Soon tasted the corn gruel. One more swallow. Her sallow tongue exploded with the taste of it. She waited after she swallowed—she could feel her body hungrily attacking this fresh nourishment.

"More?" she asked.

"Yes, yes, there's more," said Ja.

Young Soon ate several bites, concentrating on the wonderful feeling of fullness entering her now. "Where? Where did you—"

"Don't worry, just eat," said Ja.

Young Soon was sure that her sister was feeding her what meager rations her husband acquired for working in the mine that month. It was a true sacrifice for both of them.

"It is Friday, Young Soon. You've been lying here for three days teetering between life and death." Her voice caught as it always did when she was upset. She turned her head and Young Soon heard her crying. "Please don't go. Your children need you. I—I need you."

"I will live," Young Soon answered. "I will live." She wondered if the mine boss was angry she missed the meetings. "Will we still receive our rations? Is it a holiday?"

"Stop worrying about rations," said Ja. "Here is food. Eat it."

"Oh!" cried Young Soon. "The baby! The baby moved!"

For the first time Ja smiled. "Ah, the baby is enjoying his dinner."

Young Soon felt as though she was being filled inside and out. Min-Hee touched her cheek. "Oma?"

Young Soon reached for her daughter's hand and held it to her cheek. "Oma's here, Min-Hee. Have you listened to Aunt Ja?"

"Yes, Oma. Look at Brother."

Young Soon turned her head. Nam Gil was indeed sitting up on his mat! Oh, what a sight!

"Do you see what your sacrifice of corn gruel has done for us?" cried Young Soon. "Oh, my sister, thank you!"

"It is not my sacrifice," she said softly. Then she sent Min-Hee to the door to guard it and she leaned over and whispered. "It is from our brother."

Young Soon was astonished. "Kim Hwan?"

"Yes. He is hiding right now but he will come to see us as soon as I send the message that you are well."

"Oh! Oh, Sister!"

Ja soothed her forehead with the cold cloth. "Help has finally come to us," she said. "Kim Hwan has brought us food. And when you are well enough, we will boil more rice. The rice has helped your children gain strength. Only—we must do it at night while everyone is sleeping."

"Rice?"

"Yes, rice," said Ja. "Go to sleep now, Young Soon. Our brother will come to see us tomorrow night."

I caught a star after all, she thought. Her hand touched the roundness of her abdomen and she slipped into the subconscious realm of sleep.

Rural China

CHAPTER 13

It had been eleven days since they left Du Yan. Although they saw a couple villages far off in the distance, they'd still met no travelers. Father had said that the villages in the mountains were small and far apart. It seemed like another world to Mei Lin. Her shoes were worn down a bit and her feet still burned a little when she walked, but she knew they were close now. She picked up her pace a bit—they would probably come to Ho Ting today.

"Mei Lin," Fei called to her in a singsong voice. "What are you thinking? Tell me!"

"Let's gather our things," said Mei Lin. "I'll tell you as we walk."

Mei Lin shared a few of the berries they picked last night as they walked. Mei Lin had tried to tell Fei the dream four days ago. Today the emotion was building inside of her again. Liko was the only one who knew she was barren. She couldn't tell Fei–she couldn't tell anyone else—that her body was left barren after the beatings in prison.

Despite Liko's comforting words and his continued pledge to marry, she felt plagued with grief every time she looked at Ping's baby. She longed to give Liko a child, to hold her own baby and nurture him or her to life. Her intense desire to have a child mixed with the cold reality of her physical limitations had tormented her since she came home from prison. Today she was an evangelist in the countryside of China—well, she was a camper and a hiker so far. But she was still a woman and, deep inside, she longed to have a child.

"Did I look sad when I was waving at you in the dream?" asked Fei. She seemed more curious than concerned.

"I couldn't tell," answered Mei Lin. "You were too far away."

"Wait! I know! Pastor Wong told us he had a dream one time and God used it to show him that the PSB were coming. Remember that?"

"Yes!" Mei Lin exclaimed. "Yes I do remember! Oh, how could I forget that! He said after he woke up he knew that they were to leave town immediately."

"And he left!" said Fei. "I loved that story!"

"What made it so authentic is that he later found out that the police came to the house after he left and wanted to arrest him."

Fei laughed. "What an incredible story! Pastor Wong is full of great stories."

Mei Lin fell into a bemused silence. Any doubt she'd had that morning melted under the new faith that was growing in her heart. *Faith comes by hearing,* she thought. *And hearing Pastor Wong's testimony has strengthened my faith. I believe that God is talking to me!*

Fei shifted the weight of the heavy Bibles to her other shoulder. Suddenly, she catapulted forward, kicking a large stone in front of her.

"Fei! Are you all right?"

Fei groaned and rubbed her head. "What a klutz!"

"Let me see it," said Mei Lin. Fei moved her hand and there was blood on it.

"Let's get down to the creek," said Mei Lin. "You need to clean that out and get a cold cloth on it."

"Oh, here I am holding us up again," said Fei. She looked as though she were going to burst into tears.

"It's all right," said Mei Lin as she helped her friend to her feet. Fei's short dark hair was mussed and her faced smudged with dirt.

Mei Lin laughed. "You're a mess! Now don't let your faith fall where your feet just did!"

Fei forced a grin. "You're right. Let's see if Dr. Chen's fiancé is a good nurse."

Everyone knew Liko wanted to be a doctor. Even though he was a farmer and a good pastor, a lot of the people still called him Dr. Chen. It sort of acknowledged his sacrifice in giving up his more lucrative vocation to serve God.

Mei Lin pulled out the shirt she laundered the night before and soaked it in cold water.

"Your cut is kind of deep," she said, frowning. "I'm not sure, but I think you may need to have it pinched a little."

"Pinched?"

"Well, I don't see a hospital around here," Mei Lin chided. "Let's just keep this cold shirt on your head and see if the bleeding stops."

Mei Lin made a pillow out of her dry pants and Fei lay back on the flat rock in the middle of the creek to rest her head and help the bleeding stop.

"I feel so stupid," said Fei.

"Stupid isn't in the Bible," said Mei Lin, giggling. "Cheer up."

Mei Lin sat on a separate rock, one of many scattered across the creek, and rested her feet in the water. She loved the sound of the rushing water, the twinkle of light where sunrays touched the ripples. But inside, her heart burned to go forward. Her commission to seek and save the lost consumed her thoughts.

Back on the path, Mei Lin paced herself more slowly for Fei. She carried her own bag on her shoulder and the two of them carried Fei's bag together, each holding one of the straps.

"Mei Lin!" exclaimed Fei. "Look!"

They had just crested the top of a hill and right before them was the village.

"It must be Ho Ting," said Mei Lin. Suddenly, she stopped. "Are we ready?" she asked softly.

Fei shifted her backpack. "I think so," she answered.

Mei Lin drew a long breath. This was happening faster than she imagined.

"Oh, I'm so excited! Let's go."

"Let's see that cut," said Mei Lin.

Fei pulled back the cold shirt. Blood was dabbed on the wet shirt, but it appeared the bleeding had stopped now.

"Wait!" Mei Lin stopped in her tracks. "We can't go into town with all these Bibles! Let's hide all but one of them down by the stream. If the people agree to hear the gospel, we can get them later."

Mei Lin kept her New Testament but hid the rest of the Bibles inside plastic down in a dirt hole beneath some rocks near the stream. They walked into the village with lighter backpacks and lighter hearts. The houses were set up in the old style, stone and mud walls with corrugated tin roofs, the overhang propped up with wooden poles in front and back of the houses. The small houses weren't huddled as close together as the ones in Tanching. The stream they had been following the last two days curved to the right and then to the left. The stream itself appeared to be the main street of the entire village, with all of the houses lined up in front of the stream facing east only yards away from one side or the other.

Amah would like this place, thought Mei Lin. *She would say it had good feng shui.*

Beyond the village, rolling hills of sugar cane and plateaus of rice paddies grew in green symmetry. As they drew closer, they saw the familiar sight of men and women bent over the last rows of rice and sugar cane for the spring planting.

The forest road narrowed to a small path that led to the stream of water. Chickens squawked at their feet, arousing the attention of the woman bent over the stream collecting water. The woman stopped and waited for the girls to approach.

Fei looked at Mei Lin. "Our first convert?"

Mei Lin smiled. "I hope so. Who's going to talk?"

"You are," answered Fei. "She may notice my bleeding forehead and think we are asking for help."

"OK. Here goes."

Mei Lin waved and the woman waved back. *So far so good.*

"Hello," she greeted the woman. "My name is Mei Lin. This is my friend Fei."

"We rarely get visitors in our village," the woman replied. "Where are you from?"

"DuYan," answered Fei.

"I'm from Tanching," said Mei Lin.

"You've walked a long way," said the woman. "I am Jenji Wan. This is my son, Quon Wan."

The little boy hugged his mother's legs, unsure of the new visitors.

"We are wondering if—if anyone in your family is sick or troubled. We would like to pray for them."

The woman seemed taken aback. "Pray?" she asked.

"Yes," answered Mei Lin. "Our God answers prayers. He helps people. He sent us here to pray for you and for anyone else who needs His help."

The woman looked thoughtfully down at her bucket of water. "I know someone who needs prayer. But they are working right now. I will ask them to come to tea tomorrow evening. Will you still be here? Will you come?"

"Oh, yes!" cried Fei.

"What time?" asked Mei Lin.

"Seven," answered Jenji.

"We will be here," said Mei Lin. "Invite anyone else you'd like to the tea. Perhaps we can talk?"

Jenji smiled. "I would like that. But not now—my husband will be home later and we will both hear you talk tomorrow."

Mei Lin and Fei walked further on the path following the stream. Although most people were in the fields, a few young mothers and older people worked in gardens and walked about.

"That was easy," said Mei Lin. "I would imagine news will spread quickly in this small village."

"We have our first speaking engagement!" said Fei. "What will we say?"

Mei Lin laughed at that. "Fei, you are like a little girl on New Year's Day, looking for her red envelopes of money!"

"But that was so easy," answered Fei. "What do we do now?"

"Look," said Mei Lin, pointing across the stream. "Let's talk to that elderly woman."

The girls walked between two houses and then removed their shoes and carried them as they crossed the cool water to where the woman stood inspecting the small sprouts of sugar cane at the edge of the field.

"Hello," Mei Lin called. The woman didn't turn to answer her. Mei Lin thought perhaps she was hard of hearing.

"Hello," she said a little louder.

"She's not going to answer you."

Mei Lin turned around to find a stooped, elderly gentleman walking out of his house. She guessed that he would have been average height had he not been so bent over. He had white thinning hair and wire rimmed glasses that slipped down his nose as he peered over the top of them to look at her.

"What's the matter?" she asked.

"She's deaf," he answered. "Has been deaf since the accident in 1989. Who are you?"

Mei Lin and Fei introduced themselves and then asked again about the woman.

"Mrs. Woo cannot hear?" Mei Lin asked.

By this time the woman had turned and entered into the conversation. She motioned to her ears and shook her head no, she cannot hear.

"She was helping with the harvest in 1989 when someone threw a rock that hit her in the side of the head." The man clenched his fist, his knuckles white. "I wanted to flatten them for hurting her, and I could have back then—that was before my back went out."

Mr. Woo spat on the ground. "It wasn't the first rock thrown her way. They told the police it was an accident, but we knew—everyone knew." He glanced at his wife and she shook her head and looked down.

"She wants to let it go—doesn't want to cause any more trouble. But it's been hard on us since her hearing left. I want to make them pay, but—"

The man looked at his wife. Sorrow etched across her wrinkled face and Mei Lin could see that this was an old conflict that had caused a lot of hurt between the couple. She looked at Fei—this time they should not wait until tea was served.

"I would like to tell you about Someone who walked on the earth long ago and He healed deaf ears and opened blind eyes."

Mr. Woo grinned, his mood suddenly changed. "This is why you came to Ho Ting?" he asked. "To tell stories? We haven't had a visitor here since last fall."

"Yes, we came to tell you stories—true stories," said Fei. "Stories that can change your life."

"I am Chinese," said the old man. "I never turn down a good story. Come, sit down. We will talk."

Mrs. Woo took their hands into hers and squeezed them gently. Then she and her husband walked hand in hand ahead of them. The girls followed the couple into the courtyard where they sat down on stools in the shady area. Mrs. Woo went inside.

Mei Lin looked at Fei, wondering where they should begin.

"I will explain your story to my wife later," said Mr. Woo. "Let's begin."

"You start, Mei Lin," said Fei. "I want to hear you tell the story."

Mei Lin nodded, hugged her legs in front of her, and began.

"In the beginning, there was no earth. See the blue sky?" she asked, looking upward. "Jesus spoke the word, and they were created. The stream that flows behind your house and refreshes you—He created it as well. He gave strength to the water buffalo and put the desire to fly into the little birds. He made flowers to look at and plants to nourish our bodies. Then He made people. The first two people were named Adam and Eve."

"Strange names," said the man.

At that moment, the man's wife came out with boiled water in dainty teacups. Real tea was usually only served after the evening meal. Besides, Mei Lin knew it was all the Woos could afford and it was given with great hospitality. She and Fei bowed slightly in thanks to her. Her husband motioned for her to join them and she scooted forward, across from the girls, and watched their lips.

"Yes, Adam and Eve are not common names in China," Mei Lin agreed. "But God liked their names. The earth was perfect at first. There were no weeds, no fighting, and no sickness. The One who made the earth and skies liked it that way. And He loved Adam and Eve. He left Heaven every evening to come down into the garden He made just so He could talk to this couple. The garden was perfect, and God told them they could eat anything they wanted to eat. Except, they were not to eat from the tree of the knowledge of good and evil."

"Ah, such a tree might bring bad fortune to the people."

"That's right. In fact, the One who made the earth and skies said the people would die if they ate from it." Mei Lin looked at the man's face. He was truly interested in her story, so she continued.

The words flowed and she told him how the One who made the earth and skies sent His Son into the world.

"Why did the One who made the earth and skies send His Son?" asked the old man. "His Son did not deserve such treatment."

"That's true," said Fei. "But the One who made the earth and skies loved Adam and Eve. He loved all the people who've ever lived. And He loves you and your honorable wife. He loves us, too. He came because He wants us all to join Him in Heaven."

"When? How do you get there?"

"When our bodies die," Mei Lin put in. "Our bodies die, but the soul goes to Heaven. Jesus said whoever believes that He is the way to Heaven, that person will have everlasting life. Our bodies will one day die and be buried with our ancestors. But the souls of those who believe in Jesus will go to Heaven to live with Him and His Father forever."

The old man bent forward even farther and put his head into his hands. Then he tilted his head upward and looked down at the girls through his glasses, which had slid to the end of his nose. "And you believe this story is true?"

"Yes," the girls answered in unison.

"And this Jesus healed deaf ears and opened blind eyes?" he asked.

"Yes He did," answered Mei Lin. "The whole story is in the Bible."

"Bible?" he asked. He looked at his wife, using a quick hand signal and then he opened his hands side by side as though he were opening a book. She nodded as though she understood. "Will you excuse me?"

"Certainly," replied Mei Lin. He walked to the back yard near the stream where she first met him.

Mei Lin looked at Fei and then at the old woman. An idea came to her suddenly. She bent over and, using her finger, she drew the picture of a cross in the dust. She drew a stick man over the cross and wrote the name Jesus. The woman looked puzzled, but smiled pleasantly.

Her husband returned with a dusty box. He was blowing dust away and wiping it with his hands. "A cross?" he asked, looking at her artwork in the dirt.

Mei Lin nodded. "God gave us the cross and the cross gave us God. Jesus suffered on the cross and took the punishment for our sins. The Bible tells the story."

Mr. Woo looked all around him and then gently opened the dusty box. "Here," he said. "Is this your Bible?"

"I—I am surprised," replied Mei Lin.

"Mei Lin!" exclaimed Fei. "It is a Bible!"

"Then—then you already knew the story I just told you," said Mei Lin. "May I ask you where you got this from?"

The man sat down on the stool again. "I haven't opened that book for more than fifteen years. A young woman came to our village around 1982. Yes, it would have been 1982 because that was seven years before my wife's accident in 1989. Ah, that was a year to remember, wasn't it? The Tiananmen Square incident and my wife is made deaf by an angry neighbor." Mr. Woo spit on the ground in disgust. "Anyway, the woman told us the story about the God who died on a cross, too. My wife and I lived with our son and his wife. They were young, like the woman preacher, and they believed in the story the preacher told them. This Bible, as you call it, belonged to them."

"Where are they now?" asked Mei Lin.

The man turned his head and looked toward the courtyard gate. "They went out of this gate fifteen years ago, arrested by the PSB."

Fei gasped. "The PSB comes all the way out *here*?"

"The PSB checks on crop production every fall," he answered. "That's when security is tight. We're so far away from everyone they don't usually visit otherwise. Of course, our cadre keeps an eye on things the rest of the time."

"Is that why you hid the Bible?" asked Fei. "You were afraid the PSB would confiscate it?"

"Well, yes, that was a possibility. But we, uh, we never learned to read. So, we hid it so that our son could have it again when he came home. That year, 1985, the PSB happened to come early and found my son and daughter-in-law holding a meeting here for the preacher to speak. Some of the others helped the preacher escape. My son and his wife were not so lucky. Woo Fan and I were preparing tea and food in the kitchen. They did not arrest us. We told them we were not involved."

Tears filled the old man's eyes. His wife searched his face, then tapped his hand to comfort him.

"They were sentenced to twenty years hard labor. They took them to the security prison in Hubei Province." The old man coughed a little. "It's too far away for us to travel. We never saw them again."

Tears filled Mei Lin's eyes. She imagined this young couple, in love with Jesus and with each other, separated for twenty years.

"Then, they will be out in five years?" asked Mei Lin.

The old man looked at his wife and put up five fingers. She nodded.

"We hope so. We send a letter to each of them once a month. We only heard from our son once, about five years ago. He told us to remain strong in the faith." The old man coughed hard and looked the other way. His wife tapped his hand quickly and got up to take the girls' cups.

"I'm so sorry," said Mei Lin. "I was in prison, too. I know how hard it can be."

"In prison?" he asked. The man looked around him to be sure no one was listening to their conversation. Then he whispered, "Please, tell me what it was like."

"Well, not every prison in China is the same," Mei Lin began carefully. She wanted to give this father hope of seeing his son and daughter-in-law again. However, she knew that only the few strong ones made it out of prison after twenty years of forced labor. As Mei Lin told the man of the labor camps, his wife came outside with a slate so he could draw pictures for her, simple pictures that described their conversation when she missed what was said watching their lips.

Tears formed in the old woman's eyes, but true to Chinese form, she did not cry in front of them. Mei Lin told them all that she could, including the story of the prisoners who gave their hearts to Jesus while she scrubbed their prison cell floors.

Woo Lan put his head in his hands and rubbed his head. "How can they be so cruel?" he asked. "I'm afraid my daughter-in-law has died. Even her parents have not heard from her. They blame us."

Mei Lin felt such sorrow for this old couple. She thought her heart would break listening to his story. Imagine waiting for 20 years to see their son when all that every aging parent wants is to hold their grandchild.

"I am so sorry for you and for your son," said Mei Lin. "I don't want to grieve you further by talking about this."

"No, no," he said. "You are the first Bible person who's come to our village since those many years ago. Life goes on. People change. Most have forgotten about the PSB raid. The only reminder we have now is my wife's deafness." Mr. Woo cleared his throat. "She did not deserve their scorn or their attacks. One day, they will pay."

Mei Lin did not feel it was time to rebuke her elder for his anger or his desire for revenge. Instead, she asked, "Did anyone else in the village believe in God?"

"We didn't talk about your God or the Bible book because we were afraid. But we have waited—for our children and for the preacher. She never returned."

"Mr. Woo, did you ever give your heart to Jesus?" asked Mei Lin. "After all your son and daughter-in-law went through, did you believe, too?"

"Our son wants us to believe," he said. "I know that. But no one talked about the Bible or the preacher's stories after the PSB came. Like I said, most of the believers were arrested. Sometimes my wife prays to the God our son believes in. We don't know who He is and we can't read. Most of the people in our village can't read and the ones who can, we do not trust. They may report us for keeping the Bible."

Fei leaned forward. "You can believe right now, today. There's one thing. You have to forgive anyone who's hurt you."

"Our son's mother-in-law did it," he offered. "She's hated us since her daughter was taken to prison from our house for believing in Jesus. But it's not our fault—what can we do? We're poor farmers and now our son isn't here to help us in our old age."

"Will you forgive her?" asked Mei Lin. "Jesus said if we forgive people who've hurt us, He'll forgive us for hurting Him with our sins."

The old man looked at his wife. He motioned to her, explaining that they had to forgive the person who hit her in the head with the rock.

"Woo Lan," someone called from outside. "I hear you have visitors!"

"The cadre!" whispered Mr. Woo. "Everyone is coming home from the field for lunch." He quickly shoved the Bible into his wife's arms and ordered her inside with it. Mei Lin felt prickles go up the back of her neck.

"Cadre Xin!" Mr. Woo called back to him. He stood and slowly walked toward the gate. Mei Lin looked at Fei. "What shall we say?" she whispered.

"What did you tell your cadre in Tanching?" asked Fei. "DuYan is so big that our cadre won't even know I'm gone."

"I'm going to visit distant relatives and old family friends," replied Mei Lin. "But our cadre knows I'm evangelizing."

Fei shifted on her stool. "Hide us, Jesus," she prayed quickly.

"Come in, Cadre Xin." Mr. Woo cordially welcomed the cadre and directed him over to the girls, who stood to greet him.

"News travels fast in Ho Ting," Mr. Woo explained to the girls. "I would imagine that the whole village already knows you are visiting."

"Yes," said the cadre. "And I understand you will be attending a tea tomorrow evening with Jenji Wan?"

"That's right," Fei answered. "We are pleased to meet you, Cadre Xin. Will you be in attendance tomorrow evening?"

The cadre smiled, obviously pleased at the question. "The Wans have asked me to attend, yes. And what brings both of you to Ho Ting?"

"We are traveling for the summer," Mei Lin answered. "I am going to meet relatives and family friends in some of the remote villages. We thought we would stop at Ho Ting on the way."

Silently, Mei Lin prayed he would not probe further.

"It is most unusual for Ho Ting to receive guests," the cadre replied. "Jenji tells me you will be talking to sick people this evening. I will be most interested in hearing what you have to say."

At that moment, Woo Fan appeared with a small tray of tea. This time there were sesame seed balls as well.

Good timing, thought Mei Lin. It had been two years since she was beaten and thrown into prison by Cadre Fang and the PSB. She thought she was fearless, but today fear tingled down her back as she sat before this new cadre.

"Your sesame seed balls are shaped beautifully," Fei remarked. "They look like the baker's cakes in Du Yan."

Mrs. Woo smiled at that and pulled up a stool and sat down. The cadre accepted the hot water and small cakes, sipping and nibbling as he eyed the girls.

"You have no relatives here?" he asked.

"Uh, no. No relatives here. We're just passing through," answered Mei Lin.

"We will be pleased to have you join us for tea tomorrow evening," said Fei. Fei glanced a reassuring smile at Mei Lin. "We only met Jenji this morning. She was gracious to invite us."

"Cadre Xin!" Someone was calling from outside the gate again.

Cadre Xin stood up, taking one last sip of the hot water.

"Thank you, kind Woo Lan, Woo Fan."

Mrs. Woo bowed slightly to the cadre, smiling at his approval.

"Cadre Xin!"

"Until tomorrow evening, Mei Lin; Fei."

Woo Lan stood at the gate, watching after the cadre until he was sure they were gone. He latched the gate and shuffled back to the girls.

"That was close, girls."

"Yes," replied Mei Lin. "I'm afraid we put you under suspicion just being here. I'm sorry."

"No," said Woo Lan. "Don't apologize. I have prayed to the God of my son. For years I told his God that if He sends the preacher back to me, and brings my son back to me, then I will believe."

Mei Lin smiled at that, relaxing a little after the cadre's exit. "I hope you will be invited to tea as well?"

Woo Lan chuckled just a little. "Oh, yes. Your presence here will be all that anyone will talk about for weeks."

"I think we should be going," said Mei Lin. "We don't want to raise anymore mistrust toward you and Woo Fan. Tomorrow night then?"

"Tomorrow night," replied Woo Lan.

Poydan, North Korea

CHAPTER 14

"Young Soon, wake up. Hwan is here to see you."

Young Soon opened her eyes. All was dark except for the glow in the kitchen. Her one-room home was hot and humid. An intoxicating fragrance filled the air. "Young Ja, is that you?"

"Yes, I'm here," replied Ja.

"What is that smell?"

"Have you forgotten the smell of rice, Sister?"

"Oh! Oh! I *have* caught a star!"

She heard a man's laughter. "Hwan?"

"I am here, Young Soon."

Young Soon shivered, unsure of what to say. What if her brother reports them for eating corn gruel without rations?

Ja carried a candle from the stove. "See our brother," she said. "Doesn't he look like Father?"

Young Soon could not sit up, but she lifted her head slightly to get a closer look. "Oh, Ja! Am I dreaming? Is it Hwan? Or has Father come back to us?"

Her brother was suddenly on his knees beside her. He took her hand in his own. "Young Soon, I brought food. I wanted to come sooner. I'm so sorry—" his voice cracked and a sob racked his frame. "Had I come two years ago, we would all have a happy reunion. Mother and Father—our sister—and Ja's baby daughter. Oh, God, forgive me!"

Tears slipped down Young Soon's face. "Brother, who is God? We have no God but the Shining Sun, Kim Jong-il and our Dear Father, Kim il-Sung."

Hwan touched her face—ran his finger along her jaw, just as she had touched Nam Gil weeks before. She changed her tone. This was the brother she adored and now she knew—he still adored her, too.

"Do you have food every day in the military, my brother?"

Young Soon saw Ja and Hwan exchange glances in the candlelight. They knew something she did not know.

"I am not in the military, Sister," said Hwan. "I left."

"Hwan! Why? Why would you leave the good meals and the service of our Dear Leader?"

"I left because—I realized my family at home must be starving." Hwan hesitated a moment and looked deeply into her eyes before continuing. "Last fall I was deployed as a security officer to accompany a government dignitary on a trip to Norway. What I saw there changed my life. Young Soon, the rest of the world looks with pity on us. Our families are starving and the rest of the families of the world are throwing away leftover food."

"No!" cried Young Soon. "It can't be—throwing away food? Impossible!"

"It's true," Hwan urged. "It's true and Kim Jong-il is not allowing others to bring food to us."

"Shut up!" Young Soon commanded weakly. She pulled her tattered blanket up to her chin. "You are an infidel to talk of our Dear Leader that way. The world does not pity us—the world admires our revolution. The capitalist nations have no food. They envy us!"

"It is North Korea that has no food," Hwan whispered.

Young Soon gasped at her brother's accusation.

"How can we have a revolution when our people are starving?" Hwan asked quietly.

Ja leaned forward on her knees. She spoke in a low whisper. "Young Soon, it is true. Look at this."

Young Soon rolled over and the three siblings huddled around candlelight and read the newspaper article from South Korea. Young Soon noticed the pictures first. No one in the newspaper was gaunt or tired or thin. Everyone was healthy and what contraptions they had!

"Where are the pictures of the food being thrown away?" asked Young Soon.

"There are none," replied Hwan, sounding agitated. "Read this, Young Soon."

Hwan pointed to an article on the second page. Young Soon could barely breathe. Young Soon read the Korean han'gl letters underneath the picture. "People are trying to escape North Korea." She saw pictures of people trying to cross the fast flowing Tumen River, guards watching. "What will happen?" she asked.

"If they are seen crossing the river, they will be shot," Hwan said, his voice sad and quiet. "If they make it across, they will try to find the underground help in China. The underground will help refugees. If they are caught, they will be sent back to North Korea's Gulag."

"A talbukja," she gasped. "Oh, the government has promised to deal severely with these political rebels."

"No," Hwan said. "They are not talbukjas or rebels. Most of them are simply hungry people."

Young Soon thought of the man who was just shot for stealing corn to feed his hungry children. Was he a traitor like the loud speaker said? Or was he simply a hungry person? It was a judgment that Young Soon found difficult to make. The loud speaker crowded out all other thoughts—*We will protect our own style of socialism. A talbukja is the worst criminal in North Korea and will be dealt with severely. Long live the ideological state! Long live—*

"The government wants no one to escape North Korea," Hwan continued. "It is like a big prison holding hungry people from getting nourishment."

A prison. Young Soon had never thought of her country as a prison before. It was a foreign idea—a capitalist idea that Hwan had somehow picked up in Norway. She suddenly had the urge to throw him out of her house and run to the coal mine boss to report him. She rolled to her side, away from her siblings, and bit into her knuckle. Such wild disloyal thoughts.

Disloyal! The man at the cornfield was disloyal. Isn't that what they said? A traitor—was Hwan a traitor?

She rolled back toward her brother. "Hwan, who filled your mind with these capitalist ideas? Aren't you afraid someone followed you here? If the boss knows you are here, you will be shot! You've put our whole family in danger!"

Young Soon felt jarred. Her body and voice trembled. Panic went up into her throat and she stared wildly from Hwan to Ja and back to Hwan again.

"You believe him, Ja? You believe we are all in a big prison?"

Ja leaned forward and whispered so that even the children could not hear. "Yes, I believe our brother."

Young Soon looked at her children. "Both of you, go over there—by the stove. Sit there until I tell you to come."

Nam Gil took Min-Hee's hand and obediently followed orders. Young Soon turned back to Hwan.

"Look," said Hwan. "Look at this news article from Norway."

Young Soon looked at the picture. She couldn't read the Norwegian words. It showed pictures of sad, starving children on the left and pictures of healthy, thriving children on the right.

"What does it say?" she asked. The paper rattled in her hand.

"It's comparing the children of North Korea to the children of the rest of the world," said Hwan. "I tell you, the rest of the world pities us."

She couldn't turn off the loud speakers.

"Young Soon?" said Hwan.

"What should we do?" she asked.

Ja went to the stove and came back with a bowl, steam coming out of the top of it.

"First, eat this," said her brother.

"A whole bowl of rice!" exclaimed Young Soon. "Hwan, where did you find this?"

Without waiting for an answer, Young Soon rolled to her left side and put the chopsticks to her lips. Clumps of warm wet rice rolled over her tongue and her mouth exploded with its taste. "Oh, it is wonderful, it is wonderful!"

Hwan wept openly as he watched her. Ja put her arms around their brother to comfort him. In time he spoke. "You are too weak to eat beans, but I have brought beans as well," he said. "We will wait for you and your children to gain your strength."

"Wait?" asked Young Soon. "And then what?"

"We will talk later," said Hwan.

Young Soon put down her chopsticks and grabbed her brother's arm. "No. Now. Now you will tell me all that is in your heart."

"Drink some water, Young Soon," said Ja. She continued to lean on her left arm and took the water. She took another bite and then another. Then she took more water and let her head fall back on the mat again. The food felt wonderful yet it made her feel tired to eat. It was as though energy was being pulled out of her through her feet, making her legs feel heavy.

"Tell me," she urged Hwan.

"When you are strong enough to walk a long distance, I have arranged for you to escape," said Hwan.

Walk a long distance. Young Soon gasped. "How?"

"There is a river—the one you saw in this paper. Those who can get across the river will find food and jobs on the other side."

"In the underground as you call it?" asked Young Soon.

"Yes."

"But why?" asked Young Soon. "Why do these people who never met me want to help me and my children?"

"The underground people believe in a certain God who loves."

"God? You mention God again? Religion is an opiate. It paralyzes the ideology of the people."

"Yes, that's what the loud speakers say," answered Hwan. He appeared agitated but Young Soon could not imagine why. He continued. "You must be careful. Women who come to China must be especially careful. Sometimes Chinese posing as businessmen will convince Korean refugee women to stay with them and later sell them to be wives or sex slaves to Chinese farmers or foreigners."

"No!" cried Young Soon.

"Yes," he answered. "It's true. So if something happens to me and I cannot be there when you come into China, look for a building with a cross on it. Then you have found the people who believe in the God who loves. You can—"

"You mean churches?" Young Soon was appalled. "Churches numb the way people think. Didn't you hear the Great Leader warn us of such places, of church people who are 'wolves with a cross?'"

Hwan sighed and Young Soon felt he only pitied her and did not take her words seriously. *Surely they taught Hwan all of this in the military...*

"They are not wolves," whispered Hwan. "In China, you will not find a kinder people than those who meet in buildings with a cross."

C. Hope Flinchbaugh

Young Soon gasped. Young Soon heard of this religion in school through a movie, *Seonghwangdang*, which showed Christianity was a myth and a tool for invasion. And people who had this cross Hwan spoke of were spies.

"But the buildings with the cross—these forerunners of imperialism, wolves—"

Hwan put his finger on her lips. "Sister, it is not that way. You do not even need to believe in their God, but they will help you to hide from the authorities."

Young Soon felt some relief. "We do not have to believe in their God?"

Hwan shook his head.

"But they will still help us? How do we pay them?"

"They do not expect payment. Young Soon, I want all of us to escape and meet in South Korea."

Young Soon's heart raced, but her imagination did not let her down. All of the years of remembering better days with full rice bowls had kept this hope alive in her—hope for a better world ahead. Hope to hear the laughter of her children. Fear crept into her mind and her candle of hope blew out —the loud speaker was on again—marching around her mind until she could hear nothing else.

"You will starve if you stay here," Hwan was saying.

"But I am a traitor if I leave," argued Young Soon. "Have you forgotten the loyalty of my husband, Sang Ki? We lived our whole lives for the DPRK. How can I turn my back on all of that?"

Hwan looked over at Nam Gil and Min-Hee, huddled near the stove. "To stay is to turn your back on them."

Young Soon felt as though someone slapped her. Her mind was reeling. "How would we get there?"

"I have it all arranged," said Hwan. "After you cross the river where I tell you, there are people who will help us get to South Korea. It will take several months, but you and your children will have food to eat."

"Ja?" asked Young Soon. "Will you cross the river, too?"

Ja shrugged her shoulders. "My husband does not like the idea. Our food rations just began again and he does not want to lose them. He won't come here tonight because he is afraid of being caught. He didn't want me to come here, but I told him I would tell neighbors that I am here to care for you and the children. Everyone knows you are sick."

"Where are you staying?" Young Soon asked Hwan.

"There is a cave a few miles from here that used to be an entrance to the mines. It's not used anymore. I am safe but my food supplies will not last long. I could only carry so much food with me."

"Will you go with me?" asked Young Soon.

"I had no idea you were so thin and frail, Sister. I cannot wait a couple of weeks for you to gain your strength. I must leave to-morrow night."

"Oh, but we just saw each other," said Young Soon. "And how will I know where to go?"

"I will give you directions," he promised. "Tomorrow you will eat beans. I will leave enough for you and Ja to last some time if you eat a little bit each day."

"Oh, Hwan, how can I do this? My baby is due in two weeks. Then I have Min-Hee and Nam Gil to carry. How can one woman cross a river with so many children?"

Hwan took her hand. "I want you to consider this, Young Soon. Nam Gil is too sick to walk right now. But Min-Hee is small and I can carry her in the bag I used to bring the food here. I can help her cross the river and take her to people who will give her food."

Young Soon thought her heart would leap from her chest. "Take my only daughter?" she cried. "Aunt Ja's precious sweetheart?" Ja choked back a sob, covering her mouth. After a few moments, she said through tears, "Young Soon, we cannot feed her. This is her only chance for a real life. I don't want to let her go—but Hwan will take care of her. And we will all meet one day again in Seoul, South Korea."

"You will come, too, Ja?" asked Soon Young.

"The rations may not last long," said Ja. "I will keep the directions so that if the rations stop my husband may be willing to come."

"Oh, Ja, if we could all be together again and live in houses with rice and beans—can you imagine?" Young Soon could imagine. All of the thoughts she crammed down for the last seven years came flying through her mind in that one moment. Dreams of education, food, housing, and laughter—especially the laughter. Han Chun! Hadn't she known somehow when Ja watered the rising sun within her that Han Chun would grow up under a different sky? She placed her hand on her abdomen. The thought of Han Chun growing up without grass poisoning, with a full rice bowl and laughter...

"Yes, Hwan. I will follow you to the river. I will bring my sons," she said patting her stomach. "And you—you will take care of Min-Hee?"

"With all of my heart," he said. "My wife and I will keep her with us until we meet in China."

Young Soon rolled to her back and called her children to her. As they lay, one on either side of her, cradled in each arm, her mind tried to sort through a hundred things all at once. Was she allowed to even think about something besides what the loud speakers told her? She was stunned that her brother referred to North Korea as a prison—and she tried to picture people who had so much food they threw some away. How was that possible? And what was an underground and how did Hwan come to know about it?

Her stomach suddenly gurgled with the pleasure of digestion, interrupting her thoughts. She was so happy to feed the little one inside her. She kissed each of her children on top of the head.

"Your brother Han Chun will be with us soon," she said. She closed her eyes and tried to imagine his life.

"Good night, Kim Young Soon," said Hwan. He kissed her forehead in the semidarkness.

"Good night, Hwan," said Young Soon. "You will come for her tomorrow night?"

"Yes, after the village is asleep."

Rural China

CHAPTER 15

Mei Lin and Fei camped in the woods near the place where they hid the Bibles the day before. Tonight was their first meeting and Mei Lin was glad to have time alone to bathe and read her Bible and pray. She sat on a smooth stone with her back to a tree. Minutes slipped into hours and it was time to go to the village.

"I'm so glad that Fan gave us those dumplings for lunch yesterday," Fei called to her from the creek. "I was hungry."

"Hopefully, we will find someone who will take us in tonight," Mei Lin answered. "I didn't want to ask the Woos. They have put themselves at risk just listening to us yesterday."

Fei shook the water off her hands, her short hair shining in streaks under the sun. She came closer and lowered her voice. "We are truly on a walk of faith, Mei Lin. We don't know where we will sleep or what we will eat. Why, we don't even know what we will say, do we?"

Mei Lin laughed at that. "We are leaning on our Savior, for sure. He will give us the words he's been longing to say to these people since the last evangelist was here nearly twenty years ago."

The girls left the creek and followed the dirt road that ran through the center of the village.

"Nin Hao!"

Mei Lin turned to see a teenage boy approaching them.

"Nin Hao!" called Fei. The girls put their backpacks down in the dirt. "Hello!"

"Where are you from?" the boy asked.

Mei Lin smiled at his forwardness. "I am Mei Lin of Tanching." She extended her hand to the boy. "And this is my friend Fei from Du Yan. And where are you from?"

He smiled shyly. "I am Dun and I am from Ho Ting. Everyone I know is from Ho Ting."

"I'm pleased to meet you Dun from Ho Ting," said Fei. "How old are you?"

"Thirteen," he answered.

"Oh, you are tall for thirteen," said Mei Lin. "I thought you were at least fifteen."

The boy beamed with pleasure. "My cousin invited me to your tea tonight. I hope you will tell us news of what is happening in the rest of China."

"What do you want to know, Dun?" asked Fei.

"I want to know how President Hu Jintao is doing and I especially want to hear about the Olympics. Everyone here talks about the Olympics." The boy paused, weighing his next thought carefully. The girls waited.

"And I especially want to know what makes the sun rise in the sky every morning and why the rainbow appears sometimes, though not very often. I see the way of the crane in the sky but I do not understand its flight pattern. Do I sound childish to you? I'm probably talking too much, but I hear you are only visiting. I want to know so many things. We hear news only once a year here. The PSB come in the fall and right after harvest the sellers come to trade with us."

"Doesn't your village visit anywhere else?" asked Fei.

"Have you ever seen a car?" asked Mei Lin.

"Only the cadre's car," he answered. "We don't have a school and the only place we visit is at one another's houses. We are too poor to travel."

Mei Lin had never been in a town that was so secluded. The people were thirsty for knowledge and she knew they would listen with whole hearts at the tea that evening.

"Do you have to return to work in the fields?" she asked.

"No, I have to take our goats to pasture in the afternoon," he said, waving his hand toward the goats. "Will you go with me?"

Mei Lin looked at Fei. It was agreed.

So the girls spent the afternoon explaining what they knew of the preparations for the Olympics in Beijing, President Hu, and the One who made the earth and skies. Fei told the story of Noah and the first rainbow. Mei Lin used sticks in the field to explain the cross that Jesus died on. The three of them became lost in conversation until Dun's mother called him to supper.

"Would you come to supper with me?" he asked. "I would like you to meet my parents."

Mei Lin and Fei met Dun's parents and within minutes their presence in the courtyard drew a gathering of grandparents, cousins, and neighbors, all sipping from teacups while seated on stools. Surrounded by the aroma of rice and chicken, Mei Lin and Fei did their best to answer questions that ranged from the Olympic sports games to the price of rice in Tanching's central market.

"I feel like a celebrity," whispered Fei, as she munched on noodles.

"We shall see how celebrated we are when we turn the light on," replied Mei Lin.

Fei caught her meaning. "What time is it?" she asked.

"Six-thirty," replied Mei Lin. "We should go get ready for tea," she said. The girls stood to say their goodbyes to Dun's family.

"Wait," said Dun. "I want to ask you a question."

"What is it," Fei asked.

"I wish to travel with you," he said.

Mei Lin stifled the giggle rising in her throat, then pulled the boy aside. She and Fei had explained the Gospel as well as several Bible stories to Dun earlier that afternoon. Now this boy wanted to travel with them—and he wasn't even a believer yet! "Oh, it would be a help to have a strong boy like you walking with us to guard us," she said. "First, you would need to become a believer. And secondly, you must know that God is telling you to go with us. We are here because we know God spoke to our hearts to visit your village. Besides, your father and mother need you here."

Dun's expression fell. He lowered his eyes and turned and walked away.

"Dun!" Fei called. "You'll come tonight?"

He hesitated a moment and looked back at them. "I will come."

Mei Lin and Fei excused themselves from Dun's family and went to a tree near the edge of the village to pull out their bookbags and prepare.

"I never dreamed someone would want to travel with us," said Fei as she combed her hair.

"Me either," said Mei Lin. "But I think Dun's motives do not have to do with evangelism. He is a young boy who wants to see the world around him. He feels stuck in this remote village and I feel sorry for him."

"I hope he becomes a Christian," said Fei. "God will help him to learn all the things he's interested in."

Mei Lin brushed her teeth, then put her hand deep into her bookbag. The scarf!

"I almost forgot!" cried Mei Lin. She put the beautiful scarf around her neck, laying it evenly across each shoulder. A gentle breeze picked up the ends and lifted them lightly into the air.

"It's beautiful, Mei Lin. It's as though you've put on a cadre's coat instead of a scarf."

"I can feel it," said Mei Lin. "I'll be a cadre from Heaven!"

Fei laughed. "Now that's a new one! And shall we discover tonight which cadre the people will listen to?" Fei's voice had grown serious. Both of them knew that they could be hauled off to prison that night for their preaching.

"We knew before we started that this could happen," said Mei Lin. "I think we should go to the tea."

Mei Lin combed her shoulder length hair and ran a damp washcloth over her face and neck.

Fei sighed. "Mei Lin?"

Mei Lin adjusted her scarf once more and dropped to her knees to put her bookbag back in order. "Yes?"

"What do you have to do to get the Gethsemane gift?"

Fei sat on the ground across from her while Mei Lin thought for a moment. "You—you simply have to be willing to suffer. The gift is up to God."

Fei tilted her head toward the sky, her eyes closed, obviously in thought.

"What is it, Fei?"

"I don't know if I'm willing, Mei Lin. I'm terrified." Fei's voice cracked and Mei Lin saw a tear escape the corner of her eye. Mei Lin scooted closer and patted her hand.

"Sister, God does not mind if you are scared."

Fei jolted upright and looked at Mei Lin. "He doesn't? I thought He requires courage and bravery in the face of persecution."

Mei Lin chose her words carefully. "We do not have to be willing to be persecuted. We must only ask Jesus to make us willing to be persecuted. We must be willing to be made willing. Does that make sense? We have no great courage without Him."

Fei sighed. "Okay. I think I can do that. Jesus, please make me willing to suffer for You. I'm sorry I'm so scared. Mei Lin says that's OK. So I'm asking You—please make me willing."

Mei Lin leaned forward on her knees and gave her friend a hug. "You're doing great, Fei. Shall we go?"

Fei wiped the tears away again. "Who's going to speak tonight?"

"I don't know," answered Mei Lin. "Let God tell us when we get there, OK?"

Fei nodded. "Good."

The June air was dense with the smell and feel of human bodies in a crammed place. Mei Lin stopped counting people after 60. Jenji was impeccably groomed for the occasion, her hair combed perfectly into a long braid down her back and a flower tucked behind her ear. She was a quiet woman, but she blossomed with hospitality that evening, the perfect hostess, offering real tea and even mini mooncakes, usually reserved for New Years celebrations, to her guests. Her little boy followed her everywhere until someone, probably his grandmother, took him away to entertain him. Mei Lin and Fei were careful to take one of everything with gratitude toward their hostess.

Although Jenji did not have some of the more modern lighting that Amah had chosen for her going away party, her courtyard was decorated in old style lanterns with wisps of red and gold silk encased in greenery from the nearby woods. The lanterns would not be needed until later in the night, after the sun went down. Mei Lin could feel the hospitality coming from her hostess and she felt welcomed and honored.

The girls mingled and greeted all of Dun's family and thanked them again for their hospitality in serving dinner the hour before. Dun was rather quiet and Mei Lin hoped he wouldn't sulk for long.

She knew he was disappointed that they didn't jump at his request to travel with them.

"Mei Lin, I have someone I would like you to meet," said Jenji. "This is my father-in-law, Sun. Father, this is our guest, Mei Lin. She offered to pray for people who are sick tonight."

Mei Lin didn't see any visible sign of sickness except that Sun was extremely thin. He reminded her of the malnourished prisoners from Shanghai.

"Hello, Sun. I'm honored to meet you this evening."

"Hello, Mei Lin. Jenji tells me you are in Ho Ting to pray for people?"

Mei Lin smiled. "Yes, I wanted to pray for sick people this evening and tell them about the One who made the earth and skies. Would you like prayer for something?"

Sun looked around, unsure of himself. "I do not know what the cadre will say," he said with a raspy voice. "He's not here yet, so I will tell you now."

"OK."

"I have stomach problems. I cannot eat properly. There's severe pain in my stomach after eating. My family—my wife is afraid I will die."

"Has a doctor seen you?" asked Mei Lin.

"Yes, we have a doctor in the village," he answered. "He suggested that I make an offering to the kitchen god. I did this but it did not work. He told me to watch out for days of bad luck and to offer a larger offering to the kitchen god on a special holiday and it will give me a great advantage of good fortune. I will do that, but—I don't know. I'm in a lot of pain and the next big holiday isn't until the harvest."

Mei Lin felt great compassion for Sun.

Just then, Cadre Xin entered the courtyard. He walked directly over to Mei Lin. She extended her hand in greeting. "It's good to see you again, Wang Mei Lin. Sun, how are you?"

Sun wiped his frail hand against his shirt, then extended it to Cadre Xin. "Hello, Cadre."

"Eat plenty of these mooncakes, Sun. You need to keep your strength up."

Mei Lin watched Sun's face darken at the cadre's words, and Mei Lin guessed he felt misunderstood. The cadre didn't seem to notice.

"How long will you stay in Ho Ting?" Cadre Xin asked.

"Oh, we're not sure yet," said Mei Lin. She didn't want to limit her time or expand it. She was here for as long as God told them to stay. But she did not say that to the cadre.

"I hope you will find our village very—hospitable," he replied.

"Oh, the people here are very friendly," said Mei Lin.

Suddenly, a boy burst through the courtyard gate. "Cadre!" he shouted. "The Xias are fighting."

"Again?" asked the cadre. "Tell your grandmother I'll be there in a few minutes."

"I can't!" shouted the boy, obviously panic-stricken. "They started a fire again!"

Cadre Xin sprinted out of the courtyard then broke into a full run at the gate.

"I'll help you, Cadre," called Bo, Jenji's husband.

With that, the disruption was quickly forgotten and everyone went back to their tea. Obviously, the Xias had a reputation for fights and fires.

Jenji was suddenly at her side. "Now is a good time to speak," she said.

Mei Lin looked into her eyes. Suddenly, she understood that Jenji had planned this. The fight and fire were part of the evening so the cadre would not be present for the meeting.

"Yes, this is a good time," said Mei Lin.

Jenji quickly rallied the crowd to sit on the benches and Mei Lin and Fei stood in the small courtyard opposite the gate so they could watch who was coming and going.

Mei Lin didn't feel that burning inside of her as she usually did before she preached. Fei caught her eye and left the person she was talking to.

"Fei, do you have the message?" asked Mei Lin. They both very well knew the message was the gospel. It wasn't the content that Mei Lin referred to. It was the power.

"Oh, Mei Lin," cried Fei. "I feel as though I will burst if I don't speak!"

Fei's eyes were a shining glory and Mei Lin knew her friend was ready. While Jenji assembled the people on benches, Mei Lin took Fei's hand and prayed Mother Zhang's prayer. "Father, give Fei boldness to preach the power of the cross, the power of the blood of Jesus, the power of salvation in His name. We trust You for signs to follow as the people believe."

Mei Lin stood in front of the back wall, ready to assist Fei at any time. Fei briefly told the story of creation, then the story of Jesus' birth and life and miracles. Mei Lin felt energized as Fei spoke eloquently from her heart. Her faith soared at the mention of what Jesus did 2000 years ago.

"And so you see, God gave us the cross and that cross gives us God. When Jesus cried out, 'It is finished!' just before He died on the cross, He knew that the price was now paid in full for your sins and for my sins—for the sins of the whole world. He offers His love and His forgiveness to every person. You just have to want it."

Fei paused until the atmosphere in the room tingled with a holy electricity. "Do you want Jesus? Do you want His forgiveness?"

Dun's parents looked back at Mei Lin and then stood to their feet. One family and then another stood to their feet.

Mei Lin put her head in her hands and prayed. *Oh, God, oh, God, see these souls entering Your kingdom. Rejoice, Heaven! Rejoice angels! See the souls! See the precious people coming!*

The room went up in a smoke of prayer. Fei looked delighted and she walked among the people in the front, praying with them as they gave their hearts to Jesus. For the first time, Mei Lin saw Mr. Woo, stooped over and leaning on the back of the chair in front of him. Mrs. Woo sat beside him, watching the room.

Quietly, she walked over to Mr. and Mrs. Woo. She squatted in front of them and whispered to Mr. Woo.

"Are you ready to meet the One who died for you? Are you ready to meet the God your son loves?"

The old man stared deeply into Mei Lin's eyes for a moment. "I cannot forgive the people who made my wife deaf. They should pay for their crime."

Mei nodded. "Yes, they were wrong to hurt her. But God wants you to forgive them. If you want to forgive them, God will help you."

Mr. Woo sighed. "I hate them. But I do want to forgive."

"I am glad you are so honest," replied Mei Lin. "Simply pray this way: "God who made the earth and skies, I ask You to help me to forgive the people who made my wife deaf—and say their names."

Mr. Woo closed his eyes. His wife bent low to try to read his lips.

"God who made the earth and skies. You have finally sent a preacher. I ask You to help me forgive the Ma's for making Fan go deaf. I want to hate them, but I ask You to help me forgive."

Mei Lin asked, "Are you ready to believe in Jesus now?"

"Shouldn't I burn incense?"

"No, God will listen without the incense."

Mr. Woo sighed.

"Very good," he answered. Woo Lan bowed his head.

"I pray now to the God of my son, Miao. I forgive Mrs. Ma for making my wife deaf. I ask You to forgive me for my sins as well. I told You I would believe if You would send the preacher. The preacher did not return, but You have sent one just like her. I believe that You are the way to Heaven. I believe in Miao's God, Jesus."

The man stopped and his wife communicated her agreement of faith with her hands, folding them in prayer. She spoke. Her voice was a bit distorted, but clear.

"Jesus, I still remember your name. I remember the first time I heard about You I knew You were the true God. I forgive Mrs. Ma for her anger against us and for throwing the rock that made me deaf."

The husband made signs to his wife and both of them stared intently into one another's eyes as they communicated with each other and with Heaven. Mrs. Woo prayed, "Please forgive me my sins, too. I believe You died on the cross, like the one this girl drew in the dirt. Thank You."

"Yes," Mei Lin said. She never heard a sweeter prayer.

"Please bring our son home safely," she continued. "And his wife, if she is still alive."

Tears sprang to Mei Lin's eyes. Faith in Christ brought persecution to this entire family. She looked into their faces, now glowing with hope. A tear trickled down Mrs. Woo's wrinkled cheek. The rest of the people were gathered toward the front, absorbed in following Fei's prayer, unaware what had just happened to this couple. Peace was there, on both of them, and immediately she felt that she'd come to this village especially for this couple.

A gentle breeze moved Mei Lin's hair until it tickled her face. She reached to pull her hair back and the ends of her scarf blew upward, reminding her of the evening when her father threw the scarf into the air over her head.

Mrs. Woo jumped up and down excitedly, banging on her husband's arm and pointing. Woo Lan exclaimed, "Yes, yes, that's the one. How could it be?"

"What are you talking about?" asked Mei Lin.

"Oh, oh!" cried Woo Fan.

"The woman who preached here," said Woo Lan. "The preacher we prayed would return—she wore this scarf. She wore the same ivory scarf with the beautiful water and red lotus blossoms. But it can't be—she would be much older than you are—"

"Mother!" Mei Lin exclaimed as she covered her face with her hands. Her knees felt weak and she quickly sat on the small bench beside her. "Oh, Mother!"

"Your mother?" asked Woo Lan.

Tears sprang from Mei Lin's eyes. This poor man was praying for mother to return and she was in Heaven now.

"This scarf—it belonged to my mother!"

"Then it was your mother who came to our village fifteen years ago."

Mei Lin was thunderstruck. A stampede of a thousand horses could not have moved her from that spot. She ran her fingers over the scarf, remembering the warmth of her mother's shoulder as she carried Mei Lin as a little girl.

"My mother—did she have a little girl with her?"

"No, no, there was no little girl. Your mother wore this?"

"Yes, I know it was—"

Mei Lin gasped. She watched the flickers of red silk dance in the wind and, in that moment, felt one with all of the prayers that her mother and father ever prayed—prayers for the lost, prayers for the persecuted, prayers for their daughter, prayers for the village of Ho Ting. She realized that this was more than a red thread connecting them; this scarf that her mother wore from village to village as she preached was a token of Mei Lin's godly inheritance. Fei was right—it was like the cloak of Elijah being passed down to Elisha. In a split moment in time, Mei Lin knew her identity. And she felt connected to her mother's purpose in coming to Ho Ting so many years ago. She watched with wonder as the token of her godly inheritance lifted heavenward.

Now!

Mei Lin immediately knew that this was the moment for miracles. The air was electric with the glory and power of God.

Mei Lin thought her heart would leap from her chest. She pointed to Woo Fan's ears, then folded her hands and bowed her head to show she wanted to pray for her ears. The old woman nodded her head in exaggerated fashion, over and over again.

As Mei Lin put her hands over Mrs. Woo's ears, she was keenly aware of the power surging through her being. She barely felt the scarf that touched her shoulders but every ounce of her being knew it was there. She was about to pray when God spoke to her inside as though He were the preacher in the meeting.

Command! Command them to be open! Speak to the deafness and command it to go!

Mei Lin shuddered at the depth of His voice within and with joy at hearing Him so clearly, she commanded, "Ears, I command you to open. Deafness, I command you to go according to Mark 16—in the name of Jesus."

Mei Lin's hands felt hot, especially her right hand. She wasn't sure what that meant, but she did not want to take her hands off of the woman's ears until she knew for sure that God was finished working His miracle. The crowd's attention had now shifted to Mei Lin's prayer for Mrs. Woo and people gathered closer to watch.

The woman suddenly put her hands over Mei Lin's hands. "I hear something," she said in a voice louder than normal. "I hear something. I hear a roar and a lot of noise."

The woman was excited, but Mei Lin wasn't sure what that roaring meant. So she prayed. "Jesus, finish Your work on our sister so that she can hear clearly the voices of those around her."

For a moment, her thoughts shouted at her. *You are crazy! If this woman isn't healed they will all laugh at your God.*

No! Mei Lin shouted back at her weak mind. *I believe the Bible. Signs will follow them that believe. Jesus is big enough to do this.*

The heat in her hands subsided and she removed her hands from Mrs. Woo's ears.

"Mrs. Woo, can you hear me?" asked Mei Lin.

Mrs. Woo turned her head from side to side. "My head is so hot," she said. Then she looked at Mei Lin, seemingly lost in a daze.

"Can you hear me?" Mei Lin repeated.

A smile of wonder broke across her face, and Mrs. Woo's eyes sparkled with life. "I can hear you! I can hear you!"

A murmur of awe went across the courtyard.

Woo Lan stood behind his wife where she couldn't see him and asked, "Fan, what did we have for supper tonight?"

"Why, we had red beans, Mr. Woo!"

The room erupted with laughter.

Mei Lin threw her head back and laughed with them. She thought her heart would burst with joy. She'd never seen sick people healed in a meeting before. It was all new to her, but it felt so right—so very true to God's great loving heart and His last word to His church before He went back to Heaven. White hot passion for her God rose within her and she could feel the message burning inside of her—she had to tell them all about Jesus in Mark 16.

"Come," said Mei Lin. "If you want Jesus to heal your body, come. After Jesus arose from the dead, He stayed on the earth and visited with His people for about a month. Just before He went back to Heaven, Jesus gathered the people on a hillside to speak to them."

Mei Lin pulled her little New Testament out of her back pocket and turned to Mark 16. "The Bible says that just before He ascended into the skies to return to heaven, Jesus said,

> *And He said to them, "Go into all the world and preach the gospel to every creature. He who believes and is baptized will be saved; but he who does not believe will be condemned. And these signs will follow those who believe: In My name they will cast out demons; they will speak with new tongues; they will take up serpents; and if they drink anything deadly, it will by no means hurt them; they will lay hands on the sick, and they will recover." So then, after the Lord had spoken to them, He was received up into Heaven, and sat down at the right*

hand of God. And they went out and preached every-where, the Lord working with them and confirming the word through the accompanying signs. Amen. (Mark 16:15-20 NKJV)

"What you have seen tonight is true. Jesus is the true God. We will be glad to pray for you and we will see the sick get well and if anyone has evil spirits, they will be delivered."

Mr. Woo stepped forward, bent over and looking up at her, his glasses at the end of his nose again. "Will you pray for my back?"

"Yes," replied Mei Lin. Mei Lin put her hand on Mr. Woo's back and prayed, "Jesus, You healed the sick and then sent out Your disciples and told them to do the same thing. I ask You now to heal Mr. Woo."

Mei Lin waited. The heat returned to her hand and she felt so overcome with power that she thought she might fall over. She didn't know what else to do, so she kept praying.

"Lord Jesus, touch Mr. Woo."

"I feel heat on my back," he said. "It's on my head, too."

Suddenly, the Holy Spirit's voice came again. Forgive. *He must forgive.* "But he did forgive," Mei Lin answered the Lord quietly. *There are others.*

Mei Lin looked at Mr. Woo. "Mr. Woo, are there others who've hurt you? Are there others you must forgive?"

Mr. Woo shrugged his shoulder a little bit. "I don't think so."

"OK," said Mei Lin. "Let's pray this prayer. Repeat this after me and if someone's face comes to your mind when you pray, say their name and forgive them, OK?"

Mr. Woo nodded.

"Say this, 'Father, in the name of Jesus, I release and forgive—you fill in the name.'"

Mr. Woo quietly repeated the prayer, "Father in the name of Jesus I release and forgive Mrs. Xia."

Now it all fit—the family that was engaging in fights and fires was the same family that threw the rock at Mrs. Woo.

Again, Mei Lin began the prayer. "Father, in the name of Jesus, I release and forgive—you fill in the name."

Mr. Woo repeated the prayer a second time. "Father, in Jesus' name I release and forgive Mr. Xia. Oh! Oooo!" he cried out.

"What's wrong?" asked Mei Lin.

"Pain bolted up my back when I prayed that."

Mei Lin thought for a moment. "OK, that must be the root of the back pain you're having. I want you to pray a blessing for that person."

Mr. Woo obeyed. The heat returned to Mei Lin's hand and again she felt the power of God going over her whole being.

"Oh! Look!" cried Mr. Woo. Mei Lin watched in amazement as Mr. Woo lifted his head a little higher.

"Keep praying!" he shouted. "Keep praying!"

Mrs. Woo was weeping now and the attention of whole room was now on Mr. Woo.

"Lord God, thank You for what You're doing for Mr. Woo," Mei Lin prayed. She hesitated a few moments. "How are you feeling?" she asked.

"The pain is gone," he answered excitedly. "Look, I can move this far."

Mei Lin continued to pray; the heat still there. She hadn't known about the heat—but she was glad it was there. It helped her know when God's power was on someone to heal them. Mr. Woo slowly moved more and more of his upper back until he could stand up.

"Look at this!" he cried. "Look at this!"

Mrs. Woo cried harder and the rest of the room rippled with the excitement of this newfound healing and forgiveness. The heat lessened and Mei Lin knew she was finished.

Mr. Woo reached for the skies with his fingers and then bent over to touch his toes. "I couldn't do this before!" he cried. "Look at this!"

"We see, we see you," said Dun's father.

Sun stepped toward Mei Lin and she motioned him forward. "If anyone else wants prayer for healing, step forward."

A few more stepped forward. Others watched while Fei continued to pray for those who came to believe and Mei Lin prayed over those believers who were sick.

"Are you in pain right now from eating?" asked Mei Lin.

Sun nodded. "The food doesn't stay inside for long."

Mei Lin realized that this admission was embarrassing enough for an elderly man, so she waited a moment without asking any more questions, praying silently before placing her hands on Sun. She felt heat come into her hands again. It wasn't a heat that burned her, but an intense heat that told her God was near—no, He was more than near—He was here, here to heal. Here to show the people in this remote village that He sees them and He cares about their pain and sickness.

Tears slipped down Mei Lin's cheeks as she felt His love for Sun. Compassion welled up inside of her until her throat felt swollen with love for all the Ho Ting people. She laid her hands on Sun's head and she knew that the heat had to be the healing power of God. This time she could feel it transfer from her hands and into Sun.

"Sun, can you feel anything?" asked Mei Lin.

Sun nodded his head. "I am hot," he said. "I'm very hot."

"Is the pain still there?"

"Yes," said Sun, his head bowed low. "But I'm hot." Mei Lin couldn't tell if he was in a prayerful position or ashamed of his physical condition. And she didn't know what to do, so she decided to keep praying. This time she did not hear God tell her to command the pain to go. So she remained quiet, only obeying Mark 16 and knowing God's words were His promises and those promises were working this miracle. *They will place their hands on sick people, and they will get well*, Mei Lin repeated to herself.

Sun looked up. "I feel the pain leaving," he whispered.

The heat was subsiding. Mei Lin was learning. Jesus was teaching her how to preach His gospel with signs and wonders following.

She waited another minute. "How are you now, Sun?"

"The pain is completely gone," he said, his voice caught with emotion.

Mei Lin was in awe. "Go tell Jenji. She had this tea party tonight for you."

Mei Lin saw tears in Sun's eyes. "Your God did this for me?"

"Yes," she replied. "Do you believe that Jesus is the Son of God? Did you receive Him tonight when Fei prayed?"

Sun nodded. "Yes, I prayed."

"Then He is your God, too," said Mei Lin. Joy welled up inside of her as she realized that God allowed her to reach the honorable elders of the village first. These elder saints would probably see Jesus before she did.

"Go eat, Sun," Mei Lin urged. "Ask Jenji to give you something to eat and tell us if there is pain afterward."

Mei Lin paused for a moment to touch the scarf. *I can feel the strength of the prayers you prayed so long ago, Mother. I feel your prayers tonight, Father.*

Then she continued to pray for the remaining eight to ten people. Each one told her they were born again and the rest of the evening went quickly.

After she prayed for the last person, a thought came to her. She went to Fei who had just finished praying for the last person in front of her, a middle aged woman who left Fei thanking her over and over again.

"What happened?" asked Mei Lin.

Fei clasped her hands together. "Oh, Mei Lin, it's wonderful! That woman has suffered from ongoing headaches continuously for three years. Tonight the pain went away and she was healed. Can you imagine having a terrible headache for that long?"

"Thank God!" exclaimed Mei Lin. Just seeing the light in Fei's eyes brought her so much joy and she felt as though she'd known Fei all of her life, like her own sister. "You know, I was just thinking, Fei. Mark 16 says that those who believe and are baptized will be saved. We need to baptize the new believers."

Fei was all smiles. "Oh, I didn't even think of that. When shall we do it?"

"I don't know." Mei Lin listened quietly in her heart. She didn't want to plan a baptism on her own—she had to hear the Holy Spirit's plan first.

"Fei, let's announce that we want to teach about baptism. Perhaps someone will offer to let us teach in their home."

"That's good," answered Fei. "Go ahead."

"Friends!" Mei Lin called. A respectful quiet descended over the room. "We would like to teach you about what it means to be baptized. We need a place to meet and a time."

Jenji walked across the courtyard with Sun. "My father-in-law is healed. Look at him!"

Sun was eating like a teenager, his cheeks stuffed with mushroom dumplings.

"No pain!" he announced, patting his stomach. "Look! No pain!"

Sun's wife hugged his side.

"Thank you," she said to Mei Lin. "Thank you."

"It is God's power that has healed your husband, not mine." Mei Lin spoke loudly enough so everyone could hear.

"I invite you all to return for tea tomorrow night," said Jenji. "I—I don't know how much tea I'll have left, but—"

"I'll bring tea," said someone.

"And I'll bring steamed rolls," said another.

"Yes, your courtyard is larger, Jenji. We'll help you with the food."

Jenji was smiling, her little son hanging on her skirts again. "Then I invite all of you to tea again—tomorrow evening, seven o'clock."

"Seven o'clock," a few murmured in agreement.

The meeting adjourned, yet people lingered to talk to those who had been born again or healed. Several talked to Mei Lin and Fei.

Mei Lin felt a tug on her arm.

"Mrs. Woo!" she said.

"My husband and I want you to stay with us while you are here," she said.

"But you put yourself at risk," said Mei Lin. "The cadre may not approve of what happened here tonight."

Mrs. Woo looked up at her husband. "I have never felt more alive in my life, young girl. I want you and your friend to stay with us. Bring this life into our house. Bring your God, our son's God, to our house."

Mei Lin felt liquid love coming from this dear woman.

"We will come," she answered. "Thank you."

Poydan, North Korea

CHAPTER 16

Young Soon wakened to the sound of her children playing quietly. She'd slept through the day again and it was dark, but Ja had left a lantern burning on the floor near the children. She sat up and dipped her chopsticks into the bowl of rice Ja left for her.

I cannot believe I have eaten rice two days in a row!

The food both energized her and exhausted her. The more she ate, the more she wanted to sleep. Her body seemed to attack the nourishment the food gave her, leaving her feeling heavy in her legs and sort of weak in her stomach. Ja said it was because she was healing and getting stronger. She would need to be stronger—the baby was due soon, about two weeks if her calculations were correct. Young Soon still did not have the strength to get up and do much more than use the bucket Ja put nearby or sit up to eat or comb her hair. But she felt her strength slowly returning and, best of all, the baby was moving all the time now! He was certainly enjoying the rice!

Min-Hee and Nam Gil had eaten for four days now—three days while she was sick and again today. There was such a change in them today! Nam Gil and Min-Hee rolled a rubber ball back and forth across the floor—a ball that their Uncle Hwan brought them from China. They both slept through the night last night. It was glorious not to be wakened by the groans of their hunger pains.

But there was one thing she wanted even more—Young Soon waited for one of them to laugh. She longed to hear them laugh. She studied their little faces. The hunger was gone, but the sadness it created was still stamped on her children's faces. Nam Gil was fearful and edgy. He kept watching the door between rolling the ball. Min-Hee watched her mother, awaiting her approval at her success in rolling the ball.

"Very good, Min-Hee," she said softly. "You will be as good as Nam Gil if you keep practicing."

Her eyes brightened and she rolled it again. The two of them continued without making a sound, concentrating on each effort to roll it successfully.

Young Soon sat and stared at her three-year-old daughter. Her eyes could not get enough of her. After the town went to sleep, Hwan would come to take Min-Hee away and she would have to say good-bye to her—and so soon after her little one was feeling better.

Young Soon sighed. How could she give her only daughter to Hwan? Once Min-Hee crossed the Tumen River into China, she would forever be a talbukja, an infidel traitor of the Democratic People's Republic of Korea. Young Soon wondered what her husband would say. They were both so loyal to the Party when they were in school. Now…she couldn't imagine that her government would shoot a three-year-old child. But there were whole families sent to prison and kept there for the crime of one member!

Wild thoughts jutted through her mind. She tried to understand—to comprehend her daughter's journey. She imagined the Korean guards shooting Hwan and Min-Hee falling into the river, drowning without her uncle's help. It occurred to her that they may not even make it as far as the river. They may be caught by the military police before they crossed the border. Then everyone would be arrested—Hwan, Ja, the children, everyone! It was very risky. Hwan and Min-Hee could be caught at any time. Hwan made it here, but how would he make it into China with her little daughter? What if Min-Hee became scared and cried?

Yet now that she had rice inside of her again, she felt that it was right. Min-Hee and Nam Gil would not live much longer without regular meals. She felt ashamed to consider becoming a traitor but she felt even more shame that she was feeding her children bark and grass. What else could she do? She touched her protruding abdomen. Her new baby would not live without food either.

Yes, Hwan was right. She and her children must go where they could find food to eat. And Hwan's words about the DPRK being a cage to trap hungry people was slowly beginning to creep into her own thoughts. Part of her wanted to leave this old house and never look back. The desperation for food and for Nam Gil's recovery often maddened her, especially in the night when all was dark and quiet. Memories of her husband lying on this same mat, dying of starvation—it was then that her thoughts shouted, *Get out of this empty box, away from this dog's den of sickness and hunger.*

She looked at her mother's painted door. She would be leaving behind everything her parents believed in.

How can I leave our home, Mother?

"Ow!" cried Young Soon. Her hand immediately flew to her middle. Nam Gil and Min-Hee left their ball and scurried to her side.

"What is it Oma?" asked Nam Gil.

Min-Hee squatted in front of her and put her face right up to her mother's face. "Ow, Oma?" she asked.

Young Soon couldn't help herself—she laughed a little. She hadn't laughed in so long that it somehow didn't sound right to her. Immediately she put her hand over her mouth. Nam Gil looked as though someone struck him at first, but then he smiled a little. Min-Hee's gaze never left her mother's face.

"The baby," Young Soon told them quietly. "The baby is moving. Here, put your hand right here. The baby is inside Oma and he's kicking his feet."

Young Soon directed her children's hand to the right spot.

"There!" she exclaimed.

Nam Gil smiled again.

"Baby," said Min-Hee. "Baby kick!" With that, she kicked her own little foot out in front of her to demonstrate.

Young Soon reached out and drew her daughter close. She kissed the top of her head and then both of her cheeks. She pulled her in front of her again. "Oma loves you, Min-Hee."

Min-Hee patted her mother's cheeks and then scooted away to find the ball.

"Oma, you will need a midwife when the baby comes," said Nam Gil.

"Ah, do you remember?" asked Young Soon. "Do you remember when Min-Hee was born?"

Nam Gil nodded. "Father was here. Now Uncle Hwan is here. Will he get the midwife?"

Young Soon drew her first child into her arms. "Oh, Nam Gil. I miss your father so. I wish he were here to see Han Chun born. Now listen." She sat her son in front of her so she could watch his expressions. "Don't worry about the midwife. Aunt Ja will help me this time. And I want you to know something else—Oma is going to let Min-Hee go to China with Uncle Hwan tonight."

Young Soon waited for that thought to sink into her son's mind, then continued.

"Uncle Hwan and Aunt Yun will take care of Min-Hee and then, after Han Chun is born, we will travel to China to be with Min-Hee again and to stay with Uncle Hwan and Aunt Yun for a while."

"What about Aunt Ja?" he asked.

Young Soon sighed. "She and Uncle Chul-moo may come later. But it's a secret and you can't tell anybody, OK?"

"Then we'll come back home?" he asked.

Young Soon's voice softened. "Do you want to come back home, Nam Gil?"

The little boy looked down. His face was gaunt, skin still stretched over bones. Only his eyes seemed changed since he ate food. "I want to eat, Oma." He looked up with longing in his eyes. "Will Uncle Hwan have food there?"

"Oh, yes," cried Young Soon. "He will have food and good tea, even! It will be like a family party!"

"Will the Dear Leader be pleased with us, Oma?" asked Nam Gil. There was a quiver in his voice just then and Young Soon wondered if her son somehow grasped the seriousness of the decision they were making.

"General Kim Jong-il loves the North Korean soldiers," Young Soon answered. "He feeds the soldiers who guard the warehouse in our town, right?"

Nam Gil nodded. "But we don't eat and I don't think it's fair."

Young Soon's spine tingled. "Don't you say that to anyone else, do you hear me?"

Nam Gil's eyes were wide as saucers. "I want to be a soldier. I want to eat."

"Someday, when you're older," she answered. "Go—go play with your sister."

Soldiers.

Every grave that was dug for citizens who starved to death pointed earthen arrows to the soldiers whose bodies were healthy and strong, yet one never saw them gather food. Those same graves seemed to verify Hwan's words that the government is allowing the people to starve to death while it feeds only its military and elite.

Young Soon shuddered. She was afraid to think about it anymore for fear the soldiers would hear her thoughts and shoot her.

Fearful thoughts paraded through her mind until she had to get up and move around to get her mind off of things. Ja left water in the basin for her to bathe Min-Hee before the trip. Young Soon heated some water on the stove and prepared a small bag for her daughter. Her blanket was tattered, but it was hers and perhaps it would help Min-Hee feel more secure. She took her daughter's bowl from the shelf and pulled her spoon out of the drawer and wrapped it in the blanket. What else?

Young Soon looked about the room. There was so little left now for any of them. All their possessions had long ago been sold for food. Young Soon wanted to give her little girl more, but had nothing.

I have nothing now. But Hwan said I can find people in China who will help me get to South Korea. Then I'll give my little girl all she needs.

Quietly, she readied the basin of water to bathe her daughter and tried to prepare herself to say goodbye.

Rural China

CHAPTER 17

Mei Lin and Fei sat at the kitchen table while Mrs. Woo stood over her brick stove, flipping an omelet. The Woo home reminded her very much of Pastor Zhang's home in DuYan. Only, Pastor Zhang had an extra bedroom. After the meeting the first night, the girls lay on their blankets near the cold wood stove and talked long into the night, excited over the wonderful souls brought into the kingdom. Fei was especially moved to learn that they were indeed reaping a harvest of believers from seeds sown by Mei Lin's mother years ago.

This morning their pens moved furiously, each writing a letter to her family back home while sipping hot water at the table inside. She had to write carefully, using code language that the authorities would not be able to decipher should they open the letter to check it.

Dear Father,

Good news! I have met some of mother's family already! Even though I am meeting them for the first time, they are glad to be a part of the family and they saw Mother a year or so before she died. They are sad to know she is not here, but they recognized her scarf. That made me feel closer to both of you! I feel as though I am finishing a walk she started eighteen years ago. See, the invisible red thread that connects those of us who are destined to meet still operates today, regardless of time, place, or circumstance. It's so true!

Of course, they welcomed us into their home to stay for a few days while we get to know one another. Please tell Amah, as she'll be glad to know!

Our elder auntie could not hear, but that problem was fixed. We're planning on a family picnic soon. Many will be there from Auntie's town. Many want to swim for the first time.

Do not worry about us. We are enjoying our travel together. I can't wait to see you again and catch up on all the family news.

Always yours,

Mei Lin

Mei Lin was so glad to send this good news right away. Since last night, she felt she was truly finishing a walk that her mother started eighteen years ago when she was only three years old. Mrs. Woo said she would send the letters early next week with the mail carrier who came twice a month to deliver and pick up mail. She sealed the envelope for father and opened the next sheet of paper to write to Liko.

"Woo Lan!" a voice called from the courtyard.

"Ah, I can hear that man calling," said Mrs. Woo. "I wonder who is it?"

"It's Cadre Xin," said Woo Lan, as he walked out of their back bedroom. "I'll greet him."

By the time the two men entered the house, Mei Lin had put away her stationery. Cadre Xin went directly to the stove. "Is it true, Mrs. Woo?" asked the cadre.

Mrs. Woo wiped her hands on her apron and then looked the cadre in the eye. "Ask me any question you like, Cadre Xin. I'll turn around and you just ask me something."

Mrs. Woo turned around and Cadre Xin nervously glanced at the girls at the table. He cleared his throat and then asked, "How many years have you been deaf?"

"I was deaf for eleven years," Mrs. Woo answered.

The cadre looked wildly at Woo Lan and then the girls. "Why did Mrs. Ma throw the stone at you? Was it an accident?"

Mrs. Woo turned slowly around and picked up her spatula to turn the eggs. "Cadre, I have forgiven Mrs. Ma for throwing the stone at me. So whether it was an accident or not, I want to forget about it."

"Mrs. Woo!" exclaimed the cadre. "You can hear?"

Mrs. Woo swung around, all smiles. Her wrinkles faded as God filled in every crease with glorious light. "Yes, I can hear."

Cadre Xin walked over to the girls.

"How?" he asked. "And Mr. Woo—he stands straight as a stick. How can this be possible?"

Mei Lin glanced at Fei. This was indeed the moment of truth. The cadre wanted to know and Mei Lin would not hide it from him.

"The One who made the earth and skies made her well."

"You? You made the earth and skies?" he asked Mei Lin.

"Oh, no," Mei Lin answered quickly. "Our God made the earth and skies. He made people and—would you like to hear His story?"

The cadre looked at his watch. "I am on my way to my office this morning, but I had to stop by here first. Will you be here all day?"

"We will be here this morning," Mei Lin answered. She felt that was the right answer. If the cadre wanted to call the county cadre to report her, it would take him longer than a few hours to drive way out here to arrest her.

"I will be back in two hours," said the cadre. "Don't go away."

The cadre left and Mrs. Woo served the omelets. "I'm not sure what he's up to," she said. "Maybe you girls should hide."

"He could be reporting us," said Fei.

"I think one of us should hide," said Mei Lin. "Fei, why don't you hide? I want to stay here this morning as I promised. That way only one of us risks arrest. And you could escape to the next village."

"Travel alone?" asked Fei. "I don't like that idea. And I don't think you should be alone either."

"If the cadre is planning to report us, it will take hours for a county officer to drive way out here. So I'm thinking that if the cadre really wants to talk, he will come back in two hours and listen. Maybe he is genuinely interested in God."

Woo Lan sat down beside them and fingered his chopsticks, his omelet left untouched. "He is the same cadre who reported our meeting fifteen years ago. No one has tried to hold a meeting without his permission since then."

"Now, don't let these omelets go to waste," said Mrs. Woo. "As soon as you've finished breakfast you can figure out what to do."

"I agree," said Mei Lin. "Perhaps Fei and I can take some time out by the stream to pray. God will help us know what to do."

Mei Lin and Fei quickly finished their letters after breakfast and gave them to Mrs. Woo for safekeeping.

"May I go with you girls?" asked Mrs. Woo. "I haven't heard the sweet sound of the water running through the stream in years. It may seem silly, but I feel like I must hear it again. And the birds—I can barely remember their songs anymore."

"Oh, yes," Mei Lin agreed. "Please come with us. We will pray with our eyes open. It is less dangerous that way."

"Shall I bring incense?" asked Mrs. Woo. "Or is that too danger-ous, too?"

Mei Lin smiled. Mrs. Woo wanted very much to please God. "No, you will not need incense or an offering. God will be pleased to see you and listen to you without all of that."

The two girls and their elder "auntie," the name she used to de-scribe Mrs. Woo to Father, walked to the creek. Mei Lin and Fei used the water to wash their clothing in a bucket. Mrs. Woo filled the buckets. Everyone looked busy, but in reality they were praying, sometimes quietly and sometimes out loud.

"Hello!"

Mei Lin looked up from her sudsy bucket. "Hello, Dun. How are you today?"

"I'm fine," he answered.

"We missed you last night," said Mei Lin.

"Oh—I was helping the cadre. The Xias are always fighting plus there was a fire to put out."

Mei Lin nodded. "The cadre is lucky to have a boy like you to help him."

Dun smiled at that. "I hope to be a cadre one day, but in another village. I don't want to live here all of my life."

Mei Lin understood this boy's need for adventure. If all the Christians in China had Dun's ambition, most of China would probably be saved by now.

"Perhaps you'll get to leave here, soon," said Mei Lin. "I know how it feels to want to experience other places."

"Perhaps you'll change your minds and take me with you?" the boy asked.

Mei Lin was surprised at his boldness. "I wish we could," she replied. "If we were boys, it would be easier. And if you shared our faith it would be easier, too."

Dun scuffed a few rocks into the water with his feet. "I won't stay here forever," he answered. Then he turned and walked away.

Mei Lin was about to call him back when Mr. Woo appeared around the back of their house.

"The cadre is here, girls," he called. "He brought Sun. It's time to begin!"

Mei Lin and Fei carried their wet laundry to the house where Mrs. Woo insisted upon hanging it up for them while they greeted the cadre. The visitors exchanged small talk with the girls until Mrs. Woo hung the laundry and served hot tea, a rare morning luxury. The cadre had small eyes and long sideburns. He did not look like Cadre Fang and did not appear threatening either. Mei Lin saw no signs of a police raid. Still, she wondered if this questioning was the cadre's personal interest or an interrogation before the arrest. The cadre's elbows were on the table and he leaned forward, his eyes full of questions. "Sun tells me that he has been healed of his stomach pain."

"Is your pain gone today as well?" Mei Lin asked Sun.

"Yes, gone," Sun agreed. He looked nervously at the cadre and then at Mei Lin. Mei Lin could tell he was afraid and she felt great pity for him.

"How did this happen?" asked Cadre Xin. "And how did it happen that Mrs. Woo was healed?"

"I'm sorry you were called away last night," said Mei Lin. "We told the story last night of the One who made the earth and skies. He is the One that healed Sun and Woo Fan."

"Yes," Fei agreed. "God healed them, not us."

"And why isn't everyone in the world healed?" asked Cadre Xin. "Why are there hospitals full of sick people if there is a God who heals?"

"This God who heals requires that people believe in Him," said Fei.

"Do you have special permission to do this?" asked the cadre.

"You mean from the government?" asked Fei. Mei Lin heard Fei's voice crack and saw the tension across her face.

"No," said the cadre. "I mean permission from your God."

Mei Lin answered carefully. "Jesus is God's son. He said that after we tell people about Him, He would convince people He is the real God by healing the sick and doing miracles. He wants to help people who believe in Him. People get sick or can even die early because they lack knowledge. The Bible says people perish for a lack of knowledge."

"And what about offerings?" asked Cadre Xin. "Even good gods require offerings and incense—some require great sacrifices."

"Yes, a sacrifice is required," Mei Lin answered. She and Fei exchanged glances. "So God in Heaven sent his Son to be our sacrifice. That way we don't have to give sacrifices, just believe in the sacrifice that God gave us."

Cadre Xin was quiet for a moment and he looked at Sun and then at Mrs. Woo. "You must tell me the whole story."

Mei Lin felt trapped. To speak of such things in the Woo home could put them in danger. The cadre could choose to file this conversation as an interrogation and in giving the address of the conversation the Woos would be suspected of helping them.

"Cadre, Sun's daughter Jenji has invited us for tea again this evening. With your permission, perhaps we could tell the story again there."

"You are from the Three Self Church?"

"No," Fei answered.

Cadre Xin sat back in the straight back chair and shuffled his feet. "This is a counter-revolutionary meeting?"

"Oh, no," said Mei Lin. "Our God loves all Chinese, including the president and all of the PSB officers."

Cadre Xin seemed to relax a little. "We get very little news out here. Just the radio station and the messages haven't changed much from year to year."

"I understand," Mei Lin answered. "I don't want you to think we have come to your village to start a counter revolution. We are just passing through and we hope to leave by the end of this week."

"You are welcome to stay," the cadre answered as he stood to leave. Sun stood beside him. "And as for tonight, seven o'clock?"

"Yes," Fei answered.

"On one condition," Mei Lin put in. She summoned all the boldness she could muster and added, "You must not press charges against Jenji's family. You yourself have asked me to share my story tonight. Jenji has nothing to do with that."

"Of course," the cadre agreed.

"We look forward to seeing you there," said Mei Lin.

~

This time it was Mei Lin who felt she would burst if she did not speak. After the cadre came, Jenji called everyone to stop and listen. Fei stood at the back wall and watched. Mei Lin knew she was praying.

"I want to welcome Ho Ting's most honorable citizen, Cadre Xin. Cadre, would you stand?"

The cadre stood and murmurs and nods of approval went up from the crowd.

"Cadre Xin was so kind this morning to give us his permission to tell you the story tonight of the One who made the earth and skies."

Several people shifted in their seats, none daring to look at Cadre Xin. Mei Lin pressed forward. She told the story of creation and the life and death of Jesus. This time she also included the story of how Jesus Himself was baptized in the water and in the Holy Spirit.

Sun looked at her just then, a tear in his eye. Dun was there, listening intently. The people were ravenous for spiritual food and Mei Lin felt like a caterer at a Chinese New Year celebration.

"The Bible says that if we decide to become a Christian, we should be baptized, too," said Mei Lin. "To hold a baptism, everyone meets at a place where there is water. In Shanghai, new believers are baptized in a bathtub. Another believer stands beside you and helps you to immerse your body and head under the water and come back up. In this way you are saying publicly that you believe in Jesus Christ. When you go under the water, you are signifying that you believe Jesus died and was buried. When you come up from the water, you signify that you believe He arose from the dead."

Cadre Xin suddenly stood to his feet. "Thank you, Mei Lin, for sharing this story. I am sorry I cannot stay longer."

Mei Lin was shocked. It was not the Chinese way to interrupt a story. Perhaps suggesting baptism was too much for the cadre.

"Honorable Cadre Xin, we understand," Mei Lin answered. "Your work in the village is most important." Her voice did not quiver although her heart shook like a leaf in the wind, knowing full well that the cadre could report them or order the meeting to be raided. Mei Lin stuffed her hands in her pockets so no one would see them trembling.

As soon as the gate clicked behind the cadre, the atmosphere of the meeting changed. Mei Lin looked at Jenji. "Jenji?"

"My husband will speak," replied Jenji.

Jenji's husband looked like he was in his late twenties with a rugged handsomeness that comes from long hours of work in the fields. He stood up. "My father was healed last night." He looked at Mrs. Woo. "Mrs. Woo can hear again. I myself have become a believer in God's Son, Jesus, and my heart feels clean and all heavy darkness is gone. This is the God I want in my life. Last night after the meeting dismissed, I built a dam upstream, a place where we can go tonight to be baptized. We can go now if you wish."

Mr. Woo stood up. "Bo, thank you for building this place for the baptism. Some of you know that my son and daughter-in-law are in jail because they held meetings like this one."

A gasp went up from the crowd followed by the low sound of talking. Mr. Woo raised his hand to stop the crowd.

"I prayed to my son's God and told Him if He brings my son home and if He brings the preacher woman to our town again, I will believe. This girl is the daughter of the preacher woman who came to our village eighteen years ago."

Every eye was on Mei Lin now.

"Her mother died after being tortured in prison for her faith."

The crowd was visibly moved and shocked. Mei Lin waved them to silence.

"There is sometimes a high cost to follow Jesus in China," she said. "My mother paid the high price. I was beaten myself and put in prison three years ago. I would like to suggest that if you want to be baptized, we meet at midnight tonight at the dam Mr. Bo just referred to."

"I will come," said Jenji. "I believe that Jesus is the true God."

"And I will come," said Bo.

"I want to be baptized, too," said Mrs. Woo.

The whole courtyard brimmed with approvals for the baptism.

"Please stay and enjoy the food brought this evening," said Jenji's husband. "Then we will all go home and pretend to go to bed. Walk by the moonlight tonight and do not use lanterns. I will have a lantern lit at the place where the dam is built upstream. Walk the stream until you see the light."

Benches shuffled about and people mingled once more before going home.

⁓

Mei Lin and Fei left with the Woos around 11:30 for the baptism. She touched the New Testament that was in her back pocket to be sure it was still there. Mei Lin was upset with herself for not remembering to tell the villagers to stagger their walks to the dam. If everyone left at once, it would be much more noticeable to the cadre or to those opposed to the baptism. However, it appeared that the entire village was asleep. Besides, Woo Fan said the cadre lived at the far end of town, so they shouldn't be spotted.

Mei Lin wasn't sure if the full moon above was a friend or foe— they could see their way in this moonlight, but then the cadre could easily spot them, too. Quietly, she and Fei followed the Woos out of the courtyard and latched the gate.

Barking!

"Get down!" Mr. Woo whispered the order. "Like this." Mr. Woo was hunched over, his hands touching the ground. Mrs. Woo clung to his side, hunching in the same manner. After a few minutes, the dog finally stopped barking and Mr. Woo led them behind the house to the stream. The moon glimmered its long reflection over the stream. Mei Lin welcomed the babbling noise it made. Perhaps their footsteps would not be heard as easily.

Mei Lin was surprised to see a couple of other people ahead of them. They were following the stream and she felt sure they were believers, too.

Good! Not everyone will leave ten minutes before midnight.

The girls followed Mr. Woo along the stream, past the place where they hid Bibles only two days before. The moon's watery reflection faded as dark shadows of trees and bamboo stretched their arms across the water's edge. The stream widened somewhat and—

There!

The lantern could be seen now in the distance. Jenji's husband, Bo, had cut back the weeds along the bank of the stream, creating an accessible path to the dam.

"How shall we do this?" asked Fei as they walked together.

"Let's stand side by side," answered Mei Lin. "Some of the men are much bigger than you and me. I think we should ask them to kneel and dunk down forward into the water."

"And if a child or a small woman wants to be baptized, perhaps we can have them bow forward," said Fei. "Mei Lin? Are you sure it was your mother who first visited this village eighteen years ago?"

"Mr. and Mrs. Woo recognized the scarf," said Mei Lin.

"It's just like I told you, isn't it?" asked Fei. "You caught the cloak that fell when your mother went up to Heaven."

"I think so," said Mei Lin. "Look at this harvest of people! I'm sure that it was the prayers of my mother and her comrades that made preaching the gospel here so easy for us."

"And the healing," Fei added. "One lady named Lian had boils on her face and they all went away."

"Really?" asked Mei Lin.

"Yes, she told me tonight that she woke up this morning and the boils were gone."

"Amazing," said Mei Lin. "Our God is amazing. But Father never mentioned healings and miracles when my mother evangelized years ago. I wonder why this is happening now?"

"I don't know," said Fei. "But just think of it. No one knew the gospel in China when Old Mother Zhang was our age. At least no one we know. Perhaps God is adding more gifts to His evangelists in China as we grow up in Him."

"Perhaps," said Mei Lin. "I mean, there were only a few miracles by big leaders like Moses and Elisha before Jesus was born. After Jesus did miracles and healings, he said his Church would do even more than He did."

A handful of believers could be seen now, huddling at the bank of the stream. Bo was walking about in water up to his thighs, adding new branches to the dam he started the night before.

Mei Lin's heart warmed at the sight of these new courageous believers. They knew the risk, yet they were here. Mei Lin felt an immense love for each one of them and spent the next fifteen minutes getting to know their names and families. She was pleased to meet Lian, a young single woman who kept touching her cheek to show her the place where her skin was cleansed.

"I would like to meet with you and Fei sometime," Lian said eagerly. The girls took off their shoes and dipped their toes into the shallow water near the shore. "I want to know more about Jesus—and more about what you are doing and where you are going from here."

Mei Lin smiled. Lian was so excited and her smile was like a lantern that hung over the stream. "Let's meet tomorrow afternoon," said Mei Lin. "After you're finished in the field?"

Lian nodded. "That would be good. I will come to get you at the Woos?"

"Yes," agreed Mei Lin.

It was time to begin the baptism. Mei Lin and Fei waded out to the middle of the stream. Mei Lin thought of John the Baptist, wading out into the river to invite Jews to repent. She held up her little Bible and explained that this book contained God's words.

Fei opened Mei Lin's Bible and read the story about the time when a man asked Philip, "What is preventing me from being baptized?"

Fei said, "And look at you and you and you! What is preventing you from being baptized? You know you are risking prison to be here, but you came. Before we baptize you tonight, we will ask each one of you to give your testimony of what Jesus did for you. If you are shy and do not like to speak, we will ask you, 'Do you believe in this Jesus we've told you about and this book called the Bible?'"

"If you say 'yes,' then we will ask you to kneel like this." Fei demonstrated the kneeling and dunking one's head under.

Mei Lin added, "If the water is too high for you to kneel, then you may stand and we will help you bow and dunk your head under the water." Mei Lin looked at Fei, the question in her eyes.

"I'm ready," she answered.

"Who would like to be first?" asked Mei Lin.

"My father and I will be first," said Bo.

Mei Lin couldn't have been more delighted. Father and son walked together into the creek and stood side by side. Mei Lin hadn't planned on doing two at a time, but there was something very powerful taking place in this first baptism and she could feel it in the quiver of her throat and the flutter of her spirit.

"I gave my testimony this evening," said Bo. "I do believe in Jesus Christ. I feel quivery inside—like a shiver and a warm feeling all at once. My wife says I am a changed man."

"Do you believe that Jesus died and was buried and rose from the dead for you, Bo?" asked Mei Lin.

"Yes, I do," Bo replied.

Sun cleared his throat and waited a moment. Out of respect for elders, everyone was silent and waited until he was ready.

"I ate three full meals today," he said, his voice cracking with emotion. "I was sick and unable to eat three full meals in one day for months. Now, because of Jesus, I am healed. I have no pain."

Mei Lin could tell that the people on the shore had no idea how to respond to this. So she simply said, "We thank God, Sun. Thank God."

"Thank God, Sun," came the echoes from the bank of the stream, "Thank God."

"Do you believe that Jesus died and was buried and rose from the dead for you, Sun?" asked Fei.

"Yes, I do," Sun replied.

"Then according to the command of Jesus, we baptize you in the name of the Father, the Son, and the Holy Spirit."

Father and son emerged from the water, wiped their faces and embraced one another. Mei Lin and Fei squeezed one another, too. Such open displays of affection were not common in China, but never had Mei Lin felt so much happiness inside.

One by one, husbands, wives, and even a few children were baptized. Mei Lin looked around for Dun. His parents came forward for baptism, but she did not see Dun anywhere. She wondered if he missed the announcement about the baptism. He was such a curious boy; he surely wouldn't have missed the adventure of sneaking out at night.

The shy woman who was healed of the boils stood last in line to be baptized. Her testimony was the simplest of all.

"I am not worthy of such great love," she said.

Tears sprang to Mei Lin's eyes at hearing this confession. Fei, who loved the woman dearly, placed her hand on the woman's back and asked, "Lian, do you believe that Jesus was buried and rose from the dead for you?"

The woman held her face in her hands and nodded profusely. "Yes, yes!"

Lian came out of the water, her face shining like that of an angel. "Oh, thank you, Jesus!" she boldly exclaimed. "Thank you!"

At that moment, a song that Mei Lin learned in the house church in Shanghai came to her mind and so she sang it aloud.

The stream of life
The stream of joy
Flow tenderly into my heart
The stream of life
The stream of joy
Flow tenderly into my heart

After singing it a few times, the people joined her jubilance. Then she taught them the verse.

I want to sing a song
A song from heaven
The dark clouds above
The sorrow in my heart
They all disappear
The stream of life
The stream of joy
Flow tenderly into my heart
The stream of life
The stream of joy
Flow tenderly into my heart

The excitement and joy was high and Mei Lin felt like dancing. A flicker of light in the woods behind the people singing on the shoreline caught her eye. She looked at Fei who didn't seem to notice.

There it was again. Mei Lin continued to mouth the words to the song she knew so well, but her thoughts were on the mysterious light that flashed in the woods.

Poydan, North Korea

CHAPTER 18

Young Soon bent over and kissed Nam Gil's forehead. His eyes, no longer dull from hunger, searched her face like shining lanterns. "Goodnight, Oma."

"Goodnight, Son. I'll wake you up later."

"Can't we eat when the sun rises?" asked Nam Gil as he yawned.

"Of course not," Young Soon whispered. She put her fingers on his thin lips. "You are to tell no one that we get up in the night to eat rice."

Nam Gil nodded. Over and over again, Young Soon had told her son to not talk about the rice in the cupboard. He knew it was important. But the food seemed to influence both his strength and his thoughts. As soon as he was well enough to get up and walk around, he was also smart enough to ask more questions.

Young Soon refused to eat more than once a day, even though her sister thought that because of the baby she should eat more. "What if I am too sick to travel?" Young Soon argued. "Then I won't have any food in the fall. And what if I leave but Hwan cannot bring you more food and you are left here to starve again?" Young Soon was convinced that she must leave some of her food here with Ja.

She looked down at Nam Gil and ran her finger along his jaw line. She realized that, although his face was very thin, the green tint was disappearing and his skin had some elasticity again. It thrilled her heart to know he would eat a full bowl of rice tonight and his deep groans from hunger pains and grass poisoning would not awaken her tomorrow. She rubbed the hollow of his cheek and then bent over to kiss him in the same spot.

"You are getting stronger," she said.

"And you are getting fatter," Nam Gil teased.

She tweaked his nose. "The fatter the better, big brother. Han Chun will need strength to be born."

"And you, Oma, you will need strength, too?"

Young Soon nodded.

"And Aunt Ja will help you?"

She nodded again. She wondered that Min-Hee's birth had left such an impression on him. He was only five when she was born, but somehow this eight-year-old knew that his mother would need help delivering a new baby. Of course, she nearly died last month after she collapsed, so perhaps it was no wonder that the delivery of the baby was worrying him. She tried to put his mind at ease. "You're beginning to talk like your father," she said.

Nam Gil turned his face toward the wall. "I wish Uncle Hwan would have come before Father died."

She put her hand over her mouth. "Oh, yes, that would have been wonderful," she said. Tears sprung to her eyes. "I miss him so much."

Nam Gil reached for his mother and they held one another. She rocked him a little, then held him out in front of her and whispered, "You are just like your father—strong and brave and self-sacrificing. Whenever I miss him I only have to look at you and find comfort."

Nam Gil smiled at that. His smile made the sadness dissipate. Young Soon watched his smile and memorized it in her mind. She wanted to use this new picture to erase the old one of the gaunt, green-tinted child near death's door only thirty days ago. She wanted to think of Nam Gil with a smile, looking healthy and strong. Although it was too dangerous to tickle him right now, she was sorely tempted to do it anyway.

"One day, when we are with Uncle Hwan in China, I am going to tickle you," she said. "Because I want to hear you laugh."

Nam Gil looked at her quizzically.

"Don't worry, you'll find out what I mean." She kissed his head once more and he hugged his thin blanket and rolled to his side to sleep. She ran her hand over his head. His hair color had not returned yet, but Young Soon noticed there was new hair growth and it was softer than before. Young Soon would not cut out the red hair. It was better that his hair remained red. Otherwise the neighbors or, worse, the gotchebee children, would grow suspicious. Someone may try to steal the rice and beans or, worse, report them to the police.

With that thought, Young Soon went to the kitchen and, after looking outside her windows to be sure no one was around, she checked under her cupboard. There, on the bottom shelf, far in the back, was the locked box. That box held her entire life. She placed her hand on her rounded abdomen. Without that box, she knew that neither of her sons would survive.

Her biggest fear was that one of the gotchebees would smell the rice and report her to the authorities. As her fear grew, her hatred grew. The gotchebees were like hidden snakes in the grass, never seen until they were underneath your feet. *Thieves. Spies.*

Ja was softer. She argued that they were someone's children and if Father were here he would have helped them. Young Soon wasn't so sure. Would Father help another man's children while his own family starved to death? No. Young Soon was sure he would hide the rice, too.

It was nearly dark now. Every day she and Ja went to the political meeting and then slowly shuffled up the hill to find grass. Of course, they could have walked faster now that they were stronger and they really didn't need the grass, but neither sister wanted to raise the suspicions of the others.

Young Soon picked up the broom for the first time in weeks. The baby was coming and she wanted to use her new strength to clean the house for his arrival. As she swept, she looked at Nam Gil. She could see his tiny frame breathing evenly under the thin blanket. The orange glow of the setting sun cast its beam over his head, shining on the wall above the On Dol stove. Young Soon looked longingly at Min-Hee's mat. Even though her little girl was gone, she would not roll it up and put it away. Everyone in the neighborhood believed Ja when she told them that Min-Hee wandered off after her mother was sick and in a coma for three days. Everyone thought Young Soon was going crazy with hysteria over her lost Min-Hee. She could tell by the way people looked at her at the political meetings, that they almost feared her. Ja told her that one of the mine bosses said, "Who knows when that crazy woman will snap?" Young Soon and Ja were delighted—perhaps no one would suspect she was a talbukja. They would all think she finally lost her mind and went out to search for her daughter.

As far as they knew, no one in town suspected that Min-Hee was with her uncle. He'd been gone for years and some of the younger officers didn't even realize he existed. Truthfully, Young Soon sometimes felt she *would* go mad until she knew for sure that Hwan had safely carried her little daughter back to China. Young Soon sighed. She could only believe the best. To believe the worst was unbearable. And so, as she swept the last corner, Young Soon imagined her little daughter eating beans and rice in broad daylight. Hwan said the rice came from people who believe in the God who loves.

Young Soon thought about the God who loves. She had no incense to pray to such a God and she wasn't sure she wanted to try. What if he was Chinese or only cared for the people living in China? Besides, the Juche theology of North Korea taught her to be self-sufficient and not rely on silly gods. *But didn't I catch a star when Han Chun's spirit moved within me? Didn't I waken to a bowl of rice gruel!* She shook herself.

Is the God who loves only a dream? Did he hang the stars like men hang lanterns?

The quest for truth was beating in her heart, beating ever stronger since the day she nearly died. It was all so hard to understand; yet she tried to find words for what she was feeling and faith for what she wanted to believe. She must have faith in herself.

I must know what the truth is. But why are there so many doubts? Is Hwan right? Have I been lied to my whole life? Or is Hwan deceived? No, the newspaper articles proved it was true— there are healthy children in the world who are not starving. Did I make the wrong decision in sending my daughter to hide in China? Is she being fed or is it a lie? No, I have the rice and beans to prove she is being fed. Oh, God who loves, help me!

A wave of shock ran through her spine. She just asked the God who loves to help her. What if He can hear her thoughts in the way that the government says that Kim Jong-il can hear her thoughts? It was all so confusing.

The room was nearly dark. It seemed to match the state of her mind—dark and growing darker. It was dusk and the first stars would appear soon. Something inside urged her to go outside. She leaned her broom against the wall in the corner and quietly tiptoed outside to watch them arrive. Good—no one was outside. She latched the door behind her, walked around to the back of her house, and sat on the wooden bench. Her father had built this bench and then cemented it into the ground years ago as a birthday gift to Mother. Father and Mother spent many quiet nights together sitting on this bench, watching the skies after Father came home from the factory.

When Young Soon was about ten, she and her father sat together here on a night much like this one. She was intrigued by the various constellations that she was learning about in school, so together they searched the skies to see what treasures they could find there. They watched the moon creep up behind the mountains and that was when Father first told her about shooting stars.

"And if you're very quick, you can jump up and maybe even catch one," Father said.

"Really?" she'd asked. *What a childish thought!* She looked into the heavens.

"Really?" she whispered now into the darkness.

Just then a bright star appeared in the bluish purple haze of twilight.

"And you are not a star at all," she said. "You are Venus."

Two smaller stars appeared and then another one beside Venus. "I don't know who you are at all," she whispered to the new stars.

She thought about what Hwan told her about the God who loves. *Is it His hand behind each star?* She imagined an invisible hook above each one, perched on an invisible line that stretched east to west, like the rope that hung at the officers' party.

Such a grand entrance they made! One at a time they flickered on, as though each one had its own special flame. Each new star that sputtered onto the black canvas was like a new sign, pointing to a new hope, a new way of thinking. She thought of her own heart, dark like the sky, and Hwan's words like the stars of hope that twinkled into her darkness.

"Oh!" A shooting star suddenly glazed across the sky and, instinctively, Young Soon jumped to her feet and reached for it. She missed! Just as quickly she reached for her abdomen. The baby? Was it time—

The squeezing sensation increased and then subsided. Young Soon trembled. She sat and waited. Minutes passed until, again, her middle contracted, signaling her that it was time. Maybe she didn't miss that star after all. Maybe—maybe she caught that shooting star! As the tightening subsided, she tilted her head to the sky above her and whispered softly to the God who loves. "And is Your hand behind this little star? Will You hang this little star over the skies of China?"

Rural China

CHAPTER 19

Mei Lin wakened at eight o'clock and lay in bed thinking about the people of Ho Ting. Nearly every person in the village became a Christian in the last three weeks and she was tempted to stay and teach them for a while. However, something was unsettled inside of her today—a restlessness perhaps.

I think it's time to move on.

Fei was already up, so Mei Lin rolled up her blanket, strapped on her money belt, and brushed her hair. Her body was still tired, but her spirit flew above the clouds. There was so much to do today!

She went outside to use the out building. Mrs. Woo was hauling water from the stream to water her garden.

"Good morning," she called.

"Good morning, Mei Lin," Mrs. Woo answered. "How are you feeling today?"

"Wonderful, thank you," answered Mei Lin. She used the out building and then washed her hands in the stream. "Where is Fei?"

"Oh, she was up at sunrise this morning," said Woo Fan as she slowly dumped water over her red pepper plants. Then she walked closer to Mei Lin and whispered. "Fei went back to the dam to pray. She said she wanted to leave before the villagers went to the fields today. Wouldn't eat a bite of food either."

"Ah, she's fasting then."

"Fasting?" asked Mrs. Woo. She walked with Mei Lin through the courtyard and into the house. "What is fasting?"

"There are times when a Christian feels urged to stop eating for a meal or sometimes he or she may stop eating for days at a time. Fasting and prayer bring much power into the life of a Christian."

"Well, then you girls must have fasted a lot before coming to Ho Ting," replied Mrs. Woo. "The power of God has touched our whole village."

Mei Lin smiled at that. "Well, yes, we did fast. But only a couple of meals. I think we can attribute the great response to the prayers my mother prayed years ago when she visited here. We also have Christians in Tanching and Du Yan who are praying for us. Do you have any relatives in WuMa?"

"Why, yes, we do," answered Mrs. Woo. "My sister moved there after the Cultural Revolution. She still writes to us from time to time."

"Is she a Christian?" asked Mei Lin.

"She didn't say," answered Mrs. Woo as she hung the bucket on the wall. "Our mail is checked sometimes, you know."

Mei Lin nodded in agreement. "Well, there is a network of house churches in WuMa and the Christians there asked my friend to send missionaries to this village to preach the gospel to their relatives."

Mrs. Woo clasped her hands together. "Oh, do you think it would be my sister?"

"Maybe," replied Mei Lin. "There are many people praying for us."

Mrs. Woo insisted that Mei Lin sit down to eat her breakfast. "You'll have to eat Fei's portion, too," she said cheerily. "Are you planning to join her this morning?"

Mei Lin prayed over her food and then answered Mrs. Woo. "I was hoping to talk to Sun and Bo sometime today," she said. "I know Bo is in the field, but Sun is home, isn't he?"

"Yes, Sun should be home," Mrs. Woo answered. "He and his wife tend their garden in the mornings. Bo takes good care of them."

There was a wistful sadness in Mrs. Woo's voice. Mei Lin could hear the message—the Woos may never have their son nearby to take care of them in their old age.

"Trust God to take care of you," said Mei Lin. "I know it's not easy, but I'm sure that is how your son has prayed for you all these years while in prison."

"Yes, I'm sure you're right," she said. "If God can heal my ears, then surely He can bring my son home."

"There is a special gift that comes to those who suffer for Jesus," said Mei Lin. "It's called the Gethsemane gift."

"What is that?"

"Gethsemane is the garden where Jesus prayed before He was crucified. He knew He was about to experience terrible pain for our sin and God gave Him angels who strengthened Him to bear the burden of that suffering."

"I want to hear more about—"

The courtyard gate slammed just then and someone was running inside.

"Bo!" cried Mrs. Woo. "I thought you were—"

"No time," he said, heaving for air. "I had one of the children follow Fei to the dam this morning." He looked at Mei Lin. "Fei was just arrested by the PSB. They are on their way here to find you. You must go!"

Mei Lin stood to her feet, her hand over her mouth. "Fei? Oh, Jesus, help her!"

"Come on, you must go now!"

"Where?"

"I have a place to hide."

Mei Lin grabbed her blanket and her bookbag. Mrs. Woo quickly gathered her breakfast and put that and a few other morsels of food into a sack and gave them to her. She took a tin teacup from her sink and handed it to Mei Lin. Her hands were visibly shaking.

"God go with you, child." Her voice cracked.

Mei Lin's knees were weak, but she put the tin cup into her bag and squeezed Mrs. Woo's hand. "Please tell them that I was here but I left ahead of Fei and you do not know where I went. You think I left permanently because I took my backpack with me."

"Yes, yes, don't worry," she said.

"They're coming," said Bo. "Let's go."

Mei Lin had no time to think and she was grateful for Bo's quick planning. She had no idea where he was taking her, but she knew she could trust him.

Quickly she hugged Mrs. Woo. "Thank you," she whispered. "Now, go, hide the Bible."

"Thank you, Mei Lin," Mrs. Woo replied. "Now go!"

Mei Lin ran out of the courtyard behind Bo, her bookbag slapping her back.

~

Mei Lin lifted her head from her bookbag where she'd laid for a long time, probably hours, praying into the darkness. Black. Black and damp, like her thoughts right now. A dim diagonal beam of light caressed the far corner of the cave. Mei Lin knew it was still daylight outside, but it was terribly dark inside. She didn't dare venture outside until all danger of being found by the PSB had passed. Bo checked the cave well to be sure it wasn't occupied and then left her here, promising to return the next morning. Mei Lin had no choice but to trust him and remain until he brought word back tomorrow morning. She had no idea where she was, only that they'd run for more than an hour after they fled from the PSB.

Wasn't it only this morning that she felt unsettled? Her thoughts turned to the baptisms three weeks ago. That night a light flickered in the woods during the last two baptisms. Bo had seen it, too. Nothing came of it and so they forgot about it and continued their work in Ho Ting. After arriving at the cave this morning, concern for Fei nearly overwhelmed her and she prayed for her until she fell asleep.

The dark cave reminded her of the prison in Shanghai. I hope there aren't any rats here. The cave made its own kind of hollow sound inside even when nothing moved. Mei Lin listened for a few moments and then her mind turned back to Fei.

"Jesus, help her," Mei Lin whispered into the darkness. Her voice bounced off the rock walls, magnifying her prayer. She could taste the musty dampness in her mouth and considered praying silently. After a few moments she couldn't concentrate, so Mei Lin shook off her fears and again spoke into the darkness. "Fei was so afraid of persecution and now she is in the hands of persecutors, people who hate You. Please strengthen her, Jesus, so that she will not deny You. Give her the gift of faith to believe You right now."

Mei Lin thought about how Fei was afraid of persecution when they first arrived in Ho Ting. She wondered what prompted Fei to fast and pray this morning. Did I miss something? Was Heaven warning me to leave yesterday and I didn't listen? Mei Lin carefully thought through their day yesterday. No, the unsettled feeling did not come until this morning. She scolded herself for sleeping in when she should have been praying. Mei Lin's lips moved once more in intercessions for her friend. Tears of compassion mingled with sorrow for her friend. She continued until her face felt swollen from crying. She shuddered. She needed to get out of this dismal cave before its dreariness soaked into her soul.

Mei Lin stood to her feet and walked hunched over to the front of the cave to peer outside. The sun was still shining and it appeared to be midday. She inched out to the cleft of the rock which formed the entrance and looked below. Her new home was high on the rocky cliffs above the same creek that ran through the Ho Ting Village. The rocky crags east of the village used to be Bo's childhood playground. He easily helped them find their footing to the cave high in the rocks.

Mei Lin knelt at the edge of the entrance and watched below. The gurgling of the creek was a comforting sound. She sat for some time until she saw a brown squirrel scamper across a fallen log that formed a natural bridge across the creek.

Her eyes scanned the forest edges, searching for the police. Nothing moved except the turning of the leaves in the trees as the wind stroked them. Clusters of bamboo grew in spaces where the trees weren't prevalent. Long rays of sunlight shot through the ceiling of the forest to spotlight the leafy forest floor and mirrored glittery light on the water below.

If there was a path, Mei Lin couldn't see it from her position. Bo's childhood playground was like a fantasy world, unspoiled by human hands. Mei Lin sighed. She felt relieved and safe, yet her heart longed to know how Fei was doing. She hoped and prayed for her escape. How would she continue to journey to the other villages without her?

Mei Lin changed positions. She sat on a low rock at the cave doorway and leaned back against the cool stone wall. She had to think. She had to plan.

Pastor Wong would surely be disappointed if she did not complete the map. The map!

Mei Lin ran back into the dark cave and groped for her bookbag. She sat back outside on her rock seat and searched its contents. Mrs. Woo's tin cup and breakfast was on the top. She dug past her Bible and toothbrush and washcloths until her hand touched it. The scarf! Mei Lin pulled the scarf out of the bag. Besides her

Bible, Mother's scarf was her most precious possession. She needed it right now. Mei Lin wrapped her mother's scarf around her shoulders and adjusted it so that both ends were hanging evenly from both shoulders.

"Mother, I built on what you started in Ho Ting Village," she said softly. "Many were saved, healed, and baptized."

A tear slid down Mei Lin's cheek. It was always during these lonely times when she missed her mother the most. Fei had a Christian mother, someone she could fall back on for advice, comfort, and explanations to the mysteries of life. Father's sisters and mother's brother all moved away during the Cultural Revolution. Mei Lin had no one but Father and Amah. She was thankful for them, but she wondered about her mother—how she felt about certain things, like Amah's insistence on ancestor worship and how Mother thought one should respond in thought or action when experiencing hatred from guards while in prison. These were questions that Mei Lin would never have answers for until she reached Heaven.

The sun was shifting, casting its warmth on the edge of her rocky cave entrance. Mei Lin took off her shoes and dangled her toes in the spray of light and then took out Mrs. Woo's breakfast and finished it. She left the rest of the food in the bag for tomorrow and took out her map. She was to head northeast on the Village Road to the second location. There were several more villages she could go to before circling westward again to WuMa. Mei Lin traced her finger along the path. How would she travel to all these places alone? What would it be like sleeping under the stars without Fei there as a companion? Mei Lin considered her route, reading and retracing the map and studied it until the sun ducked behind the great rock that would be her shelter for the night.

Then, before the light faded completely, she took her tin cup and inched her way along the narrow path that she and Bo hiked earlier that day. After relieving herself behind a large rock, her eyes searched every inch of the forest for police. It seemed to be safe, so she quickly went to the water's edge to drink. She drank and then filled her tin cup for later. The thought came to her that she did not have a bed or firewood inside the cave. Glad for something to do, Mei Lin gathered enough hollow bamboo off the ground for a fire and tied it with a vine to her back. It was easy work—work that she did daily at home. She found enough wood for a longer burning flame and hiked back up the slope with her fuel.

The cave was darker than before and for a while she could see nothing. Mei Lin assembled her fire and put the dry matches in her money belt, still strapped around her waist underneath her pants. She didn't plan on starting a fire, but she wanted to be prepared just in case she needed it. Who knew what animals lived in this cave before her arrival? She had no intentions of being won ton soup for some wild panda bear.

After assembling her new bedroom, Mei Lin grabbed her flashlight and bookbag and went out to the entrance of the cave again. The dark purple haze told her that the sun was nearly set behind the forest wall. The beautiful scenery below now looked dark and foreboding. She'd never spent a night totally alone in the woods. Mei Lin sighed. She felt better inside the cave.

Mei Lin sat on her blanket with her flashlight on and took out the letters her father asked her to write. She hoped Bo would see that it was delivered next week.

Dear Father,

Our visit with elder auntie has come to an end. My good friend is no longer traveling with me. The dogs chased her this morning and we are separated now. She needs our good thoughts. I think about her often and hope you will do the same. I'm sure you will update her mother on her problem with the dogs.

Although I will miss her, I will travel as previously planned without her. Do not worry—I will bring home a harvest when I return in autumn. It will be a time of great celebrating for my good fortune.

Tell Amah I am using the blanket she packed. Please give Liko the other letter inside. I will write again soon.

Wishing good health and success to both of you.

Your daughter,

Mei Lin

Mei Lin knew her father would know that to "think about her friend" meant to pray for her. She stuffed the letter into the self-addressed envelope and quickly penned a separate letter to Liko.

Dear Liko,

I am thinking about you tonight, imagining you are thinking about me, too. I am thinking about what you said to me during our last walk together. Your words stay with me and they form a great house of peace so that I am not afraid. I am wondering if Father helped you fix the plow and if all of your planting is finished now.

Please keep my friend in your thoughts. Maybe you can help her family find out where she went? I'm sure her mother will want to help care for her dog bites. I will miss her on my journey.

Please give your mother my greetings and I will look for your letters to me in the big city where I am going.

Your future wife,

Mei Lin

Mei Lin wanted to tell him about the dream she had about the baby, but decided against it. Some things are better said in person. She put the letter inside the bookbag on the top, ready to give to Bo in the morning. She knew this would probably be the last chance she had to contact Father and Liko for some time.

The cave was musty, damp, and dark. There was no way for an animal or person to get to her except through the front entrance. So she put the sticks between herself and the front entrance, just in case she'd need a fire to scare away an animal—but not so close that it could be seen by a Public Security Bureau police officer.

She lay back on her blanket, using the edge of the backpack as a pillow. She smiled in the darkness. Didn't Liko pray, "Even if the devil looses every wild animal in Jiangxi Province against you, your shield of faith will be like a house of walls around you."

"Oh, God, build the walls of faith around me now."

Her thoughts turned to Fei's capture. Who turned them into the county cadres? For some reason, she doubted that the cadre turned them in. He seemed too interested in their stories and allowed their meetings to go on for three weeks. But if it wasn't the cadre, then who? Who would report them to the county cadres?

Was Fei suffering under the hands of prison guards? Again, the dampness of the cave made her thoughts trace back to Shanghai Prison where she spent nearly a year for passing out "seditious literature" in her high school. Mei Lin had no desire to go back to that place of suffering, but she knew that what she learned in prison would stay with her the rest of her life.

"Oh, God, give Fei Your help tonight. Give her Your protection or—if she is suffering—grant her the Gethsemane gift so that she is able to know You and not be terrified of the devil's plan to hurt her."

Mei Lin lay in the darkness and prayed until her eyes grew heavy with sleep.

Mei Lin wakened suddenly, her heart pounding. What was that? She reached for her flashlight and then covered herself.

"Mei Lin!"

"*Bo?*"

"Mei Lin, it's me, Bo."

"I'm back here," she answered as she sat up on the blanket.

She saw the beam of the flashlight before she saw Bo.

"I have someone with me," said Bo. "A new friend."

Mei Lin searched for Bo's face. She shined the beam past Bo. Lian! The girl who was healed of the boils and was baptized a few weeks ago had accompanied Bo to the cave.

"Hello Mei Lin," said Lian.

Bo also brought the familiar bookbag loaded with Bibles and canteens to take to the next village.

"Was it hard to find the bookbag?" she asked.

"Not at all," Bo answered. "I asked Sun to find it for me while everyone was working in the field.

He was glad to do it."

"Well, thank you, Bo. And Lian, thank you for coming," said Mei Lin. "Please, sit here on my blanket, both of you. Let me wash up at the creek and I'll be right back."

The sun was bright—a good day for traveling—and Mei Lin was thankful for that. She quickly washed up and returned to the darkness of the cave.

"Here, eat this," said Bo. He propped his flashlight so that they could dimly see one another. "Mrs. Woo packed breakfast for all of us."

"Wait," said Mei Lin. "Tell me first about Fei. What happened to her?"

Bo's face looked grim. "We don't know," he said, shrugging his shoulders. "I hope our cadre is satisfied."

"I don't think the cadre turned us in," said Mei Lin.

Bo looked dumbfounded. "Then who?"

"I don't know," said Mei Lin. "But I felt as though God truly worked on his heart. Did this arrest cause him trouble?"

"Hardly," said Bo. "After the arrest, Cadre Xin was walking around with the PSB gathering interviews and evidence to use against you and Fei. What makes you think he's innocent?"

Mei Lin sighed. "I don't know. Let's ask Heaven."

The small group bowed their heads and Mei Lin led them in prayer for Fei. Afterward, Bo opened their breakfast basket from Mrs. Woo, but Mei Lin hardly felt like eating now. She forced down a steamed roll and easily gulped down the warm tea. "Please give my thanks to Mrs. Woo."

"Mei Lin, we need to talk to you," said Bo.

"Okay," she replied. "What is on your mind?"

"What are your plans? Have you thought about what to do from here?"

"Yes," Mei Lin replied. She pulled her map out of her bookbag. "I have a map given to me by the house church leaders. Fei and I were to go to at least these five villages."

Bo held the flashlight closer to the map. "Hmm. I never heard of two of these villages."

"Exactly," said Mei Lin. They are so remote they can't be found on a map. But Jesus cares about these people."

"Why is ZhingCho circled in blue?" asked Bo.

"Pastor Wong—he's one of our leaders—said ZhingCho already has Christians in it and they would take an offering when we got there. We plan to teach, but it was placed in the middle of our journey as a type of resting place until we were prepared to leave again. There are good Christians there."

"I think you should go there first," said Bo. "And Lian should go with you."

"Lian?"

"Lian is single and she has a great love for Jesus since He healed her."

"Mei Lin," Lian put in. It was the first time she'd said anything at all. Lian had long black hair that usually hung below her shoulders. Today her hair was in a pony tail. Her bangs were recently cut and her shoulders slumped in the shadows. "I want to serve the God who cleansed my skin and changed my heart. I know I can't be as good as Fei, but Bo thought—"

"Oh, it's not that," said Mei Lin. "I just never dreamed of going with someone else."

Mei Lin hadn't thought of changing plans either. What would Pastor Wong think? She remembered what the Zhangs told her—that some of her most important assignments would be those that were not on the map, but came from Heaven.

Mei Lin looked intensely at Lian's face, highlighted by the glow of the flashlight over the map. "Jesus told us that in order to follow Him we must take up our cross daily," she said. "The only day that Jesus took up a cross was when He was going to die. Are you willing to die for Jesus? Can you travel with me on those conditions?"

Lian cleared her throat. "I have nothing else to live for. I am willing to accept those conditions."

"This journey may be very dangerous—as I guess you've seen already."

"I'm sure," said Lian. Her face was beaming and Mei Lin marveled at how beautiful she was now that the boils were gone. Her smile revealed straight even teeth.

"Lian wants to learn how to be a—a what did you call it?" asked Bo.

"An evangelist," answered Mei Lin.

"Yes, an evangelist," Bo repeated. "And you need a traveling companion."

"Yes, I do," replied Mei Lin. "I wondered last night how I would sleep under the stars all alone in a strange land."

"Now you don't have to worry," said Bo.

"What about your family?" asked Mei Lin.

"I am single," said Lian. "My mother and father do not know where I am going but I told them that I must go and see other places. I told them I was restless."

"To protect them?" asked Mei Lin.

Lian nodded. "They both see a great change in me since I became a Christian."

Mei Lin looked at Bo. "And what makes you think that Zhing-Cho should be the next place?"

"I felt that perhaps Fei might crumble under interrogation. She may tell where you were going next and that would put you in danger."

Mei Lin realized this was a possibility—but she truly hoped that Fei would hold up well under the questioning by prison officials.

"Besides," Bo added. "We want you to come back and teach us— like you're going to teach the Christians in ZhingCho."

A smile broke out over Mei Lin's face. "Oh, that would make me very happy!"

"It's settled then," said Bo.

Later, the group huddled around the Bibles Sun and Bo retrieved. Mei Lin reached into the sack and handed one of the precious books to Bo.

"For me?" he asked.

"For you," said Mei Lin. "Ho Ting Village will need a pastor."

"Me?" asked Bo.

"You," replied Mei Lin. "I wish I had more time to teach you, but I will return. And Lian will return and tell you what she's learned during our journeys. Until then, read the Gospel of Mark."

Mei Lin fingered through the pages until she found it and Bo put a leaf inside.

"All four of these books, Matthew, Mark, Luke, and John tell the story of Jesus' life. Each person told the story from their point of view. And each Gospel adds something special to the story of Jesus' life and death and resurrection."

Bo held the book to his chest. "I never dreamed my life would change so much," he said. "Thank you for this gift, Mei Lin. I will treasure it—and guard it with my life."

"And here," Mei Lin said. "Please—will you mail these when your post man comes next week?"

The three new friends prayed together. Then Mei Lin set off on her journey with a new companion and a new destination—ZhingCho.

Poydan, North Korea

CHAPTER 20

Quickly, Young Soon set to work cleaning the rice pot. It was dark outside, but by the light of the fire, she could see the green stains from the grass soup that used to be their sole food source. She did not try to rub them off. It's better that the stains are there. *Perhaps no one will suspect this pot has cooked rice for us every night for the last month.*

Nam Gil was asleep now, his belly full of beans and rice. It would not be many days until they'd leave for their journey. Young Soon wanted all three of them to be strong enough to travel. Still, she would eat only once a day and leave some of the rice and beans here for Ja.

Young Soon hung the pot on the wall and checked under her cupboard again. The rice and beans were still in the locked box. She didn't dare hide the rice under the floor—a gotchebee may hide under her house and find it there. *Filthy thieves.*

Oh! At that thought, Young Soon felt a darkness descend into her heart, so much so that it made her stop what she was doing.

Strangely, she felt in the wrong for what she thought. *I am stupid. Who cares what you call a gotchebee?* Young Soon tried to ignore the thought. The baby cried just a little and she quickly wiped her counter and went to him.

The God who loves you also loves the gotchebee. Again she stopped in her tracks. What a wild thought! Was the God who loves angry with her? Young Soon hadn't felt remorse for a bad thought since she was a young girl. She didn't like the feeling, so she tried to shake it off. By the time she sat on her mat, Han Chun was crying loudly. She quickly pulled him to her breast. He latched on and lustily drank her milk. He was very small, and no heavier than one of the small bags of rice in her cupboard. Somehow he managed a small tuft of black hair on the top of his head and the rest was mostly bald.

"My Little Star," she whispered into his hair, and then kissed the soft spot on his head. Just then a thought struck her. If Min-Hee did not make it across the river, then she would be a gotchebee. Horror struck her heart like a spear.

No! No! My child is not wandering aimlessly looking for food. She can't, she's only three. She can't—

The reality of it all collapsed over her. For the first time she realized that a gotchebee child could be her child, or her niece or nephew. A sob caught her throat. The baby stopped sucking and looked up at her, his little eyebrows creased. She nestled his head closer again and he continued to drink.

She mulled the thought over and over again in her mind. *The God who loves you loves the gotchebee, too.* Never had she placed herself on the same level of a gotchebee and certainly she'd never thought of her own daughter as one! Skinny, dirty, swollen-bellied…This time she could not stop. Young Soon sobbed. She felt her heart would break. *I am so sorry! I am so sorry!*

Just then the door opened and Young Soon jumped in surprise. The baby lost connection and coughed and sputtered. A lantern ducked inside the opened door.

"Ja!"

"I heard the baby crying," she said. She had a pile of laundered diapers in her hands. "The neighbors will not suspect wrongdoing if I come help my dying sister with her sick child, now will they?"

Young Soon thought her heart would thump out of her chest. "You scared me, that's all."

Ja laid the diapers on the kitchen counter and came to sit beside her on the mat. "Why, you've been crying, Young Soon. What's the matter?"

Nam Gil woke up. "Oma?"

Young Soon whispered, "It's okay, Nam Gil. Aunt Ja is here."

"What is wrong?" Ja's lower jaw jutted out, just like Mother's used to when she'd caught them misbehaving.

"I'm crying over the gotchebees." Young Soon wiped her face.

"What?"

"I know, isn't it strange? Today I had this thought. I thought, 'The God who loves, loves the gotchebee, too.'"

"But why are you crying?" asked Ja.

"I am crying because I feel I was wrong for not pitying them and, worse, for saying such mean things to them." Young Soon felt some relief after the confession of her wrongs.

"Oh, you're just emotional because the baby is here. New mothers always cry and—"

"No, Ja. I really mean it. I keep talking to the God who loves, the one that Hwan told us about. Remember?"

Ja nodded. "I didn't think you remembered because you were so sick at the time. I think of Him, too, and I wonder if He is real."

"Sister, do you remember the night Han Chun was born? Just before I felt the quickening, I was sitting outside on Father's bench. Father used to tell me that if I saw a shooting star I should jump up and try to catch it."

A smile played at Ja's lips. "Father was telling you stories, Young Soon."

"Maybe not! Just before the baby quickened, I saw a shooting star. I jumped up off the bench and tried to catch it. Just then, Han Chun decided to be born and I put my hand to my stomach. Now, do you think that maybe that shooting star went right into Han Chun?"

Ja's eyebrows winged upward and she broke into a full smile.

"Sister, don't laugh at me! It's true and it happened exactly as I told you. And that night I was thinking about the God who loves. I imagined that it was His hand behind every star and He was hanging them across the sky on lines like those soldiers hung the lanterns for their party last month. I think that suddenly He threw one of his stars to me and I caught it and now it is with Han Chun. I tell you, he is a special boy."

Just then Han Chun pulled off her nipple and Young Soon handed him to Ja to let him burp. Ja relaxed and smiled. "Yes, he is a special boy," she agreed. "And Min-Hee, she is a special girl. All three of your children are gifts."

Ja pulled something from her pocket and leaned closer, the baby perched high on her shoulder. "Perhaps your God who loves sent this as well. Look what my husband found today outside the mine."

Young Soon looked at the paper. "What is it?" she asked as she unfolded it.

"Chul Moo said that it was wrapped in a stretchy orange material. It wasn't there yesterday. It's as though it dropped from the sky last night, like Han Chun's star."

Young Soon read the Korean words. The caption read, *Millions Die of Hunger in North Korea Since 1990s.*

"Ja, this is counter-revolutionary material. You can't—"

Ja put her hands on Young Soon's lips. "This is a newspaper article. It tells the truth." She looked over at Nam Gil and told him to go back to sleep.

Young Soon saw pictures of starving North Korean children. She looked at her own son on his mat. The children in the pictures looked like her son did last month before Hwan brought food. One caption said, "Whole families continue to die in North Korea." Quickly, she read more.

> *Aid agencies have estimated that up to four million people have died in North Korea since the mid-1990s because of acute food shortages caused by natural disasters and economic mismanagement. The country, which adheres to the Juche theology of self-reliance, depends most heavily on foreign aid to feed millions of its people. Non-government Organizations (NGO's) complain that the head of state, Kim Jong-il, keeps their food donations for his military and will not allow them to bring their free food to the masses of starving people who need it.*

"Oh, no!" cried Young Soon as she folded the paper in front of her. It seemed beyond comprehension—four million people! And why wouldn't the General allow the non-government organizations to bring food to them? She thought of Lee Chung Ho and cringed. *He was a good father. He only wanted to feed his children.*

"It is just like our brother told us," said Ja. "I am more sure than ever that Hwan is right."

"It is so confusing," said Young Soon. "Have we been so deceived? But the Dear Leader cares for us!"

"Stop," said Ja. "Stop saying that. We have been taught to think that. If this is true," and Ja punched at the paper in Young Soon's hands, "then our mother and father, and my sweet baby Eun Ae, and your husband Sang Ki, all died because the Dear Leader, General Kim Jong-il, would not give us food."

Young Soon gasped. "But Father Kim il-Sung—"

"Father Kim il-Sung died in 1994. The famine began after his death. Didn't we eat when we were children?"

Young Soon nodded her head. The dreams of her happy childhood were all that kept her walking up that wretched hill for the last three years.

Ja handed the baby back to Young Soon, then folded the news article back up and placed it carefully in her pocket. "Now, let's stop talking about the newspaper article. Let's talk about you. You must take the children to China where they will not starve."

Tears sprang to Young Soon's eyes. Little Han Chun had fallen asleep so she cradled him in her arm. "We shall miss you, Ja." She squeezed her sister's hand.

"Will you leave soon?" asked Ja.

Young Soon nodded. "Probably within the next two weeks. But my heart is torn in two. How can I leave you behind? Won't you come with us? Perhaps Chul-Moo will come later?"

Ja shook her head. "My place is with my husband. Chul-Moo needs me. He, too, is grieved because we have no child. Perhaps the rice will increase and I will have another child."

"Oh, wouldn't that be perfect?" exclaimed Young Soon. "Only I want to be near you so I can be the good auntie, as you've been the most wonderful auntie to Nam Gil, Min-Hee, and now Han Chun. It doesn't seem fair that hunger pulls us away from one another." Young Soon sighed. "I love North Korea. It will be the first time in my life that I have missed the September 9th celebrations." Tears sprung to her eyes. "I love North Korea," she repeated. "But leaving you—that is my only regret."

"Your only regret?" she asked.

"And Father and Mother."

"I will attend their graves," Ja promised. "And your dear late husband's, too. It is time to move on, Young Soon. You must save your children. They cannot live here anymore."

Young Soon knew that Ja was right. But with all of her heart she wished Ja would go with her. It would make her journey so much easier, too. What if she got lost? What if she was shot by the guards at the border? Hwan said Chinese and Korean military guarded the border.

She had to squeeze those thoughts out of her mind or she would never gather the courage to walk out the door.

Just then she had an idea. "Ja, remember that I told you to come and take the box out of my house?"

"Yes."

"I will leave some cooked rice underneath Father's bench out back. Will you ask Lee Chung-Ho's children to bring water from my well? Promise to give them grass soup or something. They will go there and find the rice bowl underneath the bench. Will you do that for me?"

"I don't know, Sister. What if they report me?"

"You can tell them that you don't know where they got the rice. You just sent them out for water and they came back with rice."

Ja smiled. "You've really changed, Young Soon. I don't know if it's this baby or the food Hwan brought or the God who loves, but you've changed."

Young Soon smiled. The darkness ascended and light poured into her soul. Somehow she knew that the God who loves was pleased with her.

Rural China

CHAPTER 21

Mei Lin added more sticks to the small fire. Its flames cast light and then shadows against the nearby trees that flickered about their 0faces and clothing. It was dark and damp and Mei Lin had no idea where she was, only that it had taken them three days to get this far. She hoped that she and Lian would not have to walk ten days as she and Fei had walked to get to Ho Ting.

Mei Lin found her new companion to be good company and, most enjoyably, a great scout. Lian had come equipped with more than a bookbag stuffed with food and supplies—she knew the wooded area where they traveled.

If it wasn't for Lian, she'd be completely lost. Skipping the smaller villages may have been safer, but the stream followed that pathway and now, without the stream nearby, their water supply was low.

"How much farther?" Mei Lin asked quietly.

"We should be there by tomorrow afternoon sometime," said Lian. She sat on her blanket and hugged her knees as she stared into the fire. "I don't know for sure—I've only been to ZhingCho a couple of times when I was a child."

Mei Lin stoked the fire to a fair blaze, poking the blue flames beneath the heavier wood until it caught on to the wood on top. She stared into the fire for some time, lost in thought. It was too warm, really, for a fire. But the fire would scare away the animals and they'd chosen a place behind a hill that surely could not been seen by the PSB if they followed the creek. Silently she offered prayers for Fei and then for Liko and her family. She missed them tonight as she stared into the fire. In the end, she gave up the solitude of thought to continue training Lian.

"I think we should take some more time to study."

Lian eagerly opened the Bible Mei Lin handed to her. Lian was a good student. They'd read the book of Mark together and now Mei Lin read the stories of the first church that followed Jesus' lifestyle by the power of the Holy Spirit.

Mei Lin's faith was stronger now after reading the persecution endured by the first church. The first church saw thousands of people saved as they preached the gospel. They also saw miracles—and hatred from authorities that imprisoned them, beat them, or killed them.

"Lian, did I tell you that I am engaged to be married?"

"Really?"

"Yes, and my fiancé told me that miracles would happen when I went to villages."

"Well, that is certainly true," said Lian. "My skin is proof of that."

"Liko—my fiancé—told me that when we preach the blind will see. The deaf will hear."

Lian was listening intently, so Mei Lin kept going.

"Liko prayed for me. He said that he believes that people who are insane will be delivered and the lame will walk. And that I will return with a great harvest of people whose lives are changed by the Gospel."

Lian leaned back on her arms with her long legs crossed in front of her and stared up at the stars. "I can believe anything of this great God who made the earth and sky."

Mei Lin smiled. Lian's faith was probably greater than hers! Minutes later they opened the book of Acts and took turns reading the chapters. Most Chinese love a good story and this book was full of them. They read together until the fire dwindled and they could no longer see to read. Then Mei Lin added the wood they'd stacked nearby and stoked the fire again before the two settled into their blankets for another night in the woods.

Mei Lin drifted into a peaceful sleep, her heart full of faith for these Bible miracles to happen again in China.

"No!"

Mei Lin wakened with a start. A boy was crossing a river in the middle of the night and he was holding a baby. But the boy was crying and he needed help. Who was that child? Where were their parents? Lian rolled over in her sleep and Mei Lin looked down at her own blanket—the ends tightly balled inside her fists, fists that were reaching for the shirttails of the boy holding the baby. She'd reached for the children in her dream to bring them to shore.

Mei Lin threw more sticks on the fire and then wrapped herself back inside her blanket. The sights and sounds of the dream haunted her. The last time she dreamed about a baby she was giving birth. In this dream she's trying to rescue a baby and a boy. Was it the same baby? Who was the boy? Or were these just a bunch of mixed-up dreams?

Her questions formed prayers and the longer Mei Lin prayed for the children, the more confident she felt that it was God who gave her the dream, a dream of intercession for two children she didn't know. Although there was no river within miles of where she lay, her night remained immersed in its current beside the boy and the baby, praying to God that her prayers would pull them safely to the other side, wherever that was. Sunrays from the early light of dawn pierced the forest canopy before the burden of prayer lifted. Mei Lin rested easily then and drifted back into a peaceful sleep.

The next morning, she and Lian quickly packed their belongings and left. Mei Lin sipped a little of her stale water, saving the rest for later. Lian offered to share some of her food, but Mei Lin turned it down.

"I think I'm to fast this morning," she said.

"You've been quiet all morning," said Lian. "Bo told me that Fei was fasting before she was captured. Do you think we're going to be captured, too?"

Mei Lin looked at her new friend. Her face was full of questions, not fear. "I suppose I have been quiet," she answered. "I was up praying through much of the night after having a dream."

Mei Lin explained her dream and her prayer for the children she didn't know. "I know it sounds strange, but the longer I prayed the more confident I felt that I was praying for two children who really were in trouble. It reminds me of the dream I had before we came to your village—"

Mei Lin stopped in the middle of the path. "Oh!"

"What is it?" asked Lian.

"The other dream—I was pregnant with a baby and Liko picked me up in an old car to take me to deliver the baby at the hospital but Fei wasn't with us. I looked back and she was waving—I couldn't tell if she was saying goodbye or waving us to come back."

Mei Lin bent over and picked up a long stick that lay across the path. "I don't understand it at all. But I think God's trying to tell me something."

"Wouldn't it be easier to just come down here and tell you?" asked Lian. "Why does He talk in a dream?"

"I don't know," Mei Lin answered. "Maybe the dreams add feelings that I wouldn't have if He just came and told me about a baby or a boy and a baby. I know this much—the dream I had last night launched me into hours of prayer. And it wasn't hard to pray either. I felt this deep sense of danger for the children and a strong urge to pray. I didn't go back to sleep until after the sun came up."

Mei Lin was glad to walk quietly for the next few miles. She wanted to concentrate on the dreams she had and the dreams she'd read about in the Bible. She wondered why Liko was in the first dream. He certainly wasn't here with her now.

By the time the sun was high in the sky, the path widened and finally joined a dirt road. Mei Lin's feet were tired, but her hopes were high. The forest was less dense and she could tell they were getting closer to ZhingCho.

"I think the creek is east of this road," said Lian. "Do you want to walk that way?"

"You mean fresh cold water?" asked Mei Lin. "Let's go!"

The girls veered off the main road to look for the creek. The thought of fresh drinking water and a place to wash her hair and take a bath was motivation enough to hike through the underbrush. Just when they lost sight of the main road, she heard it—the gurgling of a nearby creek!

The girls walked toward the sound and spent the next two hours refreshing themselves in the cool water. Mei Lin felt the burden for the two children in her dream lifting now. She ate the mushroom dumplings that Lian brought in her backpack and hung her wet clothing on a few branches to dry.

"Should we camp here for the night?" asked Lian.

"I don't think so," said Mei Lin.

Lian looked at their wet clothes hanging on the branches.

"We can wrap those up in our towels and take them along," said Mei Lin. "Pastor Wong said there were Christians in this village who would be friendly and take us in. Perhaps we will be indoors tonight to sleep."

Lian smiled. "That would be nice," she said.

The girls rolled up their wet clothes and hiked back out to the main road. An hour later, they stepped out of the forest where there were long fields of beautiful young green rice stalks in front of them. The fields neatly followed one after the other, each rising a little higher than the last as it went up the hill. The air outside the forest was hot and Mei Lin was glad that her hair was wet and her collar soaked. It would dry in the sun while keeping her cool.

The dirt road reminded her of the one that went past the sugar cane fields and rice paddies of Tanching Village. The only difference was that Tanching had a hill with a forest on one side of the road. This road was lined with rice paddies on both sides and slowly inclined upward, winding its way through the fields. The view was breath taking and Mei Lin felt a flutter of patriotism. Her country owned a vast amount of land and although most of the farmers lacked the machinery of the west, their fields were planted in symmetrical precision and great pride was taken in their upkeep and measureless harvest. By now, most of the villagers were likely gathering in their homes for an evening meal. Mei Lin picked up her pace and Lian stayed in step with her. She couldn't wait to meet the people who farmed this beautiful terrain. Pastor Zhang had told her to look for a house church pastor named Hui Hong. He needed Bibles.

"Do you know a man named Hui Hong?" Mei Lin asked Lian.

Lian shook her head. "ZhingCho is a big place."

"How large?" asked Mei Lin.

Lian answered, "Much larger than my small village. I remember holding my mother's hand very tightly when we visited. I was afraid I'd be lost."

After walking more than an hour up the incline, they came to the top of the hill. ZhingCho was much larger than Tanching, perhaps the size of DuYan. The small city continued to stretch up the mountain in front of them and houses with courtyards and small gardens were everywhere on the left and the right. From their point of view, it seemed that the mountain never stopped. It gradually loomed upward with wide roads interconnecting to small footpaths. The homes were simple sand-colored block with curved tin roofs and crowded more closely together than the homes in Tanching. Still, each house had a small garden in the back or on the side.

Mei Lin hesitated. "Fei and I hid our Bibles before we came into your village," said Mei Lin. "Perhaps we should do the same thing now."

"My Bibles are at the bottom of my bookbag," said Lian. "No one will search our bags will they?"

"I guess not," answered Mei Lin. She looked around. There were only fields behind her and houses in front of her. She didn't see a convenient place to hide the Bibles. "My Bibles are on the bottom, too," she said. "And I don't see a place to hide them here. Besides, Pastor Zhang said there are strong house churches here. Perhaps we can find Hui Hong right away."

The girls shifted their backpacks and blankets on their backs and then began their walk through town. They walked by the first house on the right where an elderly woman watered her garden. She felt a twinge of homesickness for Amah just then and wondered how she was faring without her help this summer.

The farther they walked, the more people they passed. Mei Lin and Lian continued to walk, occasionally greeting the people as they passed.

"How do you know where to start?" asked Lian.

"Good question," answered Mei Lin. "Let's pray as we walk and ask God to show us where to begin."

A small family of ducks crossed the road ahead. A little boy with a long stick walked behind them, guiding them with his stick. Mei Lin smiled, but the boy was so engaged in his work that he didn't notice her. He made funny little clicking sounds as he urged them forward.

ZhingCho was not as large as the city of WuMa where she would meet Pastor Wong. WuMa had a bus station, train station, and many taxis. Mei Lin didn't see one motor vehicle, but she saw a buffalo pulling a cart and an ox being led by its owner to its shed. ZhingCho was not only beautiful; it had a peaceful feeling about it. Several women were talking at the corner of one house on the right and Mei Lin waved to them.

"Hello!" one of them called to them.

"Hello!" Lian answered.

"Hello!" called Mei Lin. These friendly women seemed like a good place to start.

Mei Lin looked at Lian, whose long hair was dry now, hanging loosely down her back. "Let's talk to them," she urged.

Lian nodded. The girls approached the women until they were close and did not need to shout.

"Nin Hao?" asked Mei Lin.

"We are fine, thank you," said the woman in the center. The small woman had a wide smile and her eyes seemed to twinkle when she talked. Her hair was pulled back into a bun with a long streak of gray from each of her temples to the back. All three of them were dressed plainly like the women of Tanching.

"You are visiting ZhingCho?" the woman asked.

"Yes," answered Mei Lin. "We are hoping to find friends here."

"What is your friend's name?" asked the woman. The four other ladies listened intently while the one in the center led the conversation.

"Hui Hong," said Mei Lin.

The women looked at one another.

"I—I mean, we have a friend from WuMa who recommended that we come here and stay with his friend, Hui Hong."

"Ah," replied the woman.

She seemed cautious, but friendly. Mei Lin tried again. "We are wondering if there are any religious people in ZhingCho?"

"You are Mei Lin? And Fei?"

Mei Lin felt her spine tingle. "You know my name?" she asked. Immediately she wondered if the county cadres who arrested Fei had notified this town that they were looking for her.

"Of course," the woman answered. "You know a man named Wong San Manchu?"

Suddenly, Mei Lin understood. This woman was a Christian!

"Yes, yes," answered Mei Lin. "But this is not Fei. This is Lian from Ho Ting Village. Lian has quite a story to tell you. Fei—Fei was arrested six days ago."

"Oh, I didn't know," the woman replied. Then she whispered, "We will pray for Fei. Perhaps our cadre can help her. We didn't think you were coming for another month. Come, you will spend the night at my house? We have plenty of room and my husband will be pleased to have you as well."

The woman chattered so quickly that Mei Lin found it hard to answer her. She looked at Lian, who was smiling like a child holding candy in her hand.

"Yes, we will come," answered Mei Lin.

"Hui Hong is my cousin," the woman offered. "He lives higher up on this mountain. I am Mrs. Ma. These are my friends. We attend the same church in ZhingCho. The county cadres want to establish a government church here."

"The Three Self Church?" asked Lian.

"Right," answered Mrs. Ma. "There are three churches here that are not Three Self and, although we have to be quiet, we do not need to meet as secretly as some other churches in China."

"Why not?" asked Mei Lin.

The woman smiled widely and her dark eyes danced. "The cadre is a Christian, too. Besides, the cadre tells us that the laws against religion are relaxing. The Religious Affairs Bureau is beginning to see that Christians are good, patriotic people who want to help the community."

"How wonderful," replied Mei Lin. "Is that why you thought perhaps your cadre could help Fei? I hate to think of what she's going through right now."

"Yes, he may be able to help. He has guanxi all over Jiangxi Province. We have really tried to convince the county officers that we have good intentions and we have no plans to lead a revolt against China. I think it is finally sinking in."

This testimony gave her hope that Cadre Fang would accept their house churches in Tanching and perhaps even become a Christian one day. It would be wonderful if her dear friend Ping would one day know Jesus, too, and have a decent husband who loved her.

Mrs. Ma said goodbye to her friends and then turned to Mei Lin and Lian. "We have been praying and fasting for your meetings here. Come, you will stay at my house."

Mei Lin and Lian followed the woman to the right off the main road. As they hiked uphill to Mrs. Ma's house, Mei Lin questioned the woman about her cadre.

"How long has your cadre been a Christian?" she asked.

"Oh, for ten months now," replied Mrs. Ma. "Since that time the other two churches were started."

"Has all of ZhingCho been evangelized?" asked Mei Lin.

"I wouldn't say that all of ZhingCho has been evangelized," Mrs. Ma answered. "There are more than 60,000 people in our town and only three house churches. We have been praying for the gospel to penetrate the hearts of the people of ZhingCho."

Mei Lin glanced over at Lian. She'd been a wonderful companion and guide on the road. But she was a new convert who needed teaching in order to help her own village later on. Pastor Wong thought this town would be a place of rest for them where they would teach existing churches, but Mrs. Ma sounded anxious to evangelize. In her heart, she prayed and asked God to show her what to do next.

"Where do you meet?"

"We go from house to house," replied Mrs. Ma. "We meet at different times between Saturday evening and Sunday. The cadre is a Christian, but there are government spies—especially now that they are interested in setting up a Three Self church here. Last year we met outside of town in a small shed. Our numbers have grown now and we need more room."

Mrs. Ma turned left off the straight incline and pointed. "Our home is the third one on the left along this path. My mother-in-law lives with us. Her eyesight is poor as old age is catching up with her, but she loves to tend her herb garden."

There were houses close together on each side of the path. Each house they passed had a small courtyard, one of them so high that Mei Lin could not see into it. Nearly every inch of ground around the homes was filled with gardens of one kind or another. She could smell steamed rolls coming from one house and some sort of sweet meat being fried in another. Her stomach rumbled.

"Our son is grown now," Mrs. Ma added. "He is in Peking University to study literature."

"He is very fortunate," replied Mei Lin. She did not tell Mrs. Ma that her own college education had been stopped after her imprisonment for passing out Christian literature in her high school. She dreamed long ago of becoming an elementary school teacher. Still, she couldn't imagine being happier than she was right now—meeting new friends and teaching and preaching the gospel.

Mrs. Ma's home looked like all the others—worn tan brick frames with black corrugated tin roofs. Only the courtyard walls and gardens varied in size and color. The wooden gate opened with a latch. Mrs. Ma's courtyard was small with several pairs of men's pants hanging on the clothes line and the window sills lined with boxes filled with plants—probably her mother-in-law's herb garden. The rest of the courtyard contained the normal washbasins, clothesbaskets, garden tools, and scattered benches found in most homes.

"Mother!" Mrs. Ma called. "We have guests this evening."

Mrs. Ma led them inside. The kitchen stove and table were on the left and the elderly mother-in-law was stooped over the sink.

"Mother!" Mrs. Ma repeated.

The elderly woman turned around.

"We have guests this evening, Mother. Please meet Mei Lin and Lian. Girls, this is my mother-in-law, Mrs. Cho.

Mrs. Cho wiped her hands on a nearby towel and shuffled toward them. "Ah, is this the Mei Lin we have been praying for?" she asked. "And where is Fei?"

"Fei is in prison for preaching the gospel," replied Mrs. Ma.

Mrs. Cho shook her head. "We must pray," she said simply. Then her face brightened. "You are welcome here, girls. My son will be home shortly. I hope you will join us for dinner?"

Mei Lin nodded deeply and respectfully. "Thank you. You are kind, Mrs. Cho."

The woman smiled. "We are having fish and steamed rice with vegetables and steamed rolls. Do you like that?"

"Oh, yes," replied Lian. "Thank you for inviting us."

"You may use my son's room," said Mrs. Ma. "He is working near the university this summer."

Mei Lin and Lian quickly unpacked their wet clothing and hung the pieces about their new room. After using the outdoor room to relieve themselves, they washed up and joined Mrs. Ma's family for supper.

Mrs. Ma's husband was cordial, but said very little. After supper, he focused his interest on the China Daily Newspaper while the women sat on the courtyard benches where it was cooler and talked.

"Pastor Wong thought our time here would be well spent in teaching the existing church," said Mei Lin. "And I don't think he knew that you have three churches now."

"I would agree that we would benefit from teachings," said Mrs. Ma. "But we have been praying for more people to become

Christians. There are so many people in our town and more and more people are coming to know Jesus."

Mei Lin replied, "Let's imagine that God blesses us and we see 200 people saved while we are here. Where would you put them? Who would lead them all?"

Mrs. Ma smiled. "I thought about that. I think that some of our members are strong enough to begin their own churches now. We would divide again into more churches."

Mei Lin thought about Bo. All he had was new faith in Christ and a Bible. At least he had a Bible. She had no choice but to leave, but how could he lead when he knew so little himself?

"Do you have Bibles?" she asked.

"I have a New Testament Bible," answered Mrs. Ma. "The others have copied most of it for their congregations."

Mei Lin rested her head in her hands, her elbows on her knees. She didn't want to disappoint Pastor Wong by evangelizing and not teaching. But she knew that he would want her to follow what the Holy Spirit was leading them to do. People who had so few Bibles would need teaching.

"You've come at a good time," said Mrs. Ma, interrupting her thoughts. "The July exams are over and students are free. Farmers and field laborers are finished with spring planting and are tending gardens or working part time in the market."

"You mean, we could do some meetings in the daytime?" asked Mei Lin.

"Exactly," answered Mrs. Ma. "I pastor one church. Another woman pastors the second church and a man the third. The man, Brother Kung, works all morning in the market selling vegetables and baskets made by his wife. The market is closed in the afternoons due to the heat. Perhaps we could meet then?"

Mei Lin looked at Lian. "I can guide you here, Mei Lin, but I don't know how to guide you in these decisions."

Mei Lin was thankful for her honesty. "I think we should arrange afternoon meetings to teach the church members, especially the leaders. We can evangelize in the evenings."

Mrs. Ma clasped her hands together. "Yes, that's perfect."

"How do you usually evangelize?" asked Mei Lin.

"Tea parties," answered Mrs. Ma. "We have large tea parties where we tell stories."

"Ah," said Mei Lin, smiling. "The greatest stories ever told?"

"Yes, the greatest."

It was all arranged. The next afternoon Mei Lin was surprised to find 50 people crowded into Mrs. Ma's small courtyard. It was hot and part of the courtyard had no shade from the sun. Sweat poured down the faces of the listeners and Mei Lin's heart went out to them. She decided not to give away any Bibles until she knew the leaders more personally. If the evangelism went well, the new leaders would need Bibles for their churches.

Mei Lin opened her Bible to the book of Mark. If this group were to teach new believers, they'd need to start from the beginning. Pens flew over paper in straight mandarin columns as the eager Christians tried to take down every word she read from the Bible. Mei Lin slowed down her reading to accommodate them. The first day she taught about baptisms—the baptism by water as a symbol of the forgiveness of sins to a new believer. She taught them about the baptism of the Holy Spirit, which gives us the power to overcome satan's temptations, and the wonderful power to walk with the One who made the earth and skies.

"Although Jesus was the Son of God, not even one miracle was recorded until after He was baptized by water and by the Holy Spirit. If Jesus needed to be baptized by water and by the Holy Spirit, how much more do we need to be baptized!

"Verse 22 tells us that even His teachings were strong after these baptisms. Jesus taught with authority, not guessing at what was right or wrong in God's eyes. He healed Simon's mother-in-law who was sick with a fever and cast evil spirits out of people and healed a man with a terrible skin disease. Lian, will you come to tell us the story of how Jesus touched your life?"

Lian, who was sitting on the floor by the doorway, stood to her feet. She was visibly nervous. Her hands trembled and her voice quivered. Mei Lin prayed silently while her new friend testified.

"Four weeks ago I had boils all over my face," said Lian. She placed her hand over her cheek. "Mei Lin's friend, Fei, prayed for me. At first nothing happened." Lian looked at Mei Lin. "But the next morning when I woke up, the boils were gone."

"Ah," said the man in the first row. His interest was echoed by nods and a murmur of comments throughout the courtyard.

"I do not understand why Jesus loves me so much," said Lian. Tears fell and everyone remained respectfully quiet. "But I know that He is good and I know He loves everyone."

Lian sat down. Mei Lin smiled at her to thank her without using words.

"Jesus heals today. But again, we must realize that the beginning of the miracles He performed happened after Jesus was baptized in the water and by the Holy Spirit."

An elder in the back raised his hand and spoke out. "How can we receive these baptisms you talk about?"

Mei Lin shifted her feet and hugged her Bible, pausing before she answered. "To baptize in water is easy enough. You go to a tub or a pond or someplace where believers gather around to watch your baptism. The baptism of the Holy Spirit comes as a gift from Heaven and most of the time you do not see Him fly in the shape of a dove. But like the wind that moves the trees, the Holy Spirit moves you and you will know that He has changed you inside. There is more written in the Bible about this in Acts chapter two."

Mrs. Ma stood to her feet. "Mei Lin, I think we should hold a water baptism this evening."

A low sound of approval went up from the sultry airless courtyard.

"Where should we meet?" asked Mei Lin.

"At the field pond," answered Mrs. Ma. "Seven o'clock this evening?"

The bench-sitters nodded their approval. Mei Lin expected all of them to get up but they remained seated. Mei Lin looked from the audience to Mrs. Ma and back to the audience again, unsure what to do.

"Teach us more, Mei Lin," a woman called out.

"Yes, we want to hear more," another woman echoed.

Mei Lin was deeply touched. The heat was sweltering inside the courtyard and yet these precious people did not want to go back to their shaded homes or cool living rooms. They were ready for more. Mrs. Ma passed out fans to those sitting in the sun and some who were in the shade offered to trade places with those in the sun. Then Mei Lin opened her Bible to Mark chapter two and taught again on the life of Jesus.

For the next three weeks, Lian and Mei Lin stayed with Mr. and Mrs. Ma. It became too hot to teach in the sunny courtyard every afternoon, so Mei Lin taught each morning and preached every night. She nearly lost her voice after three days of shouting, so Mr. Ma rented a loud speaker and a microphone so the crowd could hear and Mei Lin's voice could recover.

By the end of the third week, there were more than 10,000 people at the Thursday night meeting and thousands had come to Christ. Everyone was talking about the way that Jesus healed or saved a family member or set them free from some bad habit. Mei Lin could only wonder that God could do so much in such a short time.

Around midnight on Thursday night, after the meeting, Mrs. Ma and her family sat around their kitchen table with Mei Lin and Lian talking about the week's events. "We need more new churches to keep up," said Mrs. Ma. "Those of us who prayed for this are so encouraged. God has visited us more powerfully than I thought was possible on the earth."

"I feel like I'm in a different world," said Lian. "Like Heaven has come down here to earth and I don't ever want to leave."

Mei Lin's heart was pricked as she listened to her friend. Lian was growing to love the people of ZhingCho, but Mei Lin was being nudged another direction.

"I think it will be time for us to leave soon," said Mei Lin.

"Leave?" asked Mr. Ma. "Why?"

"Well, I'll admit our plans were changed after Lian's village was raided," said Mei Lin. "We came directly here because we thought we would be far enough away from the county cadres. I can see now that God had a greater plan for ZhingCho. But we are to be in WuMa by the end of next week. I don't know—something inside is urging me to get there."

Mr. and Mrs. Ma exchanged glances and then Mrs. Ma spoke. "We have made it our personal assignment to pray for your Amah, Mei Lin," she said.

Mr. Ma chimed in, "If God can change this old heart, He can change hers." Mr. Ma pointed to his chest and leaned forward and smiled. "Do you believe?"

Mei Lin was caught off guard by Mr. Ma's subtle humor. She grinned. "I believe, Mr. Ma. I believe God can change my Amah's heart."

"Good," said Mrs. Ma. "When you go, remember that we are praying with you for her."

Mei Lin reached over the table and squeezed Mrs. Ma's arm. "I will not forget," she said. "And I will not forget your kindness here, Mrs. Ma, Mr. Ma. You've all been kind."

Lian looked as though someone had thrown a rock into her stomach. "Lian, shall we get to bed? Maybe we can talk a while?" asked Mei Lin.

Lian nodded. It was late, but Mei Lin felt this talk was urgent. The two girls went to the bedroom. A neighbor had supplied a second bed and now both girls slept soundly each night. They washed up and sat on the edges of their beds.

"Lian, I'm sure I can make my way to WuMa alone if you feel you want to stay."

"Oh, no," said Lian. "I think God sent me to be your companion—to help you in the journey. But I will miss it here. Perhaps I can return some day."

Mei Lin hugged her Bible to her chest and sighed. She looked forward to seeing Pastor Wong when they reached WuMa, but her thoughts were filled with the unusual events of the last three weeks.

"Some people are saying that Kwan Mei Lin is doing miracles," she said.

"But you tell them that it is God," said Lian. "You can't feel badly about that."

"I know," said Mei Lin. "But if I leave they will see that God does not leave. He stays with them. Did you see how the church members are bringing their neighbors to Christ?"

Lian nodded.

"And did you see how Sister Long and Mrs. Ma and Brother Kung are training at least ten more pastors each? I have done what God sent me here to do. And you—you know more than Bo now and you will be able to go back to Ho Ting to teach your village."

Lian broke into a smile. "I am not very popular in my village," she said.

"Ah, the hardest place to preach is inside your own city walls," said Mei Lin. "Jesus said that. Do you feel you are to go back?"

"Not yet," said Lian. "Your journey is not finished."

"Then it's settled. Let's leave on Monday—does that suit you?"

Lian nodded. "I will wash our clothes in the morning and prepare to leave while you teach."

Mei Lin yawned. "I've never been so happy *and* so tired in my life," she said.

Lian yawned. "I feel the same. Let's go to bed."

CHAPTER 22

Nam Gil handed his mother the cooking spoon. "Oma, do you think there will be food in China? Will there be lots of trees with leaves on them?"

Young Soon finished rolling her blanket, lined with a cooking spoon and chopsticks. "Shhh. Don't talk. Go lie down with your brother."

Nervously she fingered the rope until it was tight. Her brother Hwan told her that people in China ate three full meals a day, rice twice a day. The thought of that luxury urged her forward. One thing was sure—her mind was much clearer after eating the beans and rice her brother brought. She felt stronger than she'd ever felt in her life and somehow she believed Hwan was right—the only way for her to survive was to cross the Tumen River.

She longed for Ja to go with her. Who would she talk to in China? Did Chinese even understand Korean?

Like her little boy, Young Soon had many questions lately. She tightened the rope around her bundle, determined to stay focused on her plan of escape. Still, she had to review all of the alternatives. Most of the time, families who are seen escaping across the border were shot. At best, if they were caught, she and her children would be separated and sent away to separate concentration camps to work and starve until they died. Last week one of the coal miners said that his friend Wul Run Kil, who lived in a nearby village, was caught trying to cross the land border. Her near escape was an attempt to feed her starving children. In prison, a guard heard her say she wished she had made it into China. Because she said that, she was tied to a post, blindfolded, and shot and executed the next day in front of all the prisoners. Young Soon knew the story was true because she heard it told by another neighbor who knew a sympathetic wife of one of the prison guards.

Rung Kil's old mother watched her grandchildren until she died of starvation. Her poor children wandered the streets of their village. Young Soon wished she could help them, but how could she make a difference? They lived too far away.

Young Soon cringed, fighting back these thoughts of all that was against her now. Stabbing thoughts of fear circled like black crows around her hopes of escape. Black crows were the symbol of bad luck, so Young Soon pushed all of the crows out of her mind, forcing them to be silent.

Nam Gil lay wide-eyed beside his baby brother. The two of them stared at the poster of Kim Jong-il hanging on their wall. "Will the Rising Sun, our Dear Leader, be happy that we go on the journey, Mother?"

"Kim Jong-il is too busy doing important things for North Korea," she answered. "But I'm sure he would think we are very brave," she answered. Young Soon hated to lie to her son. General Kim Jong-il and the Party would be furious with them, but if Nam Gil knew that he might not want to make the trip. Despite the famine, her son was loyal to the North Korean general, wholeheartedly following the communist jargon brought to their village through the government's radio broadcasting. She knew children who reported their parents for not being loyal to the communist party—she knew that Nam Gil would never intentionally report her. But to be safe, she would wait to tell him the truth after they made it over the border into China.

Young Soon filled her small jugs with water. Nam Gil would have to carry his own jug, she'd decided. She dumped several days worth of cooked rice into the old rice bag and nestled the bag into the cooking pan. She packed a spoon, chopsticks, and diapers and rolled all of it together in the blanket and then tied it to her back. Her own rice bowl was full of rice, hiding in the rice bag inside the cupboard. She would leave it underneath the bench tonight for Lee Chung-Ho's children.

Young Soon was glad they were traveling in summer. The nights were cool, but at least they would not freeze. When she finished packing, she sat with her back against the door, soaking in the last of the warmth of her home, willing midnight to come— the time when they would leave to make their escape. She and Ja said their goodbyes that afternoon and Ja took the leftovers from Hwan's gift box of food home with her. Young Soon could not bear Ja's tears. She could only hope that Ja and Chul-moo would join them later. Or perhaps the rations would increase and she could return to North Korea. No, there was no returning. All who leave North Korea are traitors. Young Soon sighed. If she must be a traitor to feed her children, then she will be a traitor.

She felt that Ja would be safe, though. They again agreed to tell the neighbors that Young Soon went crazy for wondering about her missing daughter and left in the night to try to find her. She hoped that would keep the police from looking for her or from interrogating Ja and her husband. She'd even played the part in the political meetings, staring straight ahead as though she were in another world. Some of the miners were calling her "the crazy woman."

All the better, thought Young Soon.

She wished she could take Mother's door with her. It was the only valuable thing left in the house besides the box in the bottom cupboard.

Midnight drew near and Young Soon nursed Han Chun once more. "No crying now, Little Star," she said. She wrapped him in one of the thin blankets and wakened Nam Gil.

"Come, Nam Gil," she said, gently shaking him. "Let Oma measure you."

"Now?" asked Nam Gil. "I am so tired, Oma."

"Now," answered Young Soon. "Stand by the door."

Obediently, Nam Gil stood sleepily against the wooden doorpost while his mother, for the last time, carved a notch with a knife just above his head. She fingered the other notch and wondered how tall Min-Hee was now. Inspired, she took the old blanket and used it as a measuring stick to find the baby's length. She put the blanket against the doorframe and marked Baby Han Chun's small length there. Young Soon chided herself for being so sentimental, but it was the only thing she could leave behind to remember that they ever lived in their house. With all of her heart she wanted to return one day to this old house. It would be wonderful if she and Hwan and Ja and their families could live here again and eat rice and beans every day. For now, that dream was a fantasy, a wisp of smoke that stings the eyes and then vanishes.

Young Soon had a small amount of food rations and some of the match sticks Hwan left for them. It had been more than six weeks since she saw Min-Hee and her arms ached to hold her again. Young Soon put on a mournful face in front of the villagers, but she had dreamed about Min-Hee twice since Hwan took her and in each dream her face was chubby and her eyes bright. In her heart, Young Soon knew she had made the right decision.

"Nam Gil, there must be no talking and no sounds, remember?"

"Yes, Oma," said Nam Gil.

Her son was brave and, she hoped, strong enough to travel now. She'd had him practice walking in circles inside the house for long periods of time. Tonight would be the big test.

Young Soon sealed the water jug and tucked it inside another blanket and wrapped it so that it tied easily around Nam Gil's waist. She tied the small food sack and cooking utensils onto her back. Tenderly, so as not to waken him, Young Soon put Han Chun in the other blanket and tied each end, making it into a sling that went around her shoulder, carrying him in front for easy nursing in case he cried. There was no light to turn off, no friends or family to say goodbye to. She was alone. Young Soon breathed deeply, gathering her nerve. She took the bowl of rice in one hand and Nam Gil's hand in the other and stepped outside her home for the last time, into the darkness of the night.

They walked to the back of the house first, and Young Soon left the bowl of rice under the bench. Then they walked further behind the rows of houses, away from the main road. An unnatural silence crept across the dark landscape ahead of them. After they passed the houses, there were no trees to block the warm wind that whipped at their legs and faces. Young Soon didn't feel the wind. She only felt the throb of fear stuck in her throat. She tried to hold onto the Young Soon of the courageous escape, the Young Soon that decided upon this long journey.

Nam Gil put his head into her side and together they walked farther away, far behind the village houses, away from the guards who watched day and night over the cornfield. Nam Nam Gilddenly stepped ahead of her, leading the way. He was still skinny and sickly, but eager for the adventure. She hoped Nam Gil's spirit of adventure would last well into the night. They had a long walk ahead of them.

After they crested the second hill, Young Soon stopped to rest behind a tree. She clicked on the flashlight Hwan gave her to use. She wanted to look at the map one more time. Hwan said the road straight ahead would be mostly empty at night and it was safe to travel until dawn. At daybreak, they needed to be close to Jo Jou, a town about several kilometers north. Once she passed Jo Jou, she would be going further from home than she'd ever been in her life. Young Soon folded her map carefully and put it beneath the folds of the blanket sling that carried her baby.

The dirt road stretched far up one hill and down the next. Nam Gil continued to remain enthusiastic about leading the adventure.

"Oma, no one is awake," he whispered back to her. "Even the gotchebees are gone."

It was incredible, really. The gotchebees usually roamed the hills of North Korea like ravenous wolves, scavenging, stealing, and begging. Although her heart had changed toward the gotchebees, Young Soon was glad she did not have to contend with them tonight. She'd have to bribe a child with some of their food supplies or he'd tell the authorities for sure that she and her children were running away. She cringed. She wanted to be a loyal Party member, not a hated talbukja. Pictures of executions flashed through her mind until Young Soon forced herself to think of something else.

She thought of the stories Grandmother told her about the Korean war, when everyone was running away to live in Seoul. Grandmother's uncle had taken her brother with him to Seoul. Grandmother was too young for the long journey and was left behind. She never saw her brother again.

Perhaps I should pray to the spirit of my mother, she thought. No, it may not please the God who loves.

Right now, she wanted someone to walk this journey with her. Someone who could help her read the map and calm her nerves. And right now, no other god seemed as strong to her as the God who loves. As she walked, she tilted her head toward the sky. The stars were mostly hidden, but she saw one or two trying to peek through the clouds. Young Soon wondered if those two stars were God's eyes peering down on her tonight. She did not know His name, but Hwan said He cared and the people who believed in this

God would love her, too. She tried to imagine receiving love from a stranger—a Chinese stranger! She did not know Mandarin, but Hwan said it did not matter. The God who loves speaks all languages. It all seemed too wonderful to be true. One thing was for sure—she would not throw food away. If there was truly so much food, then she would help Hwan bring some back to Ja someday.

Young Soon carefully stepped over the rocks now. "Slow down, Nam Gil," she softly called. "Mother cannot keep up with you!" Nam Gil turned and smiled, proud of his expert scouting.

As she walked onward, Young Soon stroked the sleepy head of Han Chun. The month before he was born, when Ja watered the spring inside of her, she felt that this child would live under a different sky. It was hope for his life, for all their lives, that gave her courage now. How her heart ached to see little Min-Hee! She imagined their embrace and picked up her pace a bit. Her feet were burning a little, but she continued to walk quickly in the darkness. The moon peeked out of the high clouds. It gave just enough light to see the edge of the road, lined with a deep ditch on either side.

Suddenly, Nam Gil nearly knocked her backward. "Nam Gil! What—"

"Oma, up there!" he whined. He buried his head in her side and, instinctively, Young Soon squatted down. The baby squirmed just then and she rocked him gently, quietly, straining to hear.

"What did you see?" she asked her eldest son.

"I don't know—in the ditch up there," he said.

"Was it a rock? An animal?" she asked.

"No—it's not moving. But it scared me."

Young Soon relaxed a little. She waited and listened for a few minutes. Nothing. Trembling, she stood to her feet. Now Nam Gil walked behind her. She clicked on the flashlight and waved its beam into the ditch.

"Ahh!" Young Soon jumped backward. She quickly clicked off the light. Nam Gil started to cry and she took his hand. A body lying on its back—eyes and mouth were black holes. The woman had been dead a long time. She held something in her arms.

"The woman died a long time ago," she whispered hoarsely to her son. "Now, think of something else."

"But—the package. Was that a baby she was holding?" asked Nam Gil.

"She probably carried clothing and a bowl and spoon, just like us," Young Soon replied. Young Soon kept her flashlight on, but pointed it in the opposite direction. Quickly, she walked away from the dead body, her son clinging to her side. "Now, I want you to tell me again what you thought about your Uncle Hwan. Wasn't he a nice man? Did I tell you he looks just like your grandfather?"

Young Soon's stomach heaved. Bile came up in her throat. It was a baby. The package was a baby.

~

Damp sweat made her shirt cling to her back. Young Soon pictured the woman in the ditch and the blood pounded in her neck and head. She breathed deeply and concentrated, trying to imagine her first step down the slope toward the Tumen River. Her eyes searched the road across the river. She could barely see the road above the banks of the river. She certainly couldn't see the ditch where Hwan told them to hide. She wondered if Hwan would check the ditch tomorrow.

Of course he will. He'll find us. He promised.

Baby Han Chun was strapped high on her shoulder in the front, sound asleep. Her small frame trembled under the weight of the moment. The little food that was left was strapped to Nam Gil's waist in a blanket. Although she did not tell him, she wanted him to have the food in case they were separated—or worse.

"Now, Oma?" asked Nam Gil.

"Whisper," Young Soon answered softly, her finger over her lips. She was gathering courage when her young son interrupted her thoughts. "We'll leave soon."

The moon could not be seen tonight, but Young Soon knew it had been hours since darkness fell. The star she reached for in the spring months was nowhere in sight tonight. The Little Star hanging inside the blanket around her neck would be the only star out tonight. She whispered one more prayer to the God who loves. Tonight He seemed far away, like the stars she couldn't see.

Hwan told her to cross when the guards on duty may be sleeping—somewhere between 2 and 4 A.M. The river disappeared into the darkness and Young Soon wondered if she'd be able to see to cross in a straight line without turning in the strong current. According to the map, she would cross where the river was the lowest. Her heart thumped in her chest. Suddenly, the long yellow beam from the Chinese guardhouse made its periodic circle across the water and the hillside. Young Soon had been waiting for it and she scoped out her pathway, noting the places where the light did not hit. She knew her moment had arrived. She waited for this moment—the moment when staying seemed more dangerous than crossing.

"Now," said Young Soon.

Young Soon reached out her hand in the darkness and took Nam Gil's hand. "We must play the game now," she whispered to him. "Do not let the light touch you and you win."

Nam Gil did not speak. His hand trembled and Young Soon wondered if he knew.

One step, take one step. There.

One step led to the next and the slope of the hill nearly propelled them to their first spot to hide.

"Good," Young Soon whispered to her son. Her little one stirred on her shoulder. She wondered if the guards would hear him if he cried. *No, not over the sound of the river,* she told herself again.

They waited together a few minutes and the long spear of light pierced the darkness above their heads.

"I win, Oma," said Nam Gil excitedly.

"Yes, you win," said Young Soon. "Now, let's play again. But we must be very careful."

Young Soon took her son's hand and ran to the shrubbery that was the next hiding place on the incline. She knew she had time to make it to the rock just before the crossing of the river. Her pulse pounded in her ears and she pulled Nam Gil behind her.

"Come," she urged him. "Come."

Nam Gil fell and she stopped, reached down in the darkness and found his shoulders and pulled him up. "Run with me," she said.

"My knee," cried Nam Gil.

"Run!" Young Soon whispered.

Young Soon heard the river before she saw it. The waters rushed in front of her. She couldn't feel the rock in the blackness.

"Lie flat," she commanded her son.

The beam of light shone across the water but this time Young Soon did not watch. She squeezed her son's hands in her own and cradled the baby's head with the other. She saw the rock!

The light passed and she grabbed Nam Gil's hand once more and ran toward it, then collapsed beside it, on the side away from the light beam.

"Oma, my knee," said Nam Gil. He was crying a little and Young Soon could tell he was more frightened than injured. She put her finger on his lips.

"You must whisper now, Nam Gil," she said softly. "Now, you must be very brave. We are going to cross the river in the dark. And this time we must not let the light touch us."

"But Oma, I cannot swim! I'll drown!"

"No, no. The water may not be too deep. This map shows that this is the lowest spot. If it becomes too deep, I will carry you in front of me. But you must promise to be very brave. You cannot cry or make a loud sound."

Nam Gil whimpered. "I cannot swim."

"Do you remember Uncle Hwan?" she said.

"Yes."

"Uncle Hwan crossed this river with Min-Hee."

"He did?"

"Yes, and he gave us the map and told us to cross, too."

"In the dark?" asked Nam Gil.

Young Soon took her son's hand and pressed it to her lips. "In the dark," she answered. "It is much more fun in the dark."

"Oma?"

"Yes?"

"I miss Father."

Young Soon drew her son close and held him. "We both miss him. Now, let's wait for light to pass two times so we can gather our strength, OK? You help me count."

Quietly, they hid in the shadow of the large rock and watched the beam of light go by two times.

"Now, Oma?"

"Now."

Young Soon ran quickly toward the place where the beam of light was not as strong and put her foot in the water. It was cold and shocking. Her limbs started to tremble and she forced herself to gain control. Nam Gil held tightly to her hand.

"I don't like it, Oma," he whimpered.

"You will obey me," she said firmly. "Now, kneel down in the water."

Young Soon fell to her knees in the pebbles and mud and her son followed. The water was up to their waists when they knelt.

"I want to go home," he said.

"No more talking, Nam Gil," Young Soon commanded. "Now we must get ready for the beam of light.

"But it will shine on us now," he said. "There is nowhere to hide."

"Yes, there is," she said. "Under here."

Young Soon ducked her head under the water, careful not to get Han Chun wet yet.

"You try it."

Obediently, Nam Gil put his head under the water. Fleetingly, Young Soon imagined teaching her little boy how to swim. He was a dear, obedient son.

"Very good!" she said. "Now, the light will come soon. Let's go farther out."

Young Soon took her son's hand and led him until the water was up to her waist when standing. "The light will come soon. We will all go under the water together when I say. You hold your nose until we come back up."

"Even Baby Han Chun?" he asked incredulously.

"Yes—here it comes."

Young Soon prepared to pinch the baby's nose and waited until the light was scanning the water in front of them.

"Now!"

Nam Gil clutched her sides and nearly somersaulted them both. Young Soon could not pinch the baby's nose but gained control and fought the urge to immediately stand up. When the water seemed black enough, she emerged.

Han Chun was awake now! His cry pierced the night and Young Soon covered his head with the blanket and dipped her body into the water up to her chin. Nam Gil was already up to his neck.

"Oma, that was fun," cried Nam Gil. "I wasn't so scared that time. But baby Han Chun is crying."

"There's a new rule," said Young Soon. She put her little finger into the baby's mouth so he would suck it and stop crying. "No more talking, OK? Let's go."

She knew she needed to move right away—the light may go searching for the voice of the baby. Three more steps and the water deepened.

Instinctively, Nam Gil hopped onto her hip, his head now higher than hers. She shifted the baby higher and stood for a moment.

The light searched the waters again. "Hold onto me but do not push or we may fall and lose one another," she whispered.

Nam Gil whimpered. "I don't like this game."

Young Soon knew that she must tell him now. "Nam Gil, this isn't a real game. It's a pretend game. I didn't want to deceive you, Son. I just didn't want you to worry. Now, hold onto Oma, don't push or we could fall."

This time Young Soon watched the light before it came to them so she could judge how far they had to go. Its beam scanned the water as before—the shore was closer than she thought!

"Hold your nose," she whispered and ducked softly under the water, holding the blanket over the baby's face.

She ducked into the water and braced against the current head first. Seconds later they emerged.

The baby sputtered and gasped for air, Young Soon pulled both of her sons higher above the water.

"Good boys," she said.

Nam Gil clung more tightly, rubbing his eyes.

"We're almost there," she said, excitement rising in her chest. She knew she could swim with both boys the short distance that lay ahead of them. She walked forward, ready to swim at any moment. But it wasn't necessary. The floor of the river rose higher. They were close now, close to the other side! Young Soon thought her heart would burst! Freedom awaited her and the hardest part was behind her.

The water was up to their knees when Young Soon whispered, "Run now, Nam Gil, run with Oma."

The run to the shoreline was a run for freedom. Young Soon knew the danger was not over, but she also knew that a new life was now beginning.

The light!

Young Soon pulled Nam Gil to her left to shield him from the beam of light.

Boom! A powerful shot rang out. Young Soon collapsed.

Rural China

CHAPTER 23

Mei Lin jolted upright, her heart pounding. The humid night air was thick and black, yet she still felt the water over her head and the impending danger of some journey. *The baby—he's in trouble!* Mei Lin reached for her flashlight.

As soon as she turned it on she flicked it off again—its beam shouted "Danger" instead of safety.

Where are you? Who are you?

Mei Lin felt the bed covers. She half expected them to be wet after her disturbing dream. The baby was cold and frightened and drowning. Something about water and that beam of light...

Mei Lin put her hand over her pounding heart. "Jesus, I ask You to save the baby. I don't know who he is or where he is, but I know he's important to You because of the dreams You've given me. Help him on his journey. Keep him safe and please—show me what I can do."

Pray. **Pray!**

The answer came to her heart, not her head. Immediately her senses awakened as though she'd had nine hours of solid sleep.

"I bind the spirit of death from reaching this baby," Mei Lin spoke into the darkness.

"What's the matter?" Lian asked sleepily.

"Nothing," said Mei Lin. "Go back to sleep. I need to pray."

Lian rolled over and Mei Lin continued to pray. Dark demons of despair edged her thoughts. "I declare John 10:10, 'The thief comes to steal, kill, and destroy, but Jesus comes to give life—abundant life!' I speak life into this baby boy who's in danger right now. And greater is Jesus who is in me than he that is in this world. God, please send your angels to war on this baby's behalf. 'For you give your angels charge concerning him lest he strikes his foot against a stone.'"

Scripture prayers seemed to be the most powerful way to pray right now, so Mei Lin emptied herself of all she knew, throwing her entire heart into prayers over the little one that Jesus cared for so much.

Tumen River, China Side

CHAPTER 24

When Young Soon opened her eyes, both of her sons were beside her, crying. Her back was burning, probably from the fall.

"You must be quiet," she said to Nam Gil. She reached for the baby to pull him to her breast. Pain shot through her arms!

"*Oh!*"

"Oma! Oma what happened?" Nam Gil whispered, but his voice was frantic.

The light had exposed her and Young Soon knew it would only be moments before they were found. Defying her own pain, she reached for Baby Han Chun and pulled him to her breast. His crying ceased as he nursed.

"Nam Gil, you must pretend you are dead," she whispered. "There are bad men who want us dead. So let's pretend we are dead and then maybe they won't hurt us."

"Oma—"

"Obey me," she commanded. Her heart ached for her elder son. Pain seared her shoulders and she could feel warmth trickling down into her sides.

Lights.

Shouting. A language she didn't know.

"Lie still."

Would those be the last words her son would hear her speak?

"I love you," she whispered softly and squeezed Nam Gil's hand.

He sniffed and shifted position.

"Lie still," she repeated.

A shout in the distance.

Noise—shouting.

The lights were gone.

Young Soon felt blood pumping out of her back now with every breath. Quickly, she moved the baby to try to relieve the pain.

Nam Gil didn't move and she was grateful. "Stay still," she said. "They think we are dead."

Young Soon rolled to her back.

"Uhh!"

"Oma?"

She had no strength to move again. Young Soon lay on her back, her baby still reaching for her breast. In that moment, she felt that nothing in the world mattered more than nursing baby Han Chun. With a will of iron, she pushed herself back onto her side and pulled baby Han Chun to her other breast.

"We must—wait—for the baby—to nurse," she said. Her breathing was heavy. Young Soon knew she could not walk. The guards must have been called away by some other duty or surely they would have found her. The burning in her back was intense. Baby Han Chun cried, and frantically grabbed her for more milk. Could she possibly give milk while she was dying?

The blackness of it all was sinking down upon her. She was dying and her two little sons had no one. Panic gripped her heart.

"Nam Gil," she said. "Take Oma's hand, dear boy."

Nam Gil took her hand and she squeezed it. Her head felt light. "I didn't want this to happen. But you must take Baby Han Chun over this river bank right here and run to the road. Remember the road we saw from way up on the hill?"

"But you're coming, Oma," he said.

"Oma got hurt," she said softly. Her voice caught and she thought she'd fall into a million pieces. Young Soon bit her lower lip and continued.

"You take your baby brother across that road and there's a ditch on the other side. You walk in that ditch until you find a hole. Uncle Hwan said to stay in that hole and he'll send friends to find us. Now, you tell him your Oma is hurt, OK?"

"Oma, I don't want to go," said Nam Gil. He wept bitterly and Young Soon made him snuggle closer to her. He was shivering wet and sobbing now.

"I want to go with you, but I can't. I was shot in the back by that big gun. Now you tell Uncle Hwan and he'll take care of you."

"I'll tell him to come and get you, Oma," said Nam Gil.

"That's my boy," she said. Her head started to spin and she felt like she would lose consciousness.

"Take Baby Han Chun. Keep him in the blanket. You can chew the rice first and give him little bites. You have the water jug, too. Always remember—I love you."

"Oma—Oma, please come with me," Nam Gil cried again.

Breathe deeply. Go back to him. Young Soon willed herself to stay alive a little longer. "Tell Min-Hee I love her. Tell Baby Han Chun he is a spring of life. You—Nam Gil you are my firstborn and so much like your father. I want you to think of your father now. Think of him. Be brave like your father."

Nam Gil was kissing her face, his tears streaming into hers. She felt him touch her one moment and felt miles away from him the next. She fought to feel him once more and then she knew she had to command him to go.

"Go," she commanded. "Take the baby—go."

"Oma—"

"I will live," she promised.

Fingers. She could feel his small fingers at her neck untying the blanket.

She wanted to guide them across the dark road. She wanted to lead them to a table full of food at their Uncle Hwan's nice home. All of her dreams for freedom were now dying because she was dying.

Warmth. He'd covered her with the blanket. *No—take the blanket, Nam Gil. Take the blanket—you need it.*

She could not call to him.

"I love you, Oma. I will take care of Han Chun. We'll come back for you."

Crying. Small footsteps.

Blackness.

~

Young Soon felt herself sinking further and further into the blackness, a long dark tunnel of blackness.

Peace.

Young Soon saw a man in white walking across the road toward her. Fear struck her heart. Her children!

"Your children are fine," he said in perfect Korean.

Young Soon could not speak. The man was more than eight feet tall, walking in a shining robe like a tree full of lanterns in the night. She suddenly realized that she was standing, no longer lying on the ground. She looked down—her body was on the ground beside where she stood, covered with the wet blanket her son put over her. This was very much like the time she nearly died of starvation when her brother came to visit. Only this time, she did not settle back into her body. The pain in her back was gone now but she did not want to leave her children.

Love for her children summoned courage within her to speak. "Who are you?"

The man smiled. "I am your guardian. I was sent here to take you to the God who loves."

Relief and joy spilled over Young Soon. Could it be possible that this smiling glistening man would take her to the God who loves? But she couldn't go. Not now.

"My children need me," she said.

"You have been taken before your time," the man answered, as if agreeing with her. "There is much warfare here—the evil here is great." He looked up above the guardhouse into the sky, watching as if he saw something she could not see. "The most we could do was make the phone ring so the guards wouldn't find your sons alive."

"You did that?" asked Young Soon. "Then why didn't you save me, too?" It seemed an ungrateful thing to ask, but Young Soon was confused. The God who loves did not have power to save her and she wanted to know why.

"Come, I'll show you." The man put his hand under her elbow and lifted her with him straight up into the sky. He pointed above the guardhouse. Young Soon could not believe her eyes. There, above the guardhouse, was a great red dragon. Its tail swept back and forth across the river and smaller evil looking creatures ran around underneath the great dragon, seemingly in much confusion.

"Look there," said the man beside her. "Those are my warriors from Heaven."

Far above the great dragon, Heaven's warriors, all dressed in white like the man beside her, charged courageously at the dragon. The dragon seemed only distracted, not defeated. Young Soon looked more closely.

"What is that written on the swords of your warriors?" she asked.

"Prayer," the man answered. "We swing with the power of prayers from the people of the earth."

Young Soon cried, "Oh, I should have prayed more to the God who loves."

The man nodded in agreement. "Yes, but you did not know His name. Others who know His name have prayed for you."

The guards in the house below did not seem to notice the Great War that was going on above their heads. Young Soon looked across the river at North Korea. From this new vantage point, the sky over her country was as black as iron and the ground below like parched fractured bronze. The sky on the China side had a hazy orange glow surrounding the hideous red dragon as it breathed fiery words in order to kill the men in white. She had so many questions.

"We must leave now."

"But my children—"

The man smiled. "Some of my warriors are with them and they are sleeping. The God who loves will take care of them here. You must come with me."

Young Soon felt pulled in both directions. The man looked at the warfare over the guardhouse and stepped back a little.

"Come," he commanded. His voice was full of authority and power and just as her son obeyed her command to cross the dangerous river, she knew she must obey this man's command to go with him.

"Yes," she replied. "I'll come."

The shining man took Young Soon's hand. Waves of life pulsated through the core of her being and she felt her heart overwhelmed with expectation of what was coming.

"Jump," he said.

Heaven

CHAPTER 25

Young Soon jumped just a little and suddenly she and the guardian were flying hand in hand. The guardian's body arched and they flew away from the border and then out over the Korea Bay, higher and higher until she could see the Yellow Sea and the Sea of Japan surrounding the peninsula. Although she knew it was still nighttime, the sky looked dark blue and then light blue. The waters were dark, yet shining. She saw clouds going past her at a faster speed than she ever dreamed imaginable.

Peace. There was so much peace. *Boom!*

A loud sound smacked into her ears and suddenly she was in a long tunnel. Pink swirling clouds were all around her. She gripped the man's hand as he flew ahead of her, confident that he was escorting her to the God who loves.

Another boom! The tunnel ended and Young Soon was flying powerfully through the galaxies! Her heart thrilled at the sight of the stars. Hundreds flashed passed her in silver streaks while the dazzling diamonds in front of her beckoned her to fly closer. A peculiar sound reached her ear. It was not high pitched or low, but a beautiful sound that drew her in, and made her yearn to go closer. There! A beautiful planet with two glacial rings around it—and it made the most beautiful distinct sound, as though it were calling her to consider its own particular beauty.

"Saturn," the guardian called back to her.

Young Soon clung to his hand, fascinated with all that was around her. There! That planet on the left had a color she'd never seen before and it spun in cadence with the pulse of the galaxy. Sounds and colors emerged and thrilled her senses as she traveled.

A round pin of light emerged on the horizon ahead. The light pierced the darkness, grew, and within seconds she was surrounded with it. Zephyrs of love rippled through her skin, her hands, her feet, until her flesh was alive with its fragrance. They stopped in front of a dazzling person.

Young Soon gasped. The wind within her was also outside of her now—swirling around the man standing in front of her, drawing her to his eyes of liquid love. His hair was brown and then white lightening; his eyes were the same—teetering between human and God. His clothing shimmered between white and gold, rippling with life as though his garments were made of water.

"You—You are the God who loves!" she exclaimed.

"I AM," he replied. "You believed. And so you are here."

His voice was like thunder and rain, and Young Soon fell at His feet.

"Come," He said, extending His hand to help her up. Young Soon hesitated.

My children—Young Soon dared not tell Him her thoughts.

"Your children will come to know Him," the guardian explained.

Young Soon glanced up at the guardian.

246

"We all know what the other is thinking here," he replied, answering her question before she asked. "Would you like me to go back to check on them?"

Young Soon nodded her head. The guardian looked at the God who loves. He nodded and the guardian turned and flew, although he did not use the tunnel this time.

The God who loves took her hand and she stood in His light. Light surrounded her, swallowed her, and filled her. A surge of power went through His hand into hers. Waves upon waves of holy glory washed over her. That's when she heard it—she heard it before she saw it.

Laughter. Children's laughter—like tinkling bells chiming to the rhythm of the wind.

She looked up at Him. "You knew?"

He smiled and nodded. "I told My angel to bring you here through the children's entrance to surprise you."

"Angel?"

"My angels have special jobs, like your guardian. Others are messengers, warriors, recorders, or worship leaders."

The God who loves led her forward and they stepped into soft green grass. A river flowed before them and the beauty was beyond anything Young Soon ever imagined. He jumped into the river and beckoned her to follow. The memory of the last river she crossed flashed before her. A small cry escaped her lips and a tear trickled down her cheek. She longed to follow, but she froze. The God who loves ran out of the water and put His hands on her head. The awful memory faded, but the sadness remained. He took His finger and wiped the tear from her cheek, then picked her up and took her into the river in His arms.

"No need to hold your breath," He told her, and He dunked both of them underneath the water. Young Soon held her breath anyway and looked into his face. He smiled under the water. "You can talk under here, too. It's not like the earth."

Young Soon tried it. She let out her breath and inhaled—just a little bit. "I can breathe!"

At that, the God who loves threw back His head and laughed. "You're washed and healed now. Let's go."

The God who loves took Young Soon's hand and led her out of the river to the other side. A gentle breeze blew through her hair and whispered, "You are free." *Free. I'm free.* The leaves on the full green trees nearby clapped their hands at the wind's announcement, causing a huge gust that instantly dried her clothing. Young Soon looked down. Her clothing was shining white, like His! And there was a beautiful blue sash tied to her waist and matching blue sandals on her feet. But it was the scenery around her that riveted her attention.

Green grass, hills, mountains, blue skies and fruit-laden trees were all around. The trees moved so that the wind seemed to sing through their branches. Flowers of all colors, some colors she'd never seen on earth, sang softly in unison. Young Soon imagined her mother painting such beautiful flowers on the doors of the houses here. As the flowers sang and their voices went higher, their colors changed! Young Soon had never seen anything so beautiful. Above the murmur of the water behind her, above the whisper of the wind in the trees and soft singing of flowers was the sound of laughter. Each had a distinct voice and yet together they blended into a pleasing harmony.

The God who loves reached His hand into the sky and a flock of beautiful bluebirds flew to Him, carrying a dazzling golden crown with red colored jewels imbedded inside the band.

"For you," he said, as he handed her the crown.

"Me?" asked Young Soon. She turned the crown around and around in her hands. Light ricocheted from every angle of its design. "Whatever for? I've done nothing deserving of this—or—or of any of this!"

"This crown is because you learned to love on earth. Therefore you are deserving to wear it here."

"Love?" asked Young Soon. "But—"

"Remember the rice you left under the bench for Chung-Ho's children?"

"Yes," Young Soon replied. "But that was such a small thing."

"You proved your love when you left rice for Chung-Ho's orphaned children. And you overcame your hatred for the gotchebee children."

Wind whipped around her hands as she held the crown in front of her. The breeze seemed to urge her to put the crown onto her head and so she did. The crown must have been loaded with happiness because she suddenly wanted to sing and dance and even laugh. She looked at the God who loves to see if He noticed.

"Come," said the God who loves. "There's more." He pulled her with Him toward the crest of a hill. The touch of his hand launched waters of liquid love that could not be seen but poured over her dry soul bringing her much joy.

"Your love is sacred," she said as they stopped underneath one of the fruit trees. "I can feel its fountain in my soul."

"It is the same fountain you felt when I introduced you to Han Chun. Do you remember?" He asked her.

Young Soon thought back to the day when her little one was not yet born. She nearly died, but the baby…"Yes, I remember," she answered. "That was You, too?"

He nodded and pointed to the fruit in the tree branches above them. Young Soon cupped her hand under a leafy branch and a large plum-colored fruit fell into her palm.

"Eat it," He instructed. "It will fill you with strength."

Young Soon ate half the fruit. She'd never tasted anything so wonderful. The juice dripped over her fingers and the wind wiped her hands clean. Strength filled her being. She offered some of it to Jesus and He ate the rest and again took her hand and led her toward a high hill.

The chimes of laughter grew louder and children suddenly appeared over the crest of the hill, the older ones carrying small ones on their shoulders. Most of them fell at the top of the hill and disappeared again, rolling down the other side. Young Soon never saw such healthy, happy children. There were Korean children and children from other nations, too.

One of the older boys ran toward them, jostling a little girl on his shoulders. "Jesus! Jesus, come watch us!" he cried.

"Jesus," Young Soon whispered. "The God who loves is Jesus."

"I'm coming, Joshua," Jesus answered.

"Come on, Young Soon!" the boy cried. "We've been waiting for you."

"Me?" Young Soon was startled.

"I told them all about you," said Jesus. He squeezed her hand.

The whole group appeared at the crest of the hill again and ran toward her, calling her by name. The children took her hand and led her to the top of the hill.

"Watch us Young Soon!"

"Yes, watch us!"

The children tumbled down the hill, filling the entire atmosphere with laughter. She and Jesus stood side by side and watched them go up and down again and again. After a time, Young Soon closed her eyes, while the wind played at her hair, and imagined her own children playing in this wonderful place. The fragrance of honey and flowers filled her head and the mirth filled her heart. She turned to speak to Jesus.

"You'll see Him again," said the guardian.

"You're back," said Young Soon. Jesus was gone but her guardian was here and, although it surprised her, it seemed appropriate. She wanted to know about her children.

"Your children were rescued by your brother," he said. "Your baby will be raised by people who love Jesus. We have arranged it."

Young Soon smiled. Han Chun, Korean Spring—now she knew that he was named after the river she went into with the God who loves, the river of sacred love that flooded her soul just before Jesus led her to the children.

"And Min-Hee and Nam Gil?" she asked. "They will be with my brother?"

The angel nodded. "We will try to bring Ja and her husband here one day, too."

Young Soon sat down on the grass. It felt like a soft blanket that sort of cuddled her when she sat down. "I wish I had told Ja more about the God who loves," she said. "Will they all come here?"

The guardian nodded. "All who believe in Jesus, the God who loves, will come here."

"I will miss them," said Young Soon.

Suddenly, Joshua ran toward her and then collapsed in front of her. "I can't wait until my mother comes," he said.

Young Soon smiled just a little. "I can't wait until my children come," she answered.

"But you can't cry," he instructed her. "Tears aren't on this side of the river."

Young Soon heard herself laughing now. "No, tears aren't on this side of the river, Joshua. Only freedom." With that, the trees waved their branches and inside the wind the word *freedom* blew over their heads in a cloudy banner.

"See?" said Joshua, pointing. "Do you want to see where I live?"

"I'd love to," she answered. She looked over at her guardian. He nodded. Joshua helped her to her feet and together they ran down the grassy slope.

Rural China

CHAPTER 26

Friday night was humid but the crowds gathering in the fields were larger than ever. Mei Lin swatted a mosquito again. She wished she'd have worn long sleeves to keep them off her arms. But it really wasn't the mosquitoes that bothered her—it was the dream last night and the edginess she'd felt in her heart since yesterday. The grace of God had lifted and she felt as though her mission here was finished, but she struggled with leaving before Monday because she didn't want to disappoint Mrs. Ma.

Mei Lin and Lian took off their shoes and waded into the water. As soon as the people saw them, they crowded around the girls with questions about the Bible or testimonies of what God had done for them. Mei Lin let Lian lead the conversations while she waded deeper to cool off before preaching that evening.

After splashing water on her arms and soaking her t-shirt a bit, Mei Lin felt refreshed. It was only 6:30 P.M. and the songs would begin in half an hour. Mei Lin didn't want to miss it, but something was bothering her. The girls waded out of the pond and walked toward the front stage, constructed last week by some of the men in the town.

"What is it, Mei Lin?" asked Lian. "You aren't yourself."

"I don't have peace," said Mei Lin.

"Should we pray?" asked Lian.

"Yes, that is good. Let's pray."

Lian prayed and Mei Lin tried to concentrate. But she couldn't—something was wrong. As Lian prayed, Mei Lin's eyes scanned the ever-widening crowd of people. There!

"Lian," said Mei Lin. She was interrupting her prayer, but she couldn't help it.

"Mei Lin?"

"Look—over there just stepping off the road."

Lian gasped. "Why, it's Dun!"

"Yes, and who is that with him?"

Lian squinted her eyes to look more closely. "I don't know. They are much older than Dun. Do you think—"

"Yes—I think that is why I have been so restless," said Mei Lin. "Dun wanted to travel with us when Fei and I first came to your village. Perhaps he was angered when we turned him down. I can't be sure."

"He didn't come to the baptism that night," said Lian. "I noticed."

"That's right! Now it all makes sense. Dun may be the one who turned us in to the PSB!"

"Then why is he here?" asked Lian.

"Adventure," replied Mei Lin.

Both girls looked at one another. Dun hadn't spotted them yet.

"Turn around," said Mei Lin.

Both of them turned around together and walked back toward the main road. "He's probably expecting us to be up front," said Mei Lin. "We'll have to hide."

Mei Lin took Lian by the arm to guide her as they walked. Her arm trembled. "I'll pray now," said Mei Lin. She prayed out loud to calm the jitters rising in her own heart. She should have known when she had no peace tonight that this meeting was being watched. Perhaps ZhingCho's cadre was a Christian, but the county cadres were not. It was time to go.

"Over there—Mrs. Ma!" cried Lian.

The girls walked quickly toward Mrs. Ma and told her everything.

"Oh, Mei Lin, I pushed you to stay. And you were right—it was time to go."

"We have to leave now," said Mei Lin. She looked down the road. The pathway to freedom was past the crowd of people in the field and back into the wooded area where they first came to ZhingCho.

"I will send my husband to get your bags," said Mrs. Ma. "Is there anything else you need?"

Lian shook her head. "I just did our laundry today and folded it and put it on the bed. He can just put the clothes inside."

"And food," said Mrs. Ma. "We'll send food."

"Where should we go?" asked Mei Lin. "And what about the people? There are thousands of them."

"They can't arrest ten thousand people," said Mrs. Ma. "You girls go across the road and mingle with the people who are coming for the meeting as you walk. When you get a chance, cross over to the other side and duck behind the rice paddies. You'll have to walk very low, maybe crawl. But crawl toward the woods. Do you know where the creek is near the road entrance to the woods?"

Mei Lin nodded.

"Go to the creek. Stay there and I'll send someone with your bags." Mrs. Ma hugged them both. "God go with you."

"Wait!" exclaimed Mei Lin. "The people. What will you do with all the people?"

"We will sing. And then we will testify. We have to keep the meeting going so you two have time to escape."

"Your cadre!" said Mei Lin. "He will get in trouble if the county cadres know he is involved."

"I will tell him," said Mrs. Ma. "God will show him what to do."

"Please—bring our flashlights," said Lian. "And matches."

"I'll be sure," said Mrs. Ma. "Now go."

Mei Lin glanced through the crowd. She did not see Dun anymore and it unnerved her. She felt she had to see him to know if they were escaping safely.

"Lian, do you see Dun now?"

"No. I lost sight of him," said Lian. Her voice trembled and she stumbled over a stone. Mei Lin caught her arm. "Have faith," she said softly. "And slow down. We need to mingle with others."

People gathered around Mei Lin and Lian as they neared the road entrance. The road was swarming with people shouldering benches and blankets, holding the hands of children as they prepared to attend another service. After they got into the middle of the crowded road, Mei Lin put her head down and let Lian lead the way. Lian led them to the other side and one at a time, the two of them dashed into the soggy field and met behind a patch of long rice stalks. Most of the field was low, like Mrs. Ma said. But perhaps they could walk hunched over and make it. Mei Lin didn't like walking over the plants—she was a farmer's daughter. But the path was not an option because they could be seen from there. She pointed toward the woods and the two of them walked hunched over.

After about ten minutes, Mei Lin stopped. Her back ached and her heart was still pounding. She knelt in the watery mud to catch her breath and stretch her back. Just then she heard Mrs. Ma over the microphone announcing the song service. Mei Lin looked at Lian and smiled. Mrs. Ma chose a song that would not offend the county cadres. Still, the deeper meaning of the music sank into her soul:

C. Hope Flinchbaugh

The stream of life
The stream of joy
Flow tenderly into my heart
The stream of life
The stream of joy
Flow tenderly into my heart
(Canaan Hymn #547, *A River of Life*)

WuMa, China

CHAPTER 27

Mei Lin knelt at the back door of the Guis' home in WuMa. It was late afternoon and now that they were here she was anxious to meet with Pastor Wong. He didn't answer his cell phone, so she went with the alternative plan—placing a pile of rocks on the back steps of the Guis' home. Lian handed her three more rocks.

"How many more?" she asked.

"Oh, at least four or five," Mei Lin answered. "I want to be sure he can see them easily when he drives by."

Mei Lin knew the county cadre was looking for her and she was beginning to feel the strain from running and hiding from danger every minute. She hadn't slept well since they narrowly escaped ZhingCho three days ago. On top of that, she couldn't get the baby in her dream off of her mind. She felt confused and disturbed inside. Right now all she wanted was a hot bath and a warm bed.

Lian handed her the last few rocks. Mei Lin stood to her feet and dusted off her knees. "Now—we will wait."

"Can we get something to eat?" asked Lian.

"Good idea," replied Mei Lin. She felt more tired than hungry, but it was the first time Lian had asked for anything since their journey began. Mei Lin put her backpack on her shoulder again. She was glad to go with her.

The girls bought noodles and vegetables from a vendor on a side street. Mei Lin bought hot tea from another vendor and together they ducked into a deserted parking lot and sat on the curb to eat. The food was deliciously hot and Mei Lin felt strengthened afterward.

The girls stopped at the bus station to try the cell phone one more time.

"Hello, Wong here."

"Oh! This is Mei Lin!"

"Do you know where to find the instructions?" he asked.

Mei Lin was surprised he did not greet her. Perhaps there was trouble. "Yes, I do."

"Good. Go there in one hour. I'll talk to you later."

Click.

Mei Lin hung up the phone. Pastor Wong was always warm and friendly. She wondered if he was in trouble or—perhaps she and Lian were in trouble!

"Let's go back to the Guis' house," she told Lian. It took a little more than an hour to walk to the Guis after making the call at the bus station.

"What is wrong, Mei Lin?" asked Lian. "You've been so quiet."

Mei Lin forced a smile. "I'm weary, I guess," she replied. "I haven't slept well since we left ZhingCho."

Lian squeezed her hand and then let go. "You have been keeping watch for me so that I could sleep," she said. "Will your Pastor Wong have a place for us to rest?"

Mei Lin sighed. "I'm not sure. He was very short with his words on the phone. I'm wondering if something is wrong."

"Isn't that the Guis house over there?" asked Lian.

"Yes. Look! The pile of stones has been moved!"

Mei Lin held back the urge to run. The stones were moved and that was a sure sign that there were instructions underneath. She and Lian easily moved the new pile to the other side.

A paid taxi awaits you one block down the street.

Mei Lin crumpled the paper and put it into her pocket. She adjusted her backpack. "Let's go."

The taxi driver took them outside the city, over a bridge, and stopped along a curb. They got out and the driver left quickly. There were about five houses on both sides of the street, each one resembling the one beside it. Mei Lin stood and waited. The sun was setting and it was getting dark. She had no further instructions and she had no idea where they were.

A door opened and a woman waved to them. Mei Lin and Lian approached the woman.

"Mei Lin?"

"Yes," answered Mei Lin. "This is Lian."

The woman looked puzzled. "And what happened to Fei?"

Mei Lin looked at the woman. She appeared to be in her mid-forties, short hair, with simple black slacks and a pale blue collared shirt.

"Fei was arrested. Lian is traveling with me now."

"I am Mrs. Han. Please, come in," said the woman.

Mei Lin followed the woman from the lower room where a car was parked inside up the stairs to a kitchen. Then there were more stairs. At the top, they entered a room.

"Mei Lin!"

Mei Lin turned around. Pastor Wong greeted her with a warm handshake. "Where is Fei?" he asked.

Mei Lin introduced Lian and explained again what happened to Fei. "I will ask Brother Tom to try to find what prison she is in," he said. "If we can collect some money, perhaps we can try to persuade the guards to free her."

Mei Lin and Lian sat on small benches beside Pastor Wong and relayed the story of their missionary journey. The room darkened and Pastor Wong turned on a light switch. Mei Lin related every detail and when she was finished, she felt strange and hollow.

"Mei Lin, are you all right?" asked Pastor Wong.

Mei Lin nodded quietly.

"She is exhausted," said Lian. "Please, do you have a bed?"

Mei Lin looked gratefully at Lian.

"Of course," said Pastor Wong. "We will talk in the morning." He stood up to leave and then opened his Bible. "Maybe these would help you to sleep better?"

"Oh! From Liko? And Father?"

Pastor Wong smiled. "Pastor Chen Liko must like to write. There are three here from him."

Mei Lin felt her face turn warm. Lian walked Pastor Wong to the door downstairs and Mei Lin was left alone in the room. Mei Lin sat on the bench near the door and opened the most recent letter from Liko. When she was in Shanghai last summer, Liko's letters to her were almost formal and she was deeply disappointed. She wondered what his letters would contain now.

Dearest Mei Lin,

We are doing all that we can to help our friend's dog bites. My thoughts turn to you every night and I wonder if I will see you again at harvest. Mother and I were so pleased to hear that your harvest is already beginning.

My heart aches for you. It must be difficult without your friend. Mother and Amah are making plans for our wedding next spring. Amah complains about the hot weather, but otherwise is fine. She keeps little Fu Yatou skipping about with one chore or another.

I long to see you again. Write to me as soon as you can.
All my love,
Liko

Mei Lin held the letter to her chin and sighed. His letters were always short, but this time his affection was warm and heartfelt. She quickly read all the letters and then placed them under her pillow to read again just before she went to sleep. Mrs. Han had already prepared a hot bath. Mei Lin submerged her body and then her head, washing her hair with the coarse soap Mrs. Han provided. She couldn't remember the last time she felt this tired.

Longing for a soft safe bed, she quickly dried her hair with the large towel and changed into clean clothing. Mrs. Han said that the main room on the third floor was usually used as a seminary. Mei Lin and Lian shared one of two small bedrooms beside that main room. She could hear Lian talking to Mrs. Han downstairs in the kitchen. Mei Lin sat on the edge of the bed and combed her hair, still damp. It felt good to be clean again.

Mei Lin placed her hand on her abdomen. She wondered what it would be like to really give birth to a child. In her first dream, the baby was holding her finger—a boy. She missed little Mei Mei from the Shanghai orphanage, but the baby in her dream was not a girl. Her thoughts turned to the dream she had the last night she was in ZhingCho. She wondered if the baby was safe or if he drowned. It was all so mysterious and yet Mei Lin felt strangely tied to this little one and she wondered if God was speaking to her heart.

Quietly, she slipped to her knees beside her bed.

"Oh, Father. I can still feel his little fist wrapped around my finger. I don't know what You are trying to show me, but whoever this little one is, I am willing to do whatever I can to help You. Please speak to Liko if you want us to adopt this boy. Or, if he is our own child...Whatever You want, whatever Your reasons are for the dreams, I'll do whatever You want me to do—anything God. I'm Yours."

Mei Lin slipped underneath the covers. She still didn't know any more about the child than she did before she prayed, but somehow leaving it all in God's hands chased away the confusion and she felt ready now to sleep.

WuMa, China

CHAPTER 28

Mei Lin wakened to the hum of prayer in the large room outside her door. She felt rested and fresh, so she stretched and then got up to peek outside her window. Only a crack of light appeared on the far horizon. Dawn was breaking and the sound of prayer was like the sound of the Chinese thrush—melodic and distinctive to a higher kingdom that permeated the clouds. She couldn't make out the words but was anxious to join them. Quickly, she washed up, dressed, and stepped into the larger room. There were about fifteen people, many on their knees, scattered about the room in no particular order. Lian was in the far corner, sitting on the floor with her back to the wall.

"We pray for those trying to escape North Korea, Lord." Pastor Wong was praying on his knees. He wore a pale yellow short-sleeved shirt, his head bowed while hugging his Bible to his chest.

"We ask You to bring them safely across the river and into our refuge centers."

Murmurs of agreement went up around the room. Mei Lin was curious—who was trying to get out of North Korea?

"Lord, send Your power to the fatherless," said a woman in a dark blue collared shirt and sandals. "We ask You to care for the ones who have no one to care for them. Help us to find them so that they can hear of Your great love and be fed a warm meal."

Mei Lin loved to pray, but today she listened. It seemed strange to her that this small seminary in south central China was praying for North Koreans who lived far to the northeast.

"Send Your angels, Lord," the woman continued. "Send Your angels to guard and protect the innocent. Keep the sex traffickers away. Hedge them about, Lord, so they are not deceived by those who would do evil to them in China."

"Yes," agreed one of the students. "Send angels to the places we cannot see or cannot go."

Prayers continued like this for some time. Then Mrs. Han led them in a Canaan hymn:

When light dawns on China
The sound of prayer rises
Prayer brings revival and peace
Prayer brings unity and triumph
Prayer soars over the highest mountains
Prayer melts the ice off the coldest hearts
Prayer soars over the highest mountains
Prayer melts the ice off the coldest hearts…

Mei Lin felt as though she were in a room full of secrets—even God seemed to hold a secret from her right now.

The students ate breakfast upstairs while Mei Lin and Lian joined Pastor Wong at the table in the kitchen.

"Did you rest well?" Pastor Wong asked Mei Lin.

"Yes, thank you," she replied. "I feel very good this morning. Why are you all praying about North Koreans?"

"People are starving to death in North Korea and many are crossing the Tumen River into China to try to find food and a new life. Unfortunately, many of the defectors are shot by our border patrols."

"That's horrible," said Lian, her eyes filled with tears.

"The defectors who aren't shot are sent back to North Korea— our government doesn't want them here. Back in North Korea, they are interrogated, tortured, and either executed or sent to a prison camp—even children."

Mei Lin gasped. "Children are sent to a prison camp?"

Pastor Wong's face looked grave. "Yes, that's why we want you to rescue a baby."

Mei Lin couldn't believe her ears. "Say that again?"

"We want you to rescue a baby near the border of China and North Korea," repeated Pastor Wong.

Mei Lin got up from the breakfast table and walked to the window. Parting the small white corner of the curtain, she looked down on the alleyway behind the house. *Now the dream is unfolding— now the revelation comes.*

"Who is this baby?" asked Mei Lin, still staring out the window.

"The mother was killed by Chinese guards when she tried to cross the Tumen River into China only a few days ago. Both of her sons survived. The older one is about seven or eight and he's staying with his uncle in China. But the baby needs a home."

Mei Lin turned to face Pastor Wong. Tears streamed down her face now—God was giving her the answers to all her questions. "Why doesn't the uncle keep the baby, too?"

"Babies make too much noise," Pastor Wong replied. "The aunt and uncle are left to raise the three-year-old daughter, whom they helped escape a few months ago, and the son. The baby could arouse suspicions of neighbors who might report them. Then all three children would be in danger."

"I don't understand," said Mei Lin. She returned to her seat and leaned across the table. The only citizens she knew who were chased by the government were Christians. "How do you know about her? Was the woman being persecuted for her faith inside North Korea?"

Pastor Wong shook his head. "No, she probably never heard of the name of Jesus. She was running for her life."

"How awful," said Lian.

Pastor Wong folded his hands in front of him. "More than four million people have starved to death in North Korea since 1995."

Mei Lin gasped. "Why didn't I hear about this before?" she asked. It amazed her that her political science teacher never spoke of it in high school.

"It is a communist government," replied Pastor Wong. "So the president has our government's sympathies. That's why the Chinese government agreed to either kill defectors or send them back to North Korea where they are executed or die a slow death in the labor camps."

Mei Lin's neck tingled with this new information. Her mind flashed through the dream pictures she experienced on her journey. "What can we do?"

"We sent some of our Christian friends there to rent property to house the refugees," said Pastor Wong. "The refugees are stuck inside all day—they are in hiding. If they go outside, they can be discovered by a Chinese citizen who will be paid a nice sum by our government for reporting any North Korean refugees."

"I can't imagine staying inside the house all day and all night," said Mei Lin. As tired as she was from her journey, she was glad to be free to walk from town to town.

"A baby is hard to hide," said Pastor Wong. "They cry at all hours of the day and night and, because the mother is dead, we must find a nurse."

Mei Lin's eyes widened. "I cannot nurse the baby!"

Pastor Wong smiled at that. "I know. We want you to take the baby to Mother Su in Shanghai. You'd have to travel by train from WonChow in the north to Shanghai."

Mei Lin looked at Lian who was softly drumming her fingers on the kitchen table, deep in thought. Their bowls of rice congee sat forgotten. Mei Lin fingered the warm teacup, turning it around in her hands. "What about Lian?"

"Lian will go back to her village as soon as she spends some time in our seminary," said Pastor Wong. "I will send two of our evangelists with her. They will take more Bibles, of course."

Mei Lin returned to her chair at the table. "Do you know that I had two dreams of a baby while on this missionary journey?"

"No," replied Pastor Wong. "So God has already shown you your assignment! Praise God!"

"But in the first dream, I gave birth to him," Mei Lin replied. "I don't know if this is the baby. And Liko was there."

"Well, Liko already knows about the assignment," said Pastor Wong. "And he agrees that you should take it if you're up for it, especially now while the county cadres are looking for you. As for giving birth—only God can show you. It could have been a dream of intercession."

"You mean, a dream to cause me to pray for the baby?" asked Mei Lin.

Pastor Wong nodded.

"Well, that's certainly happened," said Mei Lin. She looked at Lian. "Lian, how do you feel about staying here in the seminary?"

Lian looked up and smiled, her eyes shining. "I feel like I am the most fortunate woman in the world."

"When do I leave?" Mei Lin asked Pastor Wong.

"Tomorrow," he answered. "And will you teach us tonight in the seminary?"

Mei Lin nodded. "I will be honored."

WonChow, China

CHAPTER 29

Mei Lin got off the train and looked for her contact—a woman with a blue bandana tied around her neck. She adjusted her backpacks so that the blue scarf tied to the black backpack would be easily seen. She walked past the bathrooms and inside the station. People were everywhere—WonChow was much bigger than she imagined!

Someone brushed up beside her.

"Mei Lin?" came the woman's whisper from behind.

"Yes," said Mei Lin.

"Don't turn around," she said. Go to Gate 2 and sit down at the bench there. Leave your package beside you. Someone will sit beside you. They take your package and you will take theirs."

Mei Lin simply nodded and walked toward the gates.

She sat down and set the black bag beside her on her left. She kept her personal bag on her back so there would be no mistake—the Korean Bibles would be delivered without a complication. What concerned her more were the contents of the other package—the one being delivered to her.

Mei Lin checked her tickets to be sure—they even planned for her to be at the right gate! Gate 2 left for Shanghai in one hour. They'd probably board in half an hour.

A man sat next to the bag on her left, but he only carried a large plaid rice bag. As the man beside her read his newspaper, Mei Lin looked around for her contact. She saw no one, so she tried to be patient and relax. The bench was too crowded for an exchange now, so she quickly moved the bag to her right and scooted over closer to the man. He looked up briefly, and then went back to reading his newspaper.

She checked her ticket again and then put it away in her pocket this time. People were milling about, a number of them began filling up the seats to wait for the train to Shanghai. Just then, a woman sat on the edge of the bench to her right. She had a black bag in her lap and a blue scarf around her neck!

Mei Lin moved her bag to the floor and nudged it over toward the woman with her foot. The woman put her black bag between them, checked her watch, then stood up to leave. She bent over and took the black bag full of Bibles. Mei Lin glanced sideways at the man on her left. The newspaper was hiding his face. Good!

Mei Lin's hand trembled as she unsnapped the leather bag. There, inside, was a wee little baby with a downy patch of long black hair on top of his head. He startled a little at the light, but he didn't seem to have the motor control to cover his eyes. Gently, Mei Lin lifted the precious package out of the bag. Tears sprang to her eyes. His tiny face was drawn and thin, yet he didn't even cry. Holding the baby in one arm, Mei Lin checked the contents of the bag. There were two diapers and half a bottle of milk. How could she survive the entire trip with half a bottle of milk?

Mei Lin didn't dream that she would have to find milk for the baby. She looked about the room. There were counters where snack food and even soda pop could be bought while waiting. But there was nothing there for a baby!

Gently, she took his little fist and wrapped it around her finger—just like in the dream. The sweet baby clenched her finger and she closed her eyes, imagining the dream again.

"May I help you?"

Mei Lin jumped up from her seat, the baby in her arms. "Liko!"

Liko laughed and hugged her tightly. "I couldn't let you go on this trip alone now, could I?"

"Oh, Liko, I can't believe you're here."

"Actually, our friend Wong told me you were tired and perhaps could use the help."

"He did?" she asked. Mei Lin looked back. The man with the newspaper was definitely giving them more than a passing glance now. Mei Lin pulled Liko down to the bench between her and the newspaper man. She wanted to feel him close to her. Her stomach was full of butterflies.

She held the baby in front of her so Liko could see him. "Isn't he beautiful?"

Liko reached over and whispered in her ear. His breath made her spine tingle. "He'll be ours for the journey," he said.

"You have your ticket to Shanghai?" she asked.

"Right here," said Liko. "I thought it was about time I met Mother Su."

There was that twinkle in his eye and tears sprang to her own eyes. "I'm so glad you're here."

Liko took his finger and wiped a tear from her cheek. "I missed you, Mei Lin. When I heard, I had to come."

Mei Lin thought she'd burst from happiness. And it was just like her dream—Liko was helping her to transport this baby. Sadly, she remembered Fei. In her dream, they left Fei behind.

"Have you heard anything more about Fei?" she asked.

"Yes," Liko answered. He looked around and then whispered, "The DuYan house church gave Brother Tom money for her release."

"Oh, that's wonderful," said Mei Lin. "Let's pray that the prison warden will accept the bribe."

"Oh, I don't think they'll turn it down," replied Liko. "It was quite a lot of cash."

The baby wriggled a little and Mei Lin held him securely in her lap.

"I don't know what to do," she whispered, changing the subject. "He has only half a bottle of milk. That's it."

Liko rechecked the bag. "You're right. Half a bottle is nothing." Liko slid his pinky finger into the baby's fist. "He's strong for being so tiny."

Mei Lin touched the knuckles of Liko's hand, tracing their largeness over the baby's tiny fist. "I am so glad you came."

Liko put his free hand around her and drew her closer. She could feel him smelling her hair as he always did. "I couldn't stay away."

Mei Lin put the baby in her right arm and settled her head on Liko's shoulder. She couldn't tell Liko all the miracles during her missionary journey while in the train station, but she could tell him the dreams she had about the baby.

"Now it all makes sense—we've been assigned to guard him and get him to safety."

"What's his name?" asked Liko.

"I—I don't know," answered Mei Lin. "I thought I'd call him Kwan So—after my father. It's a good Chinese name. But I don't know his real name—maybe there are papers."

Both of them sat up and Liko searched the bag one more time. There, in a side pocket was a paper. He took it out and unfolded it.

"There's writing here, but it looks like it's in Korean," he said.

"Wait!" said Mei Lin. "Turn it over."

Liko turned it over and on the other side was a letter written in Mandarin.

One day when he is older, please tell him that his mother loved him and his name, Han Chun, means "Korean Spring of life." His mother died crossing the river. His family loves him and we trust him to you with many tears.

"Han Chun," Mei Lin whispered as she stroked his little cheek. "You certainly have the attention of Heaven, Han Chun." She looked up at Liko, who was still studying the letter. "We will remember to tell Mother Su. But for now, for his safety, we must call him Little So in public." Liko nodded in agreement.

Just then the bell rang. The noise startled the baby and he began to cry. Mei Lin quickly jiggled him on her shoulder. Liko folded up the letter. "We'll need to keep this for Mother Su," he said. He picked up their bags and together they got in line to board.

The gate opened, and they walked down a dark corridor and then outside. Mei Lin squinted in the sunshine. She saw two mothers, one folding up a baby stroller as she prepared to board the train. Meanwhile, Han Chun had calmed down and was looking all around while drooling on her shoulder. She smiled. He was an adorable little guy. Suddenly, two children ran between her and Liko. They were dirty and shoeless. No one seemed to pay attention, but Mei Lin couldn't take her eyes off of them. They went over to the trashcan beside the outdoor bench and rummaged through it.

"Here, take him," said Mei Lin. She thrust the baby into Liko's arms and quickly opened her personal bag.

"Hurry up, Mei Lin, they're calling us to board."

Mei Lin pulled out the food that Mrs. Ha had given her for her journey. The noodles and vegetables were wrapped in foil. Quickly, she ran to the boys, whose bottoms were up in the air, feet dangling, as they bent over the trash.

"Here," she said. The boys pulled themselves out of the can and turned around. They slowly reached out for the food.

"Why, you're Korean!" exclaimed Mei Lin. "Do you understand Mandarin?"

The boys looked at her with blank faces. She looked back at Liko. The line was moving forward to the train and he was waving her to come. Mei Lin wanted to give the boys a Bible, but she just gave them all away to the contact. Gently, she touched the cheek of the smaller one. She pulled a few yuan out of her pocket. "God loves you," she whispered.

"Komapsumnida!" the older boy exclaimed.

"Komapsumnida!" the younger echoed.

"Komapsumnida!" Mei Lin answered. *That must mean thank you.*

Mei Lin turned back and waved a little, then ran to meet up with Liko who was toting three bags in one arm and the baby in the other. Now all eyes were on the young couple and the baby.

"Trying to be inconspicuous?" Liko teased.

"Komapsumnida!" Mei Lin quipped.

"What's that?"

Mei Lin grinned while she quickly took the baby and walked up the steps onto the train. "I couldn't just let them starve, could I?"

Liko led them through the train to a compartment. "I bought a hard bed ticket for you and the baby," he said. "I'll use your ticket and sit on the seat out in the aisle until the conductor takes our tickets.

"A hard bed? But where—"

"Connections," said Liko, smiling. "I have a few guanxi, too, you know."

Mei Lin laughed at that. Liko threw their bags on the metal rack overhead and then ducked into compartment 27. The baby was looking around, eyes wide, still drooling with his fist stuck in his mouth. Mei Lin sat on the lower bunk on the left side and propped her back with pillows from behind. Two teenagers took the top bunks and were throwing a rolled up sock back and forth. An elderly woman occupied the lower bunk on the right side. The woman seemed interested in waving goodbye to someone. She put her bags at the bottom of the bunk bed and sat at the edge, looking out the window between the beds.

Liko kissed Mei Lin on the forehead and then disappeared to take his seat in the long hall outside the door. Mei Lin pushed her shoes off and they clunked to the floor. The baby was so good. She closed her eyes and prayed for the brother who was living with his uncle. *It must have been hard to give you away,* she thought. The baby could not stand up, even when Mei Lin put her hands underneath his arms. His neck seemed strong enough, but he lacked motor control. Mei Lin thought about the dreams—God cared about this child enough to show him to her in two dreams and then bring her here to rescue him. Quietly, she held him to her shoulder and prayed over his future.

The ticket master took their tickets and, after about twenty minutes, the train began to slowly move away from the loading dock. The older woman pulled off her shoes and adjusted her pillows. She wore a gray sweater even though it was late in July.

Liko appeared in the door. "How is he?"

"Happy," Mei Lin answered.

"He's a beautiful baby," said the elderly woman. "How old is he?"

Mei Lin looked at Liko. "He's three months old," said Liko.

"He's tiny, isn't he?" she said.

Liko nodded. "We're trying to remedy that." He sat down beside Mei Lin and reached for the baby. Mei Lin watched her fiancé with this little one. Liko held him out in front of him and made faces until all three of them laughed, even the elderly woman. The baby loved the attention and grabbed for Liko's nose. After several swings and misses, Liko kindly leaned forward so his nose was within reach. The baby swung his little fist until it grazed Liko's nose. "There, now you got me!" Liko shook his head until the baby's hand flew off and the baby laughed out loud. Mei Lin laughed with him.

"Listen to him!" she exclaimed. The games continued until the baby grew tired of them and Mei Lin gladly took him back into her arms. He fussed a little and nuzzled at her breast.

Mei Lin pulled back. She looked over at the woman. She was sitting back against the wall with her eyes closed.

Mei Lin glanced up at Liko. "Where's the bottle?" she whispered.

Liko went back out to the corridor to retrieve the black bag. He came back with the bottle.

"It's not even warm," he said. "Will he take it?"

"Let's try," said Mei Lin. Mei Lin put the nipple to the baby's lips. He turned his head away. She tried again—and got the same reaction.

"What do we do?" Liko whispered.

Mei Lin remembered little Mei Mei. The nurse used to warm her bottle first.

"Find a way to warm it up," said Mei Lin.

"I'll buy some noodles and put the bottle inside the bowl of hot water," said Liko.

"Good idea," said Mei Lin. Liko left the compartment and disappeared down the corridor. Mei Lin wondered what she would have done without him on this trip. It was their very first train trip together.

The baby began to fuss more loudly now, flailing his little arms in the air. Mei Lin held him over her shoulder so he wouldn't grab for her breast. Poor thing! She wondered how he survived this far without his mother's milk.

"Hungry?"

Mei Lin glanced over at the woman and nodded. "Liko is warming his milk," she said.

The woman raised an eyebrow, but said nothing. Liko came in with a steaming bowl of noodles.

"Now, we will feed you and the baby," he said, a note of triumph in his voice.

"Do I look underfed?" she teased.

"You look a little tired," he said. "But that's why I'm here." He took the bottle and placed it into the steaming bowl of noodles. The baby continued to squirm. His cries were sporadic and weak. Mei Lin felt helpless. Liko kept shaking the bottle, working with it until it warmed.

Mei Lin dribbled a few drops on her hand, the way she did it when she cared for Mei Mei at the orphanage. The temperature seemed right.

She tipped the bottle to the baby's mouth. He turned away again. Mei Lin dribbled a few drops onto his lips and he shut his mouth tightly! Mei Lin tried to poke the nipple into his mouth, but he refused.

"Whaaaa!" he cried out, turning his head.

"He knows what he wants and this is definitely not on the menu," said Liko.

Who knows how old this bottle is? Mei Lin thought. She closed her eyes and quietly prayed. "Father, You gave me the dreams. You have made it plain I'm to care for this baby boy. Will You please tell me how to feed him?"

Suddenly, she knew! She jumped up with the baby. "I'll be back."

Mei Lin went out into the corridor, still holding the baby. Her eyes scanned the metal luggage rack above the heads of all those seated on the corridor along the wall. There! The baby stroller!

Mei Lin went to the place where the baby stroller was stored and looked around for the baby. A small cry came from compartment 10. Mei Lin looked inside, holding her little one close.

"Please, may I come in?" she asked.

The woman sat on the lower bunk patting her baby's back as he lay on the bed beside her. He was almost asleep. The person on the other side was asleep facing the wall.

"What is your baby's name?" the woman asked.

"Kwan So," Mei Lin answered. It felt good to say her father's name.

"You are the woman who gave your food away to the beggar children, aren't you?"

Mei Lin nodded. "I cannot stand to see a hungry child. That's why I came to you."

"Me?" The young woman had her long hair pulled back in a barrette. She was dressed in plain dark gray pants and a pale pink blouse. She looked harmless, but Mei Lin did not know if she could trust her.

"The baby is not mine," she said. *At least that much is true.* "I am taking the baby to Shanghai for a friend of mine, the mother."

The woman listened intently. "And where is the mother?" she asked.

"Dead," said Mei Lin.

The woman's face softened. "I'm sorry." She looked at her own child and then back at Mei Lin. "Is the baby contagious? Forgive me for saying so, but he looks skinny and sickly."

"The baby is fine," said Mei Lin. "He's just hungry."

"Would you be willing to nurse Kwan So for me?" she asked. She held up the bottle. "We were trying to feed him this and he won't take it."

Just then little So let out a pitiful cry. Mei Lin nearly cried with him. "Please?" she pleaded. "I will pay you."

The woman placed a light blanket over her own baby who was now asleep. "Give me the baby," she said, motioning to the bottom of the bunk. "Sit down there."

The woman took little So into her arms and lifted her shirt. He grabbed wildly for her breast. The woman looked up at Mei Lin and smiled. So latched onto the woman's nipple, his whole body wriggling to get closer. He pulled off and coughed, half choking.

"Slow down," the woman said, laughing. "There is nothing wrong with his appetite," she said to Mei Lin. "He just needs a nurse."

Mei Lin felt she would burst with pleasure. Baby So finished coughing and eagerly went back to nursing. The woman allowed him to nurse for some time and then sat him on her knee. He immediately burped and then she put him on the other side. This time when he latched on, his body relaxed and he drank more slowly. Mei Lin wiped back a tear.

"Thank you," she said. She put the bottle on the stand beside the bed. "I will go get the money for you. I'll be right back."

Mei Lin went back to Liko in compartment 27. "Do you have more money?" she asked.

"Where's the baby?" asked Liko.

"I found a nurse for him," said Mei Lin.

Liko grinned. "You are incredible," he said. "Here, give her this."

Liko handed her 20 yuan. "See if that will suit her until the end of the trip. We have an 18 hour ride."

Mei Lin bent over and kissed Liko's cheek. "You are the kindest man in the whole world," she said.

When Mei Lin came back to compartment 10, little So was asleep.

"He drank so quickly," she said. "The poor little boy."

"Are you going to Shanghai?" asked Mei Lin

"We're going past Shanghai," she answered.

"Will you nurse him for us until we get to Shanghai?" asked Mei Lin. "Here. We want to pay you."

The woman looked at the money.

"Please, it's the least we can do," said Mei Lin.

The woman nodded. She seemed pleased with the money. "Very soon you will need a diaper," she said. "I can hear his tummy rumbling with all the milk he just drank."

Mei Lin took little So into her arms. "Thank you," she said. "I don't know what we would have done without your help."

"I would wash out that bottle if I were you," the woman said. "The milk smells sour. It's no wonder he wouldn't drink it."

"Of course," said Mei Lin. The woman had no idea she only met this little passenger a few hours ago, so Mei Lin did not fault her for offering so much free advice. Hopefully, the woman truly cared about the baby.

"I'll bring him back in a few hours?" asked Mei Lin.

The woman nodded. "I will nurse him again."

Mei Lin smiled and adjusted the baby in her arms so she could pick up the bottle. "I'll be back."

Mei Lin didn't look down at the baby until she was back on the bunk bed with Liko. Together they pulled back the thin blanket.

"He's still sucking in his sleep," said Mei Lin. She wiped away the milk that had dribbled into the corner of his mouth. He moved a little and Liko cradled his head with his large hand. "Imagine what he's been through," he said softly. Mei Lin looked over at the woman in the other bunk. She was covered with a blanket now and breathing deeply and even, obviously asleep.

The teenagers on the top bunks burst into laughter every now and then, but So didn't seem to hear. He slept without a whimper.

"Will you fold that blanket and lay it on the bed?" Mei Lin asked Liko. "I'll lay him down there to sleep."

Little So lay contentedly on the folded blanket while Mei Lin patted his back. "Now we can talk?" she asked, after the baby was sound asleep.

She and Liko sat together with pillows behind their backs. Mei Lin snuggled closer so they could whisper into one another's ear. For the next hour, Mei Lin told Liko about the miraculous healings and salvations, the baptisms, and the thousands of people who gathered in ZhingCho to hear the gospel.

"I learned something," she said, looking up into his face. She wanted to see his reaction.

"What's that?" he asked.

"I learned to believe God to send me to the village—and to send me out of the village. I should have left when I felt uneasy the day before. Now I know that if God's peace isn't there, I should leave."

"I'm glad you weren't hurt," said Liko. He kissed her cheek. "I need you, Kwan Mei Lin."

Mei Lin looked up at Liko, her stomach still full of butterflies. "I need you, Chen Liko."

They sat quietly for some time. Mei Lin spoke first. "We've never had so much time alone to talk like this. It's wonderful."

Liko smiled. "Well, we aren't exactly alone. But we have more time than when we watch the sunset on the big rock."

"I missed you, Liko."

Liko pulled her closer. She thought her heart would leap through her throat. She looked up and her cheek was at his chin. He bent his head and kissed her full on the mouth. Mei Lin responded, willing him still closer. She felt she couldn't get enough of him.

"Marry me," he said, smelling her hair again.

"In the spring, Liko. I'll marry you in the spring," Mei Lin said softly.

Appendix A

GLOSSARY

CHOKPO

Korean genealogies which originated from two beliefs of traditional Korean life: the belief that one's identity and social status was earned by the achievements of one's ancestors, and the need to have accurate descent records in order to maintain the integrity of ancestor rituals.

FENG SHUI

The Chinese art or philosophy of arranging items (furniture, graves, buildings, etc.) in a way to keep in balance—yin and yang.

GOTCHEBEES — Orphans in North Korea who are outcasts and live on the street or in holes/caves and must steal food in order to survive. North Koreans, including the government, will not help them, giving the gotchebees the stigma that they are worthless.

GULAG — North Korean prison camps which force their prisoners to perform hard labor. North Koreans are routinely sent to these labor camps for small infractions, including singing songs from other countries or saying a negative comment against the government. If one member of the family commits one of these small crimes, the entire family is sent to the labor camp for life.

HAN'GL (also spelled han-gul) — The Korean alphabet invented in the 15th century. The words may be written using a mixture of Chinese characters (hancha) and a native Korean alphabet known as han'gl, or in han'gl alone.

JUCHE — The Juche (pronounced joo-cheh'), also called Kim Il Sungism after the leader of North Korea from 1948-1994, is the official state ideology of North Korea. Its roots are in Marxism-Leninism, yet is an original theology founded and penned by Hwang Jon Yop. Hwang Jon Yop, once hailed by Kimg Jong-il and his father Kim il-Sung for his expert ideology, escaped from North Korea and is presently residing in South Korea.

KAOLIANG

Small white or brown grains made from the Chinese sorghum plant used for food like pancakes or mush. Grain sorghum can grow up to 15 feet tall and the stalks are sometimes used for fodder, fuel, and thatching.

WOK

A wide, large, pan used for stir-frying Chinese food.

ZEPHYR

A gentle breeze.

AUTHOR'S NOTE

Most of the fodder for this book was built on the testimonies of North Korean defectors whom I've personally interviewed or heard testify in congressional hearings in Washington, DC, within the last three years. You can help put an end to their isolation by passing this book along to a caring friend. Please read over the next few pages for more thoughts on what you can do to help.

Also, I encourage you to peruse two interactive wiki Websites set up to update people with news and prayer strategies for North Korea. Please visit:

www.northkoreafreedom.wetpaint.com
(news) and
www.houseofprayerfornorthkorea.wetpaint.com
(prayer strategies).

Sign into the Website by clicking, "Join This Wiki," and set up your own profile page. Give us a peek into your prayer closet, and tell us what God is showing you regarding prayer over North Korea. Feel free to e-mail me at northkorea@comcast.net. I'd love to hear from you!

CALL TO ACTION

The Lord is looking for laid-down servant lovers to run into the darkness and call in His lost Bride. I truly believe that there is a deep spiritual connection with our Mozambican revival in one of the poorest countries of the world and the North Korean harvest in one of the darkest countries of the world. The cup of suffering North Korea has willingly taken will one day yield a cup of joy. The interwoven lives of the persecuted church in China and Korea awaken my heart to dream even more the glorious dreams of God's heart for His persecuted Bride. We must stand with North Korea to be a voice for the voiceless and a face for the silent suffering of millions.

Dr. Heidi G. Baker
Founding Director, Iris Ministries

Too often we forget what goes on behind the closed doors of countries like North Korea. Often things that are hidden from day-to-day life get ignored by those of us who *can* do something and make our concerns and our voices heard. It is shameful that such aggression and violence toward the ordinary people in North Korea is tolerated by other nations who know better. Hope Flinchbaugh wants to draw your attention to the plight of the people of North Korea and hopefully we will all respond.

Kathie and David Walters
Good News Ministries, Macon, Georgia

Hope Flinchbaugh has skillfully interwoven two stories she carries deep in her heart—the beauty of the vibrant housechurch Christians of China and the grossly oppressive and warped society of North Korea, where unspeakable atrocities and suffering occur every day. *I'll Cross the River* will both encourage and challenge you to follow Christ unreservedly and to make an impact on our needy world.

Paul Hattaway, Author of *Heavenly Man*
Missionary to Asia

Tragically, because of the lack of access to North Korea, most people living in the free world have no idea of the horrible suffering of the people in North Korea. Even those few who travel to the country are carefully watched by "minders" and have no access to see the general population. Through her book, Hope Flinchbaugh has given us a picture of life for the average citizen who must struggle daily to survive, cut off from the rest of the world and enslaved by Kim Jong-il in what could arguably be described as the world's biggest prison. Hope, who has led a prayer team to help me with my work on this issue, rightfully reminds us that helping the North Korean people is as much a spiritual battle as anything else. Her central character, Young Soon, reminds us of the triumph of the human spirit. Emboldened by love, redemption, and forgiveness, Young Soon overcomes in a land gripped with fear, suspicion, and condemnation. She embodies both the despair and courage of over 10,000 North Korean defectors who have fled their homeland. These defectors are a living testament that no matter how many years of darkness North Koreans have faced, the light of the human spirit can never be extinguished.

Suzanne Scholte
President, Defense Forum Foundation
Chairman, North Korea Freedom Coalition

I'll Cross the River touches my heart—I am so impressed. I believe this book represents the situation of North Korea exactly so people can understand the most closed country and the lives of North Korean citizens. Please pray for God to bless them.

Jung Min Noh, Broadcaster/Reporter
Korean Service Radio Free Asia, Washington, DC

I'll Cross the River is a timely and provocative novel based on true stories researched by journalist Hope Flinchbaugh, who's written extensively about persecution and revival in the nations of China and North Korea for magazines such as *Christianity Today* and *Charisma* and *Christian Life*. With stunning accuracy, Hope details the real-life drama and unthinkable choices involved with being a woman in the oppressive communist nation of North Korea.

Pat Robertson, Chairman/CEO
The Christian Broadcasting Network

Speak up for those who cannot speak for themselves, for the rights of all who are destitute. This gripping story plunges into the continuing holocaust in North Korea as the mad leader starves and destroys his own citizenry. The author brings you into the courage, humanity, and pathos of Chinese Christians, who risk prison and martyrdom, becoming unlikely heroes, giving rescue and aid to the desperate fugitives who risk their lives to flee this hell on earth.

Charles Stock
Pastor, Life Center

I pray that the story in this book will birth in you the heartbeat of God for this nation. Hope Flinchbaugh—whom I know personally—once again has captured the heart of a nation by going deep into the lives of its people. Our hearts become knit with theirs as we experience with them their oppression and their salvation!

Pastor Kathy Balcombe
Revival Christian Church, Hong Kong

For most of the past 54 years North Korea's manmade famines and disasters, regime brutality, corruption and repression, national trauma and dysfunction, as well as the unparalleled religious repression that has virtually annihilated a once-dynamic and vibrant church has been largely hidden from the world. Isolation has been the dictator's best friend! I am so thrilled that a writer as skilled and as passionate as C. Hope Flinchbaugh has chosen to write on this subject. Because she bases and builds her plots around the testimonies of North Korean refugees, she manages to give her readers a painfully accurate insight into North Korean suffering. By exposing the truth, she is also contributing to the end of isolation.

Elizabeth Kendal
World Evangelical Alliance Religious Liberty Commission

Powerful and compelling, *I'll Cross the River* captured my heart with the reality of the suffering of our North Korean brothers and sisters.

Carl A. Moeller, PhD
President & CEO, Open Doors, USA

Since the 1950s, millions of Chinese and Koreans have suffered horrendously and countless numbers have died due to the dogma of atheistic communism and the policies of evil rulers. Due to this satanic ideology, Chinese Christians in the past and to this day are suffering as they obey Christ's Great Commission. While China has reformed and improved since the implementation of the "Open Door Policy" in the 1980s, North Korea is still in a dark nightmare of starvation, brainwashing, and brutal oppression of the whole populace, somewhat akin to China's Cultural Revolution and the massive famine that was the result of the "Great Leap Forward" campaign.

It is vital that Christians in the West understand what is happening now in North Korea and the plight of refugees who escape to North China. I hope this book will motivate you to prayer and action as we reach out and help our brethren.

Pastor Dennis Balcombe
Hong Kong, Revival Christian Church
Revival Chinese Ministries International

Ways You Can Get Involved

It's hard to read this information and then close the book. What can you do?

1. Start a prayer team for North Korea in your state. Can you see God raising up one prayer team from every state in the United States? E-mail me and I'll help you begin a prayer team for North Korea—and you don't even have to leave your house.

2. Sign up to stay informed. Receive newsletters from the North Korea Freedom Coalition by emailing Suzanne Scholte at skswm@aol.com.

3. Join the North Korea Freedom Coalition. Go to and click "About Us" and "Become a Member."

4. Get this book into your local library. Ask the librarian to order it for the shelves. And pass it on—you may send a

missionary to North Korea by loaning this book to others (who will read this book and volunteer to help) or giving it as a gift to your friends.

5. Generate interest! Start a book club in your church youth group or senior meetings. American soldiers e-mailed me that they are reading my previous novels in a book club on base in Afghanistan and South Korea. Send a soldier, *I'll Cross the River.*

DEFENSE FORUM FOUNDATION AND NORTH KOREA FREEDOM COALITION

Suzanne Scholte is president of the Defense Forum Foundation (DFF) in Washington, DC, and chairwoman of the North Korea Freedom Coalition. DFF sponsors a number of projects to help promote North Korean human rights including:

1. Sponsoring a North Korean defector's airfare and hotel accommodations so the defector can visit the United States to give testimony to our government leaders.

2. Helping a defector in South Korea broadcast into North Korea and send in information through shortwave radio.

3. Supporting a balloon launch—Dollar bills (for food) and/or newspaper articles (for much needed information) and/or Bible Scriptures (for spiritual help) are placed into helium balloons and sent across the border from South Korea into North Korea.

4. Supporting new churches founded by North Korean defectors in Seoul.

5. Financing the rescue, hiding, and prayerful escape of a North Korean refugee through the Underground Railroad out of North Korea and China.

You can make a tax-deductible donation to the Defense Forum Foundation by sending a check to DFF and earmarking it for any of these North Korea programs you wish to support. Send the check to:

Defense Forum Foundation
3014 Castle Road
Falls Church, VA 22044

For more details or to join the North Korea Freedom Coalition, please write a letter to the address above or e-mail Suzanne Scholte at skswm@aol.com. Let her know you have read this book!

THOUGHTS ON CHINA

What is happening in North Korea is the most avoidable human rights tragedy occurring in the world today. China wants to be seen as a world leader, a country prepared and proud to host the 2008 summer Olympics, a coveted international event. But China refuses to help their human family in North Korea. There are three immediate solutions available for China:

1. The United Nations High Commission for Refugees (UNHCR) wants to help North Koreans but China won't allow the UNHCR to find refugees. The Chinese do not allow the UNHCR to interview refugees and the entry to the UNHCR office in Beijing is blocked. North Koreans must sneak into the UNHCR office in Beijing because China will arrest Koreans trying to enter. (Unfortunately, the same is true for all international embassies and consulate offices in China.)

2. The humanitarian community is committed to helping and has helped rescue 10,000 refugees *secretly* through an underground railroad. Imagine what could be done if China *helps* the humanitarian community?

3. North Koreans who defect are automatically citizens of South Korea under the South Korean constitution. The United States of America has repeatedly offered to resettle refugees who want to resettle in the United States. But China, rather than work with United States and South Korea, force the starving people to return to North Korea where they are certain to be tortured, imprisoned, and possibly executed.

BOOKS BY

C. HOPE FLINCHBAUGH

- ❖ *I'll Cross the River**
- ❖ *Across the China Sky*
- ❖ *Daughter of China*
- ❖ *Spiritually Parenting Your Preschoolers*

*If you enjoyed reading about Young Soon's Heaven experience, you can read an additional chapter on my Website about her. The chapters were based on true stories of people who have gone to Heaven and returned to tell us what they saw, and I personally went through the tunnel that Young Soon traversed during a near-death experience in the 1980s. Please visit www.seehope.com and click on "Heaven" to read more.

Additional copies of this book and other
book titles from DESTINY IMAGE are
available at your local bookstore.

Call toll-free: 1-800-722-6774.

Send a request for a catalog to:

Destiny Image₀ Publishers, Inc.
P.O. Box 310
Shippensburg, PA 17257-0310

*"Speaking to the Purposes of God for This
Generation and for the Generations to Come"*

**For a complete list of our titles,
visit us at www.destinyimage.com**